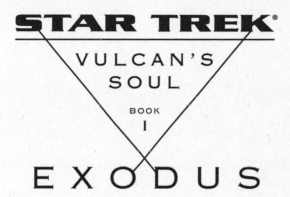

STAR TREK®

VULCAN'S SOUL

BOOK I

EXODUS

STAR TREK®

VULCAN'S SOUL

BOOK I

EXODUS

JOSEPHA SHERMAN & SUSAN SHWARTZ

BASED UPON STAR TREK
CREATED BY GENE RODDENBERRY

POCKET BOOKS
New York   London   Toronto   ·Sydney   ShiKahr

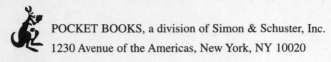 POCKET BOOKS, a division of Simon & Schuster, Inc.

1230 Avenue of the Americas, New York, NY 10020

 STAR TREK is a Registered Trademark of ® Paramount Pictures.

This book is published by Pocket Books, a division of Simon & Schuster, Inc., under exclusive license from Paramount Pictures.

Library of Congress Cataloging-in-Publication Data

Sherman, Josepha.
   Vulcan's soul. Book 1, Exodus / Josepha Sherman and Susan Shwartz.
     p. cm.—(Star trek)
   "Based upon Star Trek created by Gene Roddenberry."
   ISBN: 0-7434-6356-0
   1. Spock (Fictitious character)—Fiction. 2. Interplanetary voyages—Fiction. 3. Space ships—Fiction. I. Shwartz, Susan, 1949– II. Title. III. Series.

PS3569.H4315V88 2004
813'.54—dc22   2004044778

First Pocket Books hardcover edition July 2004

10 9 8 7 6 5 4 3 2 1

Jacket design by John Vairo Jr.

Manufactured in the United States of America

For information regarding special discounts for bulk purchases, please contact Simon & Schuster Special Sales at 1-800-456-6798 or business@simonandschuster.com.

To Elly and Peter
and
To Margaret Wander Bonanno, ancient Vulcan historian
S.M.S.

To, in no particular order, Susan Shwartz, Linda Bulmer,
Tamora Pierce, Linda Phonner, and Karen Klinck
for being there for me when I needed it most
J.S.

ONE

2364

*History is the intellectual form in which a culture
decides for itself the meaning of its past.*
—JOHAN HUIZINGA

None of the Vulcan, Romulan, human, Cardassian, and Klingon
diplomats assembled had notified their governments officially of
this meeting in the center of the Romulan Neutral Zone. Easier by
far, thought Ambassador Spock, to get forgiveness than permission. Humans might have invented that saying, but its applications
were universal.

The only problem was that Spock was not totally certain that
forgiveness, in this case, would be all that easy to attain. Not for
this meeting.

He suspected that various presidents, praetors, legates, chancel-
lors, and a host of other titles would disapprove even more strenu-

ously of where he and his colleagues had chosen to meet. Scans indicated that the echoing, circular chamber located approximately 300.58 meters beneath the jagged surface of an airless asteroid had begun its existence as a bubble in molten rock approximately 3.2 billion Earth years ago. Those same scans had also proved that the desolate chunk of rock had once been part of a planet, shattered by some catastrophe and flung free.

The symbolism was explicit. Those who did not learn from history were destined to repeat it. That was a maxim Spock had found both in Surak's *Analects* and in human philosophy.

Would old enemies prove apt students of histories not their own?

Spock found it difficult to assess that probability. For now, at least, the assembled diplomats, aides, warriors, and covert operatives eyed one another with a sensible caution, but no rage. At least, not yet.

To some extent, wariness was only to be expected. For Vulcans, rage was illogical. For Romulans, it was counterproductive. For Klingons, Cardassians, and humans, however—well, Spock not only assumed that the weapons scanners each side had insisted on bringing in were the best available and working effectively, he had checked their effectiveness himself.

But even the efficacy of the weapons scanners installed on this chunk of rock did not matter: What need had the participants in this conference of physical weapons when they had thoughts and words, the deadliest weapons of all?

Gathered around a black stone table that had been ancient before their ancestors had ever walked upright, let alone fought each other, the members of this shadow council all seemed willing to tolerate their enemies' presence. At least for now, they were willing to listen.

Spock's eyes met those of his own longtime personal antagonist. His father, Sarek, might have chosen never to meld minds with him, but Spock thought that, for once, they were in perfect understanding. It was logical to exploit the willingness of these participants in a most secret conference to talk and to listen, but that willingness was fragile. One wrong word, one false step, even a misunderstood glance could destroy it.

Sarek raised his eyebrow minutely at his son. *Now it begins.* Rising from his black stone chair, Vulcan's senior ambassador held up his hand with its fingers parted in formal Vulcan greeting. Instantly, he gained the attention of every diplomat—and every guard—in the room. Even more than his son, Sarek was legendary for the just, wily, and occasionally ruthless methods he had employed lifelong to win his diplomatic battles. Even the Romulans, knowing he was no friend of theirs, had conceded that Sarek, as eldest of the participants, was the logical representative to make the opening statement.

"We come to serve," Sarek began, pitching his voice to carry throughout the echoing stone bubble. Instantly, attentive, wary eyes targeted the august old Vulcan.

"Let the site of our meeting serve as a warning and an inspiration to us," Sarek told the men and women assembled around the stone table.

Reinforcing the symbolism, Spock thought. *Well done, Father.*

Spock had seen the geologic assays of this asteroid. They showed minute traces of types of radiation indicating that the cataclysm that had destroyed the planet had been deliberate. Thus far, however, no one had been able to learn whether it had been destroyed by its enemies or its own inhabitants. Even now, some radiation remained in the desolate rock. It would not prove harmful, Spock knew, if this clandestine meeting with Romulan negotiators was kept brief. That knowledge was shared by every one of the diplomats, officers, and scientists present. But even if concern about radiation levels had not been a considerable incentive for concluding these talks quickly, the destruction of bases on both sides of the Neutral Zone made speed a necessity.

"I am not here," Sarek continued, "to make resounding speeches about historic moments. *We* are not here for that. Instead, I urge the representatives assembled today to choose the logical path. We must reason together to prevent our own homeworlds from being shattered on the forge where this planet's culture perished."

Sarek's reflection in the gleaming black walls was only slightly distorted by the ancient inscriptions that no one had ever been able to decipher. His heavy white robes of office, gleaming with iridescent cabochon gems of white, the red of Vulcan's soil, and the green of its children's blood, seemed simultaneously to weigh him down and sustain him.

For an instant, the image in the shining stone seemed to waver. Spock tensed in case Sarek needed assistance. His father was barely two hundred. When had his shoulders become so thin?

That was one of many questions Spock asked himself.

Another question was whether it had been smugglers, war refugees, or Romulan archeologists turned tacticians who discovered the hollow beneath this asteroid's barren surface. How many cultures—over how many years—had spent their time polishing the jagged rock into some semblance of civilization?

At this moment, not even scientific inquiry matters, Spock cautioned himself. *It is illogical to multitask now. More: It is unacceptably hazardous. Your duty is to focus on Sarek's words and how they are being received.*

Frail or not, Sarek had lost none of his shrewdness. He had

made his opening remarks brief and was now bringing them to a close.

"We regard the shared knowledge of this place and the shared willingness to meet within it as evidence of a motivation to wage peace that I find highly satisfactory. And, may I add, profoundly logical."

The old Vulcan bowed to the senators, warriors, and diplomats assembled, then to the keen-eyed observers before he seated himself once more.

The Klingon observer, Kaghvahr son of Kyrosh, pounded his gauntleted fist on the table.

"Wage peace, son of Vulcan? It would be more logical," he growled out the word, "if you showed us our enemy! To destroy the honorless creatures who have turned planets into fragments—now, that would be truly glorious!"

Romulan Commander Toreth of the *Khazara,* a small woman of around Spock's age, eyed the Klingon as if he were on the same evolutionary level as the *targ* that crouched beside Kaghvahr's chair.

Again, Spock traded glances with his father. For the second time that day and the third time since Senator Pardek of Romulus had informed Spock that powers in the Romulan Star Empire favored a meeting (always provided that the Praetor did not have to take official note of it), father and son were in agreement.

Illogical of me to have been surprised that Sarek accepted the suggestion—even if it does turn out to be pretext for a battle. My father is, after all, a true disciple of Surak: if a chance for peace exists, he acts upon it. Fascinating: He wages peace with the zeal of a Klingon warrior or the cunning of a Romulan senator.

Because Sarek was regarded as less partisan—and certainly less inflammatory—than Spock, whose advocacy for Vulcan-

Romulan unification had earned him opposition from the less log-ical, Sarek had been the choice to carry the request for a meeting to select officials in the Federation.

Admiral Uhura herself had suggested this asteroid as a suitable meeting place for "you and your opposite numbers." *Her* opposite numbers had accepted the suggestion without a show of outrage or even much surprise, which led Spock to believe that the "pow-ers" that Pardek mentioned included members of the Romulan Senate.

Spock surmised that Uhura's comment about his "opposite numbers" was as metaphorical as many other of the intelligence officer's observations over the years. For many years now, Spock had had associates in the Romulan Star Empire as well as in the Federation. However, the representatives now seated across from him had violently replaced most of the Romulans Spock had fought alongside and came very close to regarding as friends, even if their governments were hostile. Now other Romulan offi-cers, politicians, and spies faced him, servants of the people who had replaced his . . . former associates in power. A human or Klingon could not have sat across from them without comment. A Romulan would have declared feud. As a Vulcan, Spock had no trouble treating them with the courtesy required by a diplomatic mission. Even though, as a sapient being who had lost . . . col-leagues, he knew the costs of trusting them, the risks of not trust-ing them might prove to be even greater.

In pursuing this meeting, Spock had put his credibility "on the table," as Uhura probably had already said someplace where Spock had not heard her. Also on the actual or metaphorical table, however, was Sarek's reputation. Both had been sufficient—just barely—to bring Romulan and Klingon ships, cloaked not just to conceal their presence but to prevent them from firing immediately on each other, into orbit around this asteroid, while Starfleet gave it a wide berth.

It was highly unfortunate that the Treaty of Algeron, which had emerged from the Tomed debacle of 2311, barred the Federation from developing its own cloaking technology: the Federation was now in the uncomfortable position of being in debt to the Klingon Empire for transportation. Only the chancellor's respect for the Starfleet captain and crew who had died at Narendra III and the officer who had risked her life and sanity to warn the Federation of the covert Romulan assault had won their cooperation. But Spock had heard mutterings that yesterday's roast *targ* was today's thin soup: the Klingons' gratitude might well be outworn.

That the Federation was still embroiled in a protracted border conflict with the Cardassians did nothing to ease the mood of the gathering. The Cardassian delegation was led by a stocky male in late middle age named Tekeny Ghemor, a legate and member of the Central Command. Seated beside him was a warship commander, the sharp-eyed Gul Akellen Macet, who watched the room as if assessing the individual strengths and weaknesses of its occupants.

And then, of course, there were the Romulans. Their negotiators might regard Sarek with respect, but they watched Spock as if he were about to perpetrate some new deceit. As if, in fact, he were one of their own. At least this one time, their suspicion was unnecessary, but Spock accepted it as an indication of the mistrust, and therefore the respect, in which the Romulan Star Empire held him—that part of it that did not want to kill him on sight.

Spock observed his Romulan observers, reflected in the chamber's curving basalt walls so that they seemed twice their number. Commander Tebok, an angular man in whose face arrogance and anger warred, sat beside Commander Toreth. If Spock could judge from the stiffness of her back, Commander Toreth was no friend of the too-cultivated senior officer seated on her other side: Admiral Mendak of the *Devoras*. Uhura had given him a report on Mendak: she suspected that he also held high rank in the intelligence agency one of Spock's most cherished enemies had founded.

Behind each senior Romulan officer stood guards, their faces obscured by helms whose resemblance to ritual gear from before the Time of Surak invariably reminded Spock just how much history Vulcans and Romulans shared.

He let his eyes travel away from the officers to the one Romulan civilian, a representative of the senate of the often-ignored Romulan people. With the exception of Spock's own consort, Pardek was the most formidable—and unlikely—survivor Spock had ever known. Where the others were lean and in warrior training, he was short and stout. His heavy brow ridges and sallow complexion made him appear stolid, but, since the time they met during the Khitomer Accords, Spock had found him a stimulating conversationalist and a thoughtful associate.

"When I found our outposts destroyed," said Commander Tebok, "I logically assumed"—his emphasis on the adverb evinced faint hostility—"an act of aggression on the part of the Federation. When I encountered *Enterprise,* however, your commander, Captain . . . Jean-Luc Picard assured me that the Federation, too, had suffered significant damages."

Tebok raised a cynical eyebrow. "But there is not even a legend that *humans* do not lie. So I told your captain that we were back. If anyone here"—he turned his eyes on the Klingons—"has forgotten that we are a force to be reckoned with, you will have a painful lesson to relearn."

Spock had no need to calculate the odds that Tebok's meeting with *Enterprise,* of all ships in the Fleet, was any sort of coincidence. Romulan doctrine left very little to chance.

What was that human adage? *Once is happenstance; twice is coincidence; three times is enemy action.* In dealing with Romulans, it was logical to assume that enemy action, if it had not already occurred, was imminent.

The assumption was logical, perhaps, but not reasonable. That was why Sarek and Spock were here—as well as to keep the Klingons from seizing an opportunity to settle old scores.

Seated next to Spock were Ambassador T'Pel and her aide, radiating the frozen Vulcan propriety that had driven Spock from his home. Completing the Federation's negotiators was a human diplomat, Samuel Robert Fox, tall, foursquare, and as stubborn as his diplomat grandfather before him, the Ambassador Fox who had spent his career crafting peace on Eminiar VII. Not to mention the guards Uhura had sent, who were a fact of life.

On Spock's other side, in the center of the Federation delegation, was its leader, Sarek of Vulcan. It was a privilege to work with his father and see how his more than a century of diplomatic experience had given him presence and a devastating shrewdness in addition to the logic that was as keen—Spock sought for an appropriate simile—as a Romulan Honor Blade.

Because father and son had traveled together from Vulcan, they had agreed to share an aide. Young Shinat, a dark-skinned Vulcan from near the planet's blazing equatorial region, had been called away from the council chamber on an errand.

Bare is back without brother.

Another human metaphor that his brother-by-choice had taught him—and as meaningful as it was inaccurate. His back was not bare. He had old and trusted associates. His consort Saavik, back on

Vulcan, was supervising damage control with the Klingons and acting as a liaison with Uhura. Deemed "too high-profile" to attend this meeting, Uhura, like Spock's sparring partner Dr. McCoy, had reluctantly admitted she was "not as young as I used to be."

No: logically, Spock's own nature had brought him to this place. Regrets were as illogical as the claustrophobia that lurked at the frontiers of his thought when he recalled that this conference room was hidden beneath hundreds of meters of rock. He had been in deeper, more secure sanctuaries, like Sargon's crypt. But none of them had been cause for more than a moment's concern during his nightly meditations.

Pardek, less rigidly disciplined than his military colleagues, touched the high collar of his cloak. His face turned a deeper olive, and he drew deep breaths as if, momentarily, he expected life-support to fail. Toreth glanced at him in brief scorn for his loss of control. A claustrophobic Romulan: fascinating.

"What do you suggest?" Ambassador T'Pel's crisp question cut across Commander Tebok's speech like a phaser bolt. Her question was logical, despite the bluntness that made Tebok bristle with offense and the Klingons mutter reluctant approval.

As Spock prepared to intervene, Shinat returned. At the door, he paused and bowed carefully at all of the ambassadors, before he walked over to Spock and Sarek. "A message from Vulcan for you, Ambassador," he said in an undertone.

T'Pel raised an eyebrow. "Inspecific," she commented, then turned away. But T'Pel had insisted on bringing her own aide; any message for her would certainly come through what humans called "proper channels."

Sarek extended his hand for the padd Shinat had brought him in lieu of a properly calligraphed communiqué. Taking it with a nod of thanks, he tilted it so that Spock, too, could scan it.

It was a recall order.

"You are requested to contact Vulcan immediately upon receipt of this message," Shinat added.

"Both of us cannot be spared," Sarek said softly. Their departure would shatter the conference past any hope of reviving it at a later date. T'Pel lacked the ability to reach out across the gulf of thousands of years, while Fox, although a satisfactory negotiator, was neither Vulcan nor had the deep understanding of Vulcan tradition that had allowed some outsiders to win an acceptance that, even now, some Vulcans still begrudged Spock. Starting with the one seated beside him.

Protocol and courtesy required Spock to allow Sarek to decide which of them should answer this summons. He lowered his eyes, lest his father see how much Spock wanted to be the one to return.

When he raised his head, Sarek caught his eye and raised an eyebrow. Was that indulgence Spock read in his glance? Sarek had always read him far too well for his comfort. It was illogical for Sarek to weaken Vulcan credibility by reprimanding Spock in public, however.

Sarek bent toward him. "You earned this," he told Spock. "You therefore should be the one to go."

Spock rose with not-quite-unseemly haste. If he thanked his father, he knew Sarek would rebuke him: there was no sense in thanking logic.

He bowed to the people seated around the great table. "I am recalled," he said. "I ask forgiveness."

Fox concealed surprise beneath what humans called a "poker face." T'Pel's eyebrows rose before she looked away, skeptical and somewhat offended that she had not been consulted. Offense seemed her natural manner. She would be a disagreeable colleague for his father.

"Coincidence?" Admiral Mendak suggested with the silken irony characteristic of him. Perhaps his intelligence sources—or the human captives Spock suspected he controlled—had acquainted him with the human adage about coincidence and enemy action that Spock had recalled 3.56 minutes ago.

Pardek, by contrast, seemed amused. He whispered to Commander Toreth, who shrugged, sly humor in her face.

Spock took one deep breath. Perhaps Pardek had the right to mention Spock's consort. Had hostilities not existed between the Federation and Romulus, he and Pardek would have been guest-friends. But his speculation about why Spock was being recalled was as inaccurate as it was inappropriate.

Spock bowed and turned to go. When Shinat made as if to accompany him, Spock signaled for him *and* Uhura's security forces to remain, so emphatically that the room was shocked to silence.

"You're the one irreplaceable piece of this puzzle," Uhura had told him when the conference had started to take shape. But no one was ever irreplaceable, and some things took precedence over his old friend's schemes. This call had a 97.63 percent probability of being what Spock expected. That being the case, Sarek, T'Pel, and Ambassador Fox would have to manage damage control as well as the negotiations themselves without him.

He knew Sarek liked to dismiss hope as a human construct, but *if that is indeed the case, why did you agree to these talks, my father?* Spock thought, however, that if Sarek knew what he hoped to hear, he would have to concede that it was logical for his pulse rate to rise to a breathless 350 beats per minute. Nevertheless, because the physiological reaction stemmed from emotion, it was unacceptable.

Spock steepled his fingers briefly and subvocalized a mantra of control. Then he sealed himself into the secure privacy zone Uhura's staff had set up in a rock alcove.

He tapped the screen and found himself facing his consort's image. Spock's heart and respiration accelerated once more. Logic demanded, he told himself, that he feel . . . satisfaction at seeing his wife.

"My husband," Saavik greeted him, meeting his eyes, then lowering her own. For 3.02 seconds, they kept silent. His consort's eyes brightened, and Spock felt his own eyes warm in response.

After a moment, Saavik looked decorously away and downward.

"I calculated that Sarek would cede the recall order to you. I am pleased to know that I was correct."

Spock tried to suppress the tiny smile he reserved for her.

"They have completed the preliminary translation," Saavik added. *"Your presence is vital."*

"I will requisition a shuttle from Admiral Kaghvahr," Spock said.

"Transport has already been arranged," Saavik informed him serenely. *"I have already spoken with the admiral's staff. His ship has a lock on you and will beam you out once we end this conversation. The shuttle will plot a course toward the next starbase, where convoy to Vulcan has been arranged."*

"Superfluous," Spock said.

Saavik raised her brows. *"Attacks have now occurred on both sides of the Neutral Zone. We still do not know their cause, and I assign a 75.669 percent probability to Captain Picard's hypothesis that the Romulans do not know either. Therefore, I consider the risk level unacceptable."*

Disputing security with Saavik, especially *his* security, was usually futile.

"I shall depart immediately," said Spock.

"I shall await you at the appointed place," Saavik told him. Her eyes went smoky.

Spock touched the screen as if it had been her face. They would finish *that* conversation in private.

Then the Federation seal replaced the familiar, beloved features, and Spock scrambled all records of the encrypted message.

As he stepped out of the privacy zone, the crimson of Klingon transporters engulfed him, to re-form him slowly on board Kaghvahr's private shuttle. Cloaked, it left the asteroid at warp seven. Approximately 8.67 hours later, the shuttle was surrounded by the convoy Saavik's vigilance had provided.

Even before Spock materialized outside the most secure installation of the Vulcan Science Academy, the heat of his homeworld rose to welcome him.

Saavik stood before him, a cool shadow in the oppressive light. Too quickly, she strode from the deeper shade of an overhanging roof onto the ruddy sand to meet him. Too briefly, she touched his fingers and gazed into his eyes.

"They are waiting for you," she said, and led him within.

The translation team he expected to see was assembled: philologists, archeologists, computer scientists, a Seleyan adept, and Ruanek, their resident expert on the Romulan language. Characteristically, he had appointed himself guardian of the artifact. Spock agreed with the Romulan's decision: Ruanek definitely had the curiosity; and, as an exile from the Two Worlds, he had the right.

Seeing Spock, Ruanek hastened forward, his eyes blazing with all his old impulsiveness. Twenty years on Vulcan sufficed— barely—to allow Ruanek to keep his face impassive; within the privacy of his thoughts, the Romulan exile was probably dancing with eagerness and the curiosity that Vulcans and Romulans, even this long after the Sundering, still shared. His wife, Healer T'Selis, who served as the representative of the adepts, philosophers, and priests on Mount Seleya to this project, touched Ruanek's sleeve with two fingers. Presumably, she was suggesting more control. Presumably, she would have little effect.

"Your father's suggestions helped us break the encryption algorithms," Ruanek told Spock, making a laudable effort to speak more slowly. "Once we completed the translation, we knew the time was right to contact you."

Spock nodded. Combined with the artifact's own arcane and ancient technology, the encryption algorithms that concealed the artifact's message had been so complex, so elegant that they had earned even Ambassador Sarek's admiration before he set off for the . . . Even in the heart of the Vulcan Science Academy, Ruanek would not permit himself to mention the secret conference from which he had extracted Spock. Even after twenty years of exile, he retained a respect for secrets.

Nevertheless, Spock felt his eyebrow rise before he could suppress it. It was too much to have expected that either Ruanek or, for that matter, Saavik herself could have withheld any information from Sarek that he wished to have. Both owed him too much and both cared for him too much. Besides, withholding information from Sarek would not just have been illogical, it would have been unkind. Sarek had found this new type of data storage fascinating.

Spock made a mental note to meditate on the subject so that he could regard any input from his father as beneficial: no doubt, Sarek would give him a private critique when he returned to Vulcan.

Ruanek gestured toward the worktable on which the artifact rested. Resembling a priestly crown from the days before Surak, it gleamed with green gems, wound with wires of copper, gold, and hyponeutronium. It was no ornament, though, but one of the most sophisticated recording devices he had ever encountered: it recorded thoughts, memories, sensations, and emotions without harming its wearer.

Ruanek handed Spock a padd, and Spock scanned the long-awaited translation. The original language, he saw immediately, was indeed Old High Vulcan. Fascinating.

Some of the awkwardness of this initial translation had to be attributable to the difficulty in penetrating the artifact's encryption. As for the rest of it—whoever had created this message used language in extremely private ways, as if the words themselves were codes for the emotions Spock sensed roiling beneath.

This preliminary translation was not satisfactory! Spock wanted to say. He wanted to know so much more, and he wanted to know instantly.

Before Saavik or Ruanek could stop him, he reached out for the coronet and set it on his head. As filaments darted out from its bloodmetal flanges and pricked his temples, he stiffened in shock, but restrained himself from crying out.

Spock had shared his mind before. He had carried Kollos's mind for a time, and melded with everything from humans to a Horta with only minimal discomfort.

Now, however, a rush of sensation and emotions assaulted him. He steeled himself to endure the barrage. Because this record dated from before the great success of Surak's teaching, it was only logical that its author was not just emotional, but passionately so.

This must be what McCoy had endured in carrying his *katra,*

Spock deduced in a second of revelation. Then, the message in the ancient coronet overpowered all other thoughts.

Dimly, as if his eyes were already in someone else's control, he saw Ruanek and Saavik race forward. T'Selis stepped in between them and Spock.

"Kroykah!" she commanded softly.

She brought up a medical tricorder and scanned Spock before meeting Ruanek's anxious eyes and Saavik's face, which had frozen into a mask of control. The Healer shrugged. It was all the reassurance she could in conscience provide.

Disappointed that you didn't volunteer first? Spock thought at his wife and his friend. He knew them so well. Why hadn't they volunteered? Because they hadn't dared? Not likely.

Because he would never have forgiven them? Also unlikely. He wanted to find an answer, but he was finding it harder and harder to pursue his train of thought, harder to . . .

Where was he? This didn't look like the Vulcan Science Institute he remembered.

Who were these people? Why was one of them shouting? How strange they sounded. Surely, they could not be native to ShiKahr. They had no legitimate cause for alarm, not on his account. He tried to tell them so, but so many thoughts were warring in his head that he could not speak.

He managed to raise an ironic eyebrow before his consciousness was engulfed.

And Spock *remembered* . . .

TWO

MEMORY

Karatek took up the recorder, admiring its ambiguous beauty. Its inventors had wrought it in the form of a coronet of the te-Vikram priest-kings, blood-green gems and precious metal concealing a highly effective technology that the rest of Vulcan would have warred over, assuming they had known about it.

The coronet's sensor panels were hotter by far than the heat of his body, bred as it had been on the deserts of the Mother World, which he would never see again if all went well.

"If I forget thee, O Vulcan, let my eyes lose their fire, my blood lose its flame, and my intellect its keenness."

The coronet's heat was as welcome as Karatek's ship, the *Shavokh*, was cold. In the last pirate attack, three decks had suffered hull breaches and been repaired at tremendous risk to those who survived, as his youngest child—Lovar, even his *katra* lost! —had not.

Because supplies were short and the Exiles no longer needed

the space, those decks were put on envirosave, and life-support throughout the entire ship had been reduced. Now every person on board who wished to maintain even a minimal level of fitness had to exercise for hours daily to preserve body mass and strength. Their breath chilled their lungs as they fought for it, and no one remembered what it was like to be truly warm.

But what did physical discomfort matter when Vulcan-in-Exile was still alive? Even if that was a rhetorical question, Karatek thought with a warming spasm of resentment, it was an important one and needed to be considered.

Not all the generation ships that had abandoned Vulcan 80.45 years ago had survived this far. This far from Vulcan—and from refit capabilities—the great ships had worn out faster than any of the defense scientists and other experts, himself included, had projected. And, Karatek estimated, pausing to make the calculation, there was a 76.99 percent chance that none of them would survive for the time it would take to reach the next planetary system with *Minshara*-class planets. In the privacy of his thoughts, he preferred not to calculate how long that journey might take.

Logic and exact calculations aside, planetfall seemed impossibly far off. So everything must be preserved, from recycled parts to the emotions of this exile—the anger and the hope and the bitterness. Let the future and more distressingly logical generations toward which Surak's true followers strove to diminish their people study this record and see from what rough beginnings they had evolved.

Holding the glittering recorder, Karatek indulged himself in the sensation of warmth that spread from it out along both of his hands. Ironically, the recorder resembled a coronet from the most ancient of days when all Vulcan, not just a few tyrannies, had Ruling Kings.

The crown's sparkling blood-green crystals were set in hyponeutronium. The treated alloy, a spinoff from the weapons program that had been the focus of Karatek's own career, was not just incredibly durable, but capable, when treated properly, of superconductivity. Gems and metal, combined, however grudgingly, with the science of the adepts at Seleya and Gol, formed part of a psionic system that fused machine and wearer.

United to Karatek's mind, this recorder could enable him to create the most vivid record possible of his comrades, his life, and his acquaintance with Surak, the visionary whose teachings had sent 85,974 Vulcans off into the eternal night into Exile.

It was logical that Karatek, as one of the 694 surviving members of the Exiles' Council, be one of those who risked themselves to leave such a record. Logical, but not wholly without risk. Captured documentation from some of the scientists—assuming the magi and inquisitors of the renegade te-Vikram priest-kings deserved the title "scientist"—who had invented this recorder's prototypes had been grisly. Some early versions of the recorders had melted, their metal fusing to experimental subjects' skulls. Other subjects had been lost, their minds trapped forever within the gleaming crystals that now housed their memories in the Hall of Ancient Thought where not even the te-Vikram could be denied access.

Did the Halls of Ancient Thought still stand? Did Vulcan still exist as more than a collection of radioactive asteroids and dust, in orbit around its bloody sun?

Even though Karatek knew those questions would never be answered, at least not in his lifetime, he could not stop himself from asking them. Now, however, there was no logic in looking into the recorder's glittering crystals without taking action—and even less logic in further delay.

He drew in three deep, rhythmic breaths. This latest model of the recorder had enhanced fail-safes built in. If a circuit showed signs of malfunction or sensors detected severe psychic distress, the recorder would shut down. The peril, their last surviving Healer-adept had trained him to remember, lay only in overuse. Although Karatek had used the recorder before, he had never worn it for as long as he now planned. He thought he remained well within his physical and mental endurance levels. If he did not, however, well, the need was sufficient.

Karatek shut his eyes, preparing his mind. He recalled Vulcan. The embattled world that circled its huge, angry red star so far from them might not survive. That thought had waked him on the lonely watches of the ship's night more times than he wished to recall. But even if the Mother World had died, the soul of Vulcan—these people, this heritage, these memories—would last if Karatek had to pour his own blood into the ship's engines in a final sacrifice.

His hope, his willingness, and his furious desire to survive might be illogical, but they were so.

And if the Exiles were not the only Vulcans in the galaxy, if the warring tribes and factions fortunate enough to remain on the Mother World managed not to reduce it to radioactive asteroids in their ceaseless, senseless civil wars, it would be the duty of Vulcan-in-Exile, one day, to leave whatever refuge they had found and bring these memories home. His duty and that of his descendants.

Even if they never survived to make planetfall, some other race, more logical in its choices, might find the *Shavokh,* or one of the other surviving remnants of Vulcan's exile fleet, derelict in space and, finding these records, learn from them.

As Surak had taught them, what was, was. But there were always possibilities.

Surak himself had seen that. Karatek had been with him for some of that time. He remembered, and now it was time to pass on those memories. Yielding to the logic of this situation and the decision he had made, Karatek placed the recorder on his head.

Immediately, the invasion he had trained himself to accept assaulted his consciousness. He let his defenses fall: resistance would damage brain and synapses.

There is no pain, he chanted silently. *There is no pain.*

And then, there was not. Images and thoughts formed in his mind, flowed into the crystals, and would be preserved as long as their lattices survived.

"I am Karatek, physicist, once of ShiKahr, a citizen of Vulcan-in-Exile, on board the Shavokh . . ."

How sweet the rush of sensations was: the Forge at dawn, the sweetness of the desert wind, the sweep of a *shavokh* across the sky, the rustles, bells, cries of a procession of pilgrims—as if he stood in ShiKahr, watching the Gates. A tear slid down his cheek: the logical consequence of such memories.

On such a day, Surak had walked out of the desert, wrenching Karatek's life as well as that of the battered Mother World into new patterns.

Karatek remembered . . .

The swift, one-person riser brought Karatek to Vulcan's surface just as the all-clear sounded. He stepped outside the Vulcan Space Institute's defensive shields onto the sand, ochre shading into the true crimson of the deep desert.

The sky was clear. In his thoughts, Karatek praised the foresight that had buried ShiKahr's factories that labored to build the ships that would one day carry Vulcans from their own skies out to the stars. Not only had they reduced pollution to such a degree that, from the Gates of ShiKahr, Karatek could see the Forge more clearly than at any time since he had taken his *kahs-wan,* it had protected them from the sneak attacks that had turned similar facilities at ShanaiKahr into a glassy pit.

The haze from those last explosions had subsided. Now, as Karatek began to record the daily test results for atmospheric radioactivity and biotoxins, his badge glowed the green of healthy blood. Today, he would not require decontamination treatments. The wind that had blown radiation from the new craters on the Forge had turned: it was safe to be outside without protective gear. No ash from battle or from Seleya, in its active eruptions phase once more, clouded his view, and the hot wind was sweet. Karatek glanced out again toward the distant Forge.

A faint whine alerted him to ships patrolling overhead. He raised a hand to salute ShiKahr's guardians. He had worked on those ships' propulsion systems, the first generation of the mighty engines that he hoped would one day propel the Great Ships now under very slow construction. If only the funding continued to flow!

It had been bad enough when only the te-Vikram priest-kings opposed the decision of the Vulcan Space Initiative to settle here in ShiKahr, the last city before the Forge on the road that leads past Mount Seleya to the Sea. Since ancient times, Karatek thought, pilgrims could count on robbers: the te-Vikram were only the latest, and possibly the worst, in a long line of predators. It was not their attacks on travelers that concerned Karatek about the te-Vikram; it was their assault on thinking minds.

To Karatek's mind, a greater problem was the new political party that was gaining power in the Vulcan Assembly. They were technocrats, which many thought made them the Vulcan Space Initative's natural allies—but they were also utilitarian and pragmatic. They would fund the building of ships if they were warships or if they enabled Vulcan miners to exploit the resources of the outer worlds. But ships that could make the great voyages out beyond Vulcan's star system, engines that might be developed at later times that could leap the speed of light: unless they saw a practical—indeed, a near-term financial—reason for such ships, the technocrats opposed them.

The te-Vikram wanted to destroy the VSI. The technocrats wanted it to serve their own ends—bigger and better warships; bigger and better weapons. They were as bloody-minded as the te-Vikram, rational as they sometimes sounded in debate.

The ships passed out of range, leaving Karatek in silence. Then the faintest of shadows fell across him, and he looked up. Night, day, and sweet water . . . why, it was a sundweller, its fragile, iridescent wings unfurled to take advantage of every possible breath of air, glinting as they reflected Nevasa's light. Sundwellers spent their lives soaring through Vulcan's thin atmosphere, mating in the air, dying aloft, with only fragments of their gleaming wings ever uniting with the desert. Not even the hungriest *shavokh* would hunt a sundweller. Karatek honestly had thought they were extinct, extinguished by time or poisoned by the wars raging on his beloved, beleaguered world.

Ancient legends held that seeing a sundweller was an omen. It meant your fate was changing, or dramatic times were coming, or some such superstition that Karatek, scientist that he was, scoffed at. He could explain the physics of a sundweller's flight, the biology that powered its fragile metabolism; but he could not explain why seeing one gave him such a shock of joy, and he refused to analyze it.

Overhead, the sundweller banked, turned, and swooped. Karatek watched it until even the faintest gleam of sunlight on its wings vanished. He would tell his wife, T'Vysse, about the sundweller tonight. She had a poet's soul. She too would rejoice.

He smiled at the Gates of ShiKahr, over which the sundweller had flown. The current cease-fire meant more people were passing through, either out to the shrines in the deep desert or on their way to the sea or on their way to those of the inland cities on this continent that still would receive guest-friends from afar. That too was a breach of custom that Karatek, modern as he was, regretted.

Beyond the Gates, two immense flanged pylons of cracked green stone, half-buried in the sand, trudged a caravan, its cargo loaded onto guarded armored carriers that resembled nothing so much as gigantic metal versions of deep-desert *myrmidex,* creeping across the waste.

Heading unescorted through the Gates was a group of pilgrims bound for the waters and the shrines at Seleya. Today, blue-white lightning danced on its snowcapped peak. Karatek checked the scanners once more: there was a 73.22 percent chance of an eruption in the next five days.

Scientist though he was, Karatek liked to think that those pilgrims included a family, much like his own, Seleya-bound to give thanks that an only son born to older parents had survived his *kahs-wan.* He heard the tinkle of bells and the shrill ring of systra accompanying the ladies, veiled and deadly, who swayed on russet-furred *vai-sehlaten* gengineered for riding. Their fangs would be capped with bloodmetal and would glitter with inset gems.

On a previous occasion, Karatek had seen a procession of priests, accompanying a penitent victor in a wedding challenge. He had watched maimed veterans wearing the sigils of captains of hosts or clan-heads, plus all their other honors, bearing jade or gold ritual weapons as they marched onto the Forge to surrender for the only time in their lives. He had even seen one of the heavily guarded wains of the te-Vikram, headed for the Forge and the Womb of Fire beyond it.

One day, if the war ever ceased and if the ships ever got off the ground, Karatek hoped to cross the desert himself to Gol, to study the progress of the scholar-priests in unlocking the arts of the mind.

But that would be another day's adventure. For now, Karatek was happy building ships. Usually, he managed not to think of what the tremendous engines, the shapely hulls, and the raw power of the weapons would be used for.

The day was quiet. Usually, he saw at least one group of protestors—anything from religious environmentalists to political fanatics to the te-Vikram, who combined both elements with a perversion of ancient Vulcan history and weren't, Karatek thought, above some viciously effective terrorism. One more well-placed assassination, and the constant low-grade skirmishes could explode into total war. It might be the last war on Vulcan: no one knew better than Karatek how powerful the weapons were in both sides' armories. Vulcan had seen far more than its share of war. How had the Mother World managed to survive this long?

A shadow distracted him from the darkness of his thoughts.

Right beneath the sundweller's glide path, a tiny blur formed on the sand.

Karatek narrowed his eyes: the blur shimmered, then resolved. Three men wearing hooded robes almost ragged with long use approached ShiKahr's Gates on foot. They were not just unguarded and unarmed; they carried not so much as a water flask or a blanket against the chill of the desert nights.

Only four types of men walked the desert thus: pilgrims, madmen, ritual suicides, and prophets. The groups were almost indistinguishable from one another.

Had Karatek not just mused that the world had changed, and not for the better? Here was his opportunity to redress that in some small way.

Slapping his palm against the sensors to signal that he was off shift, he hastened toward the security checkpoint beside the ancient Gates. There he found the newcomers. They were arguing with three guards. Though the guards retained the helms of ancient designs (enhanced by a heads-up display), their ceremonial *lirpa*s were stacked against a wall, and their *ahn woon* were wrapped about their waists beside their com gear. So far, none of the three had drawn shockers or stunners.

Karatek stopped and blinked so forcibly that the Veils almost covered his eyes. Immured as he was underground for most of the day, he actually recognized one of the men from those newsnets that still covered demonstrations. The cropped hair, lighter than the Vulcan norm; the thoughtful eyes that were the color of still water, deep-set in a face pale despite its exposure to the deep-desert sun; the fine features so in contrast with a warrior's frame. Day and night, it was Surak himself.

Karatek had read his monographs, written in the days when Surak had been a scientist rather than—depending on the speaker's politics—a political nuisance, a zealot, or a philosopher. On a planet littered with creeds, philosophies, and factions, Surak's party was one of the most recent, one of the smallest, and surely the most strange.

He had last been spotted heading into the desert from an unauthorized exit point. A cursory search had been conducted, but official hopes were that he'd been eaten by *le-matya*s.

Now, two guards approached him, electronic binders in hand. The lights that signified activation—albeit on the lowest pain threshold—winked green and blue. Creeping up behind them, quiet as a hunting *le-matya* despite his height, was a sallow, angry man. Taller and thinner than Surak, he had stretched arms out toward the guards in a violently businesslike way.

"Do you know who we are?" shouted the third man, younger than the others.

"Obviously, they do, Varen," said Surak. "Or they would not seek to detain us. Skamandros, stand down: violence is simply illogic by physical means."

One of the guards (the one, in fact, holding the cuffs) whirled, horrified to find Skamandros almost upon him. Karatek stifled a laugh. This was like some of the stories he'd read as a boy, before his parents reminded him he had scholarships to win.

No learning is ever wasted, he reminded himself before he drew a deep breath and shouted, "I offer these strangers guest-right!"

THREE

NOW

JANUARY 2377
ONE YEAR AFTER THE END OF THE DOMINION WAR

It was, Spock thought, looking calmly about, quite a charming scene despite the distraction of the milling, noisy crowds. The grounds of Starfleet Headquarters were green with new grass and newly replanted bushes, and all the broken windows had been replaced. In fact, the whole complex looked as if there had never been a war at all, and the fountains were playing normally once more, their water sparkling in the sunlight.

To one side of the great lawn, a large viewscreen had been set up, carefully placed so as to not block the guests' view of the region.

It was indeed a worthwhile view. From here, where all the guests stood, the land sloped gently down, giving them a clear sight out over the bay and the perfectly rebuilt orange arch of the

Golden Gate Bridge, and on to the rolling brown and green hills of the old Marin County. Those hills bore only a few crater scars, already a fuzzy green with new growth.

The weather was agreeable enough as well, Spock thought, the type of day that he understood was a normal one for autumn in San Francisco. It was a little chilly for a Vulcan, but his dark ambassadorial robes, gleaming with their Federation insignia and Vulcan sigils, kept him warm enough. "Normal" in this Earthly climate meant sun, clear blue skies, cool temperatures—pleasantly so, at least for the humans in the gathering—and, since it was early in the day, none of the fog that formed with almost precise timing out over the Pacific Ocean every day in the late afternoon.

It was quite logical for Starfleet to have moved the event outdoors. Even considering the vast size of the headquarters' main hall, it still would have been uncomfortably crowded. For this, Spock thought, was a sight that had never yet been seen in all the years of the Federation. There were ever-growing throngs of senior diplomats of many species in their robes, suits, flowing shawls, or their own fur—a rainbow of colors mixing, blending, or clashing—and officers of the Federation, also of many species, in their somber red dress uniforms glittering with insignia of rank.

What made it out of the ordinary, though, was that this wild mixture of Federation members was joined by members of the Federation's two uneasy imperial allies: the Klingon Empire and the Romulan Star Empire.

The Romulans, as was typical dress for them in official functions, were a sober lot in their broad-shouldered uniforms of dull silver crossed by sashes of rank. The Klingons, by comparison, were a cheerfully gaudy group with their red, black, and bright silver House baldrics glittering with signs of clan and rank. A few of the Klingons were even bearing tall red and black House banners.

Spock permitted himself the tiniest upward crook of one corner of his mouth, in pleasure. What made this event unique was the fact that all were gathered here in peace and even good spirits.

Perhaps there is yet hope even for Unification.

A subclan of five small Oriki, looking like bipedal, chittering meerkats in cheerful red and yellow robes, scurried past him, then stopped short in recognition and, all five of them, gave him a credible imitation of the Vulcan salute. Spock, who had served a major role in bringing their planet into the Federation, politely returned the salute, and heard their delighted chittering continue as they scurried on.

The Oriki are always *in good spirits,* Spock thought, *regardless of the situation. Fascinating.*

Two Andorians, their blue faces standing out against their startlingly scarlet ambassadorial robes, nodded to Spock with professional courtesy, their antennae tipping in his direction. One Andorian was a tall, lean *thaan,* the other a tall, lean *zhen.* "Ambassador Spock."

He recognized them after a split second. "Ambassador th'Telos, Ambassador zh'Shaav."

Th'Telos, clearly attempting the unfamiliarity of small talk with an effort, quipped, "It is truly amazing to see no fighting in so large and mixed a group."

And zh'Shaav added, her antennae rippling as she spoke, "Will it last, I wonder?"

"There is, as the humans say, always hope," Spock replied.

Accepting the logic of his observation, the Andorians walked off without further comment.

"Ah, Ambassador Spock!"

Spock, his robes sweeping about him in dignified folds as he turned, saw the reason for their retreat. It was George M'beni, tall and lean as the Andorians, but as always eager as a child. M'beni was Earth's ambassador to Nikari, and made a perfect ambassador to the perpetually optimistic Nikariki. But right now, as he practically beamed at Spock, his intense cheerfulness seemed almost as overwhelming to the Vulcan as the endless chittering of the Oriki.

"Quite a sight, isn't it?" the human exclaimed. "I'd say every dignitary who could wangle an invitation is here, from all the Federation worlds, as well as the delegations from Romulus and Qo'noS. It's the first time I've seen Headquarters look downright crowded. Fortunate that everyone's on his, her, or its best behavior."

"It is," Spock agreed politely.

They would, logically, all be minding their manners, given that they were all gathered here to commemorate the war and celebrate what everyone here honestly hoped would be a bright future. But Spock had already been waylaid by enthusiastic Klingons, enthusiastic Starfleet officers, the Oriki, the Andorians, and now, it would seem, enthusiastic fellow ambassadors.

Fortunate for me that I have had those years of training in self-control while serving aboard the Enterprise. *Dealing with Jim and Dr. McCoy—especially with Dr. McCoy—has stood me in good stead.*

A slender figure in a Starfleet captain's red collar moved to Spock's side: Saavik, rescuing her husband from the emotional M'beni, who politely bowed and moved away. Ignoring the undeniably emotional little thrill of pleasure suddenly warming him at Saavik's hand on his arm, Spock murmured to his wife, "Should you not be with the other Starfleet officers?"

"Marriage to a Vulcan ambassador overrules Starfleet protocol."

Their different careers took them away from each other for far longer and far more frequently than either would have wished. But separations had never yet weakened their bond for each other.

Parted and never parted.

Never and always touching and touched.

The words of their marriage vow echoed in Spock's mind.

"Amazing," Saavik said. "No one has so much as threatened to draw a weapon on anyone."

"Nor has anyone begun shouting for better terms."

"It won't last."

Spock raised an eyebrow. "You, my wife, are becoming what humans call a cynic."

One corner of her mouth curled up in what only another Vulcan could have identified as a grin. "And you, my husband, have already become what humans call a cockeyed optimist."

"Perhaps, perhaps not. My wife, let us, *as the humans might say,* simply watch the show."

"Gentlebeings," a clearly amplified voice proclaimed with professional good cheer, "look up!"

Now the second reason for them all being outdoors was made clear. Overhead, three sleek flights of ships—Federation, Klingon, and Romulan—roared by, each in perfect close formation.

A great deal of diplomacy had gone into which planet's squadron should go first, and how many ships should constitute a squadron. The Klingons had agreed to leave it to chance, and the Romulans, great gamblers that they were, had agreed. So first, by the luck of the draw, zoomed four sleek silver ships of the Federation in perfect diamond formation, then four fierce dark green vessels of the Klingons, also in diamond formation ("Anything you can do, we can do better"), and last, the deadly blood-green Romulan ships in their own formation. That it closely resembled diamond formation was, of course, merely coincidence.

As each squadron in turn dipped down toward the sweeping orange arc of the newly rebuilt Golden Gate Bridge, one ship from each government peeled off in the human custom of the "missing man" formation. The Federation personnel stood at attention. The Romulans and Klingons had been briefed about the meaning of the gesture; both cultures understood far too well the custom of giving honor to fallen heroes. The Romulans saluted, clenched fists to chests, all of them as one, in perfect precision, and the Klingons threw back their heads and gave wild howls of tribute.

Spock and Saavik exchanged glances, saying a great deal without words. For that instant, the three powers had actually been acting and feeling as one.

"Wouldn't it be wonderful if the moment could last?" Saavik asked. "If we could all stay so amazingly unified. Of course," she added, "that is logically not possible."

There was less than a .00035563 chance of such an intense feeling of unity lasting any longer than it took for the ships to zoom out of sight. But Spock had spent so much time and effort in bringing the three powers at least this far that he felt obliged to defend them.

"It is logical to postulate that some form of the alliance will continue," he said. "The Klingon Empire, under Chancellor Martok, continues to favor a partnership with the Federation, at least. And the Romulans, we both know, are pragmatic enough to see a continued alliance as useful."

Saavik, half-Romulan herself, raised a wry eyebrow. "At least for now. Assuming that nothing goes wrong."

"Worry about the future," Spock told his wife, "is a human trait."

She smiled ever so slightly and retaliated by seemingly accidentally brushing a finger across his hand. To a touch telepath, that was as powerful as a passionate kiss, and it sent an involuntary little shiver down Spock's spine.

"That," he said, "is not the issue."

"It can be," she said demurely with a sly little sideways glance. "I do have leave right now, after all, and I believe you are not on assignment just now, either, my husband."

He crooked up an eyebrow. "Fascinating."

"Is it not?"

But suddenly there was a roar of static that stopped their gentle flirtation and silenced the crowd. "Look!" someone yelled.

An image was forming on the great viewscreen, crackling and flickering with interference. Part of the celebration, surely, sent in from some distant Federation world.

But then the crowd cried out in shock, the Romulan voices fierce above the others, as one figure suddenly was clear on the screen:

"A Romulan woman," Saavik said sharply.

"A Romulan officer," Spock added, then corrected himself. "More precisely, a proconsul; that is a proconsul's uniform."

The woman was disheveled, her uniform torn and stained, and a long green streak of blood trailed down the side of her face. Smoke and flames surged up around her, hiding the rest of the image.

"I am Proconsul Terik," she reported against a background of steady explosions and gunfire, "of the Romulan Star Empire colony Nemor. This day, at Third Hour, a fleet of alien ships was sighted crossing out of the Neutral Zone into Romulan territory, heading toward Nemor. When they were challenged by Nemor's forces, the alien vessels offered no communication but directly opened fire."

At her gesture, the scene shifted to a taped view looking out from the colony into space.

What are those ships? Spock wondered. *The design . . . it is not like any I know, and yet . . . there is something almost familiar . . . something out of history, perhaps . . .*

Spock dropped surmise, watching, as shocked as everyone else, as the aliens took out each Romulan ship that challenged them, destroying the ships with blasts of eerie green flame, with what seemed contemptuous ease.

The image returned to the despairing proconsul. "The attackers do not appear Klingon . . ." ("They are not!" the Klingons roared.) ". . . or Federation, and certainly not Vulcan. No one on our colony has ever seen such bizarre ship configurations—and no Romulan has ever died like this!"

A horrendous blast shook the image, and for a moment it was lost to wildly shifting bands of interference. Then it cleared, at least enough to show Proconsul Terik grimly facing the screen. "That last attack destroyed the colony's shield generators," she said. "Our land-based defenses cannot hold out much longer. It is the end for us. I send this message to Praetor Neral on the homeworld: He must know what happened here! All the Empire must know! This cowardly attack against a colony world must be avenged."

Terik's eyes widened. Her face hardened in resolution. "Life to the Empire!" she cried.

A blazing nova of green flame engulfed her world—and then the screen went dark.

The crowd exploded into chaos, everyone shouting at once, and the Romulans' shouts were even fiercer than that of the Klingons.

But before anyone could say anything constructive, a new image formed on the screen. The crowd fell deathly silent, staring. This was the eerie, shell-like face of an unknown alien—

No, Spock thought. What they were seeing was some form of ceremonial mask, a perfect, featureless oval of so dark a green that it was almost black, and ornamented with etched zigzags from top to bottom like so many lightning bolts. The mask covered the alien's face so completely that only the occasional hints of dark blue eyes could be seen.

The alien's voice boomed out, cold and utterly without emotion, "I am a Watraii. You do not know this name yet, but you shall. You will come to learn it and to fear and respect it as well. For we are a wronged people, a race denied its rightful home. Hear me, you who watch. My people lay claim to the homeworlds of our kind. We lay claim to nothing less than the worlds you call Romulus and Remus."

"No!" a Romulan cried.

"Impossible!"

"This cannot—"

"How dare they—"

"Who are—"

"Ours is a right and just claim," the alien who called himself Watraii continued relentlessly. "Hear and understand: These two worlds you claim are *not* your property or heritage! You are mere beggars, homeless wanderers—you are not native to our worlds!"

That much, Spock thought, was true—but that did not justify the destruction of innocents.

"Those worlds once belonged to the Watraii," the masked figure continued fiercely. "It is *our* people who are the wronged ones, *our* people who were forced into exile by the usurpers and killers who now call themselves Romulans. But hear me, all of you, and know I speak for the Watraii. These worlds will belong to us again!"

The screen went blank.

The crowd erupted into a wild new roar of shouts, screeches, screams, yells, and trumpetings. Over it all, the Romulans could be heard shouting in what seemed genuine outrage, "Lies! Foul lies!"

Are *they lies?* Spock wondered. *If they are not . . .*

Were he human, he would no doubt have been despairing right now. If the aliens really could prove that the Romulans were guilty of atrocities, it would end the hope of any Romulan-Federation alliance. The Romulans didn't have the might to fight a war over what to them would be a horrible loss of honor—and the resulting chaos might not just destabilize their government, it might destroy them. But if the Watraii had no just claim after all, if it turned out that they had destroyed the colony without even the flimsy argument of revenge—that could lead to a hopeless war as well.

We cannot let either catastrophe happen. Those who live today cannot be blamed for what happened in the long-ago past. We cannot let destruction come in any form, for any reason, not to the Sundered, our own cousins, not to the Federation, not to any of our allies.

Spock and Saavik exchanged a second quick, understanding glance. For all the fine words of alliance that both sides were declaiming right now, he and she knew perfectly well that the Federation was not going to get involved in this, especially not right after a war. Besides, there were too many hard memories between both sides, and too many in the Federation who wouldn't want to help Romulans.

But . . . there is someone who might be able to help. In fact, the only one who might.

As soon as he could, Spock slipped away to contact Admiral Uhura.

FOUR

MEMORY

"You can't do that!" The tallest guard whirled just in time to stop the lean man Surak had called Skamandros from edging up behind him and catching his neck in viselike fingers.

A second guard took young Varen and began to fit his wrists with binders. Prudently, he offered no resistance.

The tall guard chuckled. "That's a good one, *T'Kehr* Karatek. I thought they kept you scientists too busy down there working on the gods only know what sort of demon's snare to remember the old ways. Didn't you, Subcommander?" He turned to his superior officer, who was moving in on Surak, binders in hand.

As Karatek met his eyes, the subcommander deactivated the binders' charge.

"Will you still dare to arrest them now that I stand as their host, Ivek?" Karatek asked. Subcommander Ivek and he were old acquaintances: schoolmates, in fact, and friends until the last war, when an argument over politics had divided them.

"Your own subordinate's reaction gives you away. I know you know that law is still on the books," Karatek told him. "But, if you don't believe me, call in to headquarters. You never did have much of a memory. And history was never your subject."

"There is no logic in shaming a man as he seeks to perform his duty," Surak spoke up in the pure High Vulcan for which ShiKahr had been famous before the Vulcan Space Initiative had focused on technology, not ancient learning. "To save the sub-commander the trouble, here is the relevant citation: 'Once a freeholder and citizen offers fire and water, claiming a stranger as guest-friend, he stands surety for the guest-friend's conduct and his debts.' "

Ivek burst out laughing. "You! Here we all hear that Surak is supposed to be the great one for logic! So, here we are, trying to arrest you. Karatek here has offered to take you in; and you reprimand *him,* then quote me the law? That's not just illogical, that's incongruous!"

"I but speak the truth," said Surak. "Laughter in the face of truth is superfluous emotionalism."

Ivek subsided, flushing green at the reprimand. *The blade of Surak's wit carries two edges,* Karatek thought.

The newcomer raised his hand, his fingers parted. "Live long and prosper, Karatek of ShiKahr. I am Surak. I come to serve. Your offer honors me."

"And your service honors me," responded Karatek, raising his hand and struggling somewhat with the formal salute that few educated, city-dwelling Vulcans used these days, except when taking oaths. Generations ago, the greeting had meant that you held no weapon in your hand. But now that most weapons were fired from a distance, many sophisticated people claimed the old greeting was obsolete—to say nothing of dishonest. There were many people whom one did not wish to live long and prosper or to enjoy peace and long life.

Did Surak know what he was saying? Karatek thought he did. But did *Karatek?* Clearly, Ivek at least had some doubts.

"Karatek, think about what you're doing!" Ivek hissed at him. "These men have come to ShiKahr to break the peace as they've broken it halfway across the North Continent."

"A more accurate estimation of our distance traveled is 42 percent. 42.85 percent, to be more precise," Surak said. "Subcommander Ivek, if you accept that we are under *T'Kehr* Karatek's recognizance, may I ask you to release my associates?"

"My life answers for their acts." For the first time, Karatek spoke the ritual words in comprehension of the risks that lay behind them. Once uttered, his promise could not be withdrawn.

Ivek shook his head at his comrades. "You heard the *T'Kehr.* He always was a rash one, even when we were in school. It's his blood on the sands if these people . . . disappoint him. So we'll just let him unbind these . . . these guest-friends of his. Peace and long life indeed, Karatek. It would make more sense to wish you good luck, but I daresay this philosopher you're taking in off the sands would say luck wasn't *logical* either."

"People make their own futures," said Surak, inclining his head to the guards. "They call you *T'Kehr?*" he asked. As he turned to Karatek, the scientist was struck by the intensity of his eyes in his controlled face. "May I ask . . . ?"

"Senior research scientist at the Vulcan Space Initiative, though I've been doing a lot of engineering these days. High-performance engines."

"Then your claiming my associates and me as guest-friends is indeed a desirable outcome," Surak said.

"Perhaps you will explain tonight," said Karatek. "But only

after you have received water and fire, as the law says, and you've had a chance at a meal and some rest."

Varen, years younger than the other two and of the sort whose courage and strength flared up brightly, then subsided, looked up at Karatek's words. Visibly, he suppressed a smile. Even Skamandros unbent slightly.

"If you will lead the way . . . *T'Kehr?*" Surak suggested to his host. Behind him, the guards straightened to attention, while Ivek, their commanding officer, shrugged.

What have I let myself in for? Karatek wondered.

He suspected that Surak would consider second thoughts illogical.

Smaller than the classic villas built during the height of the nomad raids, Karatek's house had high walls that resembled those much older dwellings. The entry bridge that arched over a deep trench lined with sharp stones creaked beneath their feet. Traditionally, those creaks served as a warning to those inside, but it was a warning augmented now by modern locks and sensors embedded in the fire-hardened wood gates, reinforced by panels of metal weathered almost blood green and etched by sandstorms.

The gates opened as Karatek's small party approached. He led them past the protective outer wall, through a shaded entryway's pleasurably cool shadows, and into the courtyard around which his home was built. He had only the one courtyard that must serve for guests as well as for more private family life; these days, however, most Vulcans' time was so caught up in work or the war effort (frequently related) that the ceremonies of welcome, of meal preparation, of relaxation had all but vanished from their routines.

At the far end of the courtyard was a garden of blood-green plants, some spiny, some blossoming, interspersed with standing stones. On one side of the garden, the sand was raked into traditional patterns. On the other, Karatek saw heat-shimmer rising above the raised firepit with its broad lip that could serve as a table.

In the center of the courtyard was the fountain, symbol of the presence of water that made this home possible. Seated on a heavy bloodstone bench beside it was Karatek's wife, T'Vysse.

Didn't her modern history classes meet at this hour? Karatek thought. It was a matter for reproach, he confessed to himself, that he no longer knew T'Vysse's schedule as well as his own. So, Ivek had apparently not regarded Karatek's promise of guest-friendship as closing his inquiry. He must have taken it upon himself to call T'Vysse at the Academy.

"My wife," Karatek intoned properly. He walked to her side and touched his fingers to hers with more warmth than was strictly necessary. Logic be damned to the Womb of Fire, a man had a right to enjoy coming home, and he'd been sleeping in his office for the past three days. As always, he marveled that his wife's patience still held. Their marriage bond had been a family arrangement that could have been dissolved at any time after both Houses had been supplied with heirs. Instead, it had blossomed into something that delighted and awed Karatek every time he looked at T'Vysse.

She was tall and slender, with hair that gleamed like obsidian, secured by jade clasps. Her face was serene, her movements collected. And, as she straightened the fold of sleeve his gesture had disarranged, she awarded him a look that clearly promised that later on, they would have Words.

Later for you too, my own, he thought, meaning something altogether different. Her fingers moved against his, a sign she understood.

"I am T'Vysse, consort of Karatek," she told his three companions. "I welcome thee to the sanctity of our home."

The old, formal words. Trust a historian to know them, or, at the very least, to have looked them up fast.

Surak went formally to one knee, bowing his head. Not as deeply as for a matriarch or a priestess, but enough to show respect.

T'Vysse inclined her head, put out her hand, but did not touch her guest's head: that benediction was reserved for priestesses. From the carved stone lip of the fountain, she took up three stone cups. They were ancient, carved from a tree petrified so long ago that none of its descendants survived, and so thin that the setting sun shone crimson through them. Filling them with water from the fountain, she held them out to Surak, Varen, and Skamandros.

"Fire and water be thine, my guests," she said in the Old High Vulcan of ceremony. "Thee shall be taken to guest rooms where fresh clothing awaits while a meal is prepared."

Karatek cast T'Vysse a puzzled look. They had only the one guest room; the other bedrooms were for their children, the two sons and the daughter whose loss to a terrorist "incident" still made T'Vysse flinch at loud noises.

"Our children are with my parents, lest they disturb our guests," she explained. Which translated as T'Vysse's unwillingness to let them anywhere near these strangers until she had observed them for herself.

T'Vysse met Surak's eyes unflinchingly. "Are there people I may call on your behalf?" she asked.

Why, that little *le-matya!* Karatek thought. She had to know that Surak's family lived on the other side of ShiKahr. No creature on Vulcan guarded its young with more ferocity than the *le-matya*. Did T'Vysse truly consider these strangers to be such a threat? If so, her suggestion of a call to Surak's family might be considered a form of warning.

"I do not think they would welcome such a call," Surak admitted. "But I thank you for the courtesy."

Which, judging from the way T'Vysse lowered her eyes, indicated that Surak knew precisely what she had had in mind.

She turned away. This was Karatek's cue to lead his "guest-friends" to the rooms that had been hastily cleared out. Surak could have the spare chamber, while, Karatek decided, Varen and Skamandros would share the room that ordinarily housed Turak and Lovar. Neither Karatek nor T'Vysse would open what had been his daughter's room to strangers.

In the coolness before full dark, Karatek awaited his guests in the courtyard. Flames leapt in the firepit. A cauldron whose handles were cast in the shape of wild beasts was filled with the broth that would be their first course and bubbled over the fire. On the firepit's lip were spread hand-woven cloths on which rested flagons of sweet water and ceramic bowls and plates. Yellow and green legumes were arrayed on a round iridescent platter beside a basket of flatbreads and a glass tray of melon slices arranged to resemble a sandblossom.

T'Vysse stood before the flames, setting out skewers of food. Spiced succulents and mushrooms, mostly, Karatek observed.

"Surak and his followers do not eat meat," she whispered to him.

Now, when had she found time to research that? The wisest thing his parents had ever done was arrange his bonding to her, he thought, and reached out to touch her face.

Hearing footsteps, she pulled away.

From Surak's room came Karatek's three guests. They wore

fresh sandsuits and had evidently washed the dryness of the desert from their skins with a plunge into the thermal pools around which the house's bedrooms had been built. Varen's eyes brightened at the spread table, the peaceful courtyard.

"The broth is *plomeek*," T'Vysse assured him. "Though the spices are a family secret."

Surak bowed. He waited for her to be seated, then bowed his head as Karatek broke the pale yellow flatbread that would be served with the broth.

Varen and Skamandros fell upon the food as eagerly as if they had eaten little during the past few days, which was probably the case.

"We encountered a sandstorm, which delayed us by two days, and our supplies ran short," Varen explained.

Surak, who must have been equally hungry, raised his bowl in time with his hosts. His family was a noble one, and, as Karatek observed, he retained its exquisite manners.

As if reading his thoughts, Surak raised an eyebrow. "My family considers me a dangerous radical."

"And are you?" Karatek found himself asking.

"A radical in my approach, certainly, to our planet's difficulties. It is a violent world, and we have evolved into a violent people. That was logical before we mastered the arts of reason—to whatever degree that we have mastered them. I simply attempt to take that mastery to the next step."

"It is no longer enough to be effectively violent: we must seek to control violence. To cast it out," Varen broke in. Then, he cast down his eyes. "I ask pardon for the interruption."

Surak nodded. "We eat no meat, as your consort"—he bowed ceremonious respect to T'Vysse—"appears to have learned. We carry no weapons. And, hardest of all, we attempt to master the root cause of violence, our emotions."

"The mastery of passion," T'Vysse mused. "Can it be done? What do you think, sir?" she asked Skamandros.

"I am Surak's shadow," he said, his voice hoarse, his eyes intense. "My name used to be Ayhan, but I changed it in honor of my teacher."

"I will change my name once I find the one that truly suits me," Varen declared.

"Would it not be as logical," asked T'Vysse, "to live so that your name reflected you, and you alone?"

Karatek was only an engineer, he thought, quicker to think than to speak. It was a wonder he had found the words to claim Surak and his companions as guests. Holding his water flagon, he leaned back as T'Vysse, with a teacher's skill, drew the men into conversation or, in her skilled hands, the most exquisitely courteous interrogation Karatek could imagine.

No, Surak's principles were not just intellectual: they were an integral part of his life. And expressed so persuasively it drew a pang from his host. Surak ate no meat, not just because meat was the result of the end of a life, but because it was too wasteful of resources on a scarce world. Besides, Surak added, glancing politely aside, if you spent any time in the desert, you realized that meat-eaters had an odor that drew predators.

"Like the creatures of the deep desert," Surak said, his voice resonant, "we Vulcans are predators. But, unlike the *le-matya* and the *shavokh*, we perceive that the desert itself is as precious as food or water. Therefore, it is logical to preserve it. How best to preserve it? By realizing that warfare is illogical, a waste of life and of Vulcan's scarce resources."

"And yet, our people still produce more warriors than scientists," T'Vysse murmured.

"Even surgery is violence," said Surak, "but violence harnessed to the cause of healing. If one can wage war, how much more logical is it to wage peace? I have made it my mission to persuade scientists to wage peace instead of war, by removing themselves as the means of keeping Vulcan fighting."

"You speak as one who knows the desert well." Karatek made himself take his part in the conversation.

"I was a computer scientist 10.3 years ago," Surak replied. "When I perceived that the machines I built were being used to drive the machines of war, I forsook my family and my laboratory. I went first to Seleya, but my emotions were so strong that my teachers thought they might melt the snow on the mountain's peak. They were, of course, speaking hyperbolically. Now I see their words as a rebuke to the emotionalism with which I confronted them. They did what they could: they sent me into the deep desert to burn the passions out of me. So, I realized that Seleya was not the answer, any more than the arts I had learned in the Science Academy. I walked from Seleya to Gol, but the adepts there failed me, too: it is not withdrawal from our world that will save it, but instead, the desire to go out and transform it."

Surak's face glowed in the firelight. Its finely cut features were almost delicate—too fragile a lamp to hold so much fire.

While I tinker with defense contracts, thought Karatek. *Who is at war now? The Northeastern Alliance against the priest-kings of this latest dynasty of the te-Vikram, and everyone against the bandits? This was not how I wished to spend my life.*

Karatek forced himself not to bristle. Suspicion had afflicted Vulcan along with war: one's neighbor was one's enemy. So far, strangers still were welcome, although, judging from how ShiKahr's security force had greeted Surak and his companions, not for much longer. But strangers as strange as this? They might well be spies. At least they were civilized these days. In ancient times, Surak might well have been cast blinded from the Bridge at Seleya, the traditional punishment for sorcery.

Surak's words were only words, not threats, he told himself. But one did not need to be an ascetic or a historian like T'Vysse to realize that his line of reasoning was revolutionary.

"Our work has changed since you set your own research aside," he said. "You are my guests. Perhaps you would care to tour the Vulcan Space Initiative and see the models of the ships—ships for peaceful use—that we are creating."

Surak almost smiled, a brightening of the eyes and the attention. "I had hoped for such an invitation," he admitted. "But beginnings are important. Do you offer this because you feel you owe it to a guest-friend, or because you feel it is the logical thing to do?"

What would it mean for the VSI to have Surak as a guest-friend?

Karatek found himself smiling. "I think," he said, "that we have a great deal to talk about, your people and mine."

FIVE

NOW

KI BARATAN, ROMULUS

The great Council Chamber of the Romulan Senate in the capital city of Ki Baratan on Romulus was a starkly elegant room in a building that was over two hundred years old—the pride of the architects (who, since they'd been unfortunate enough to live in a more violent age than the current civilized regime, had not lived to build anything ever again).

The Council Chamber was a huge room with a high-arched ceiling from which hung long rows of lights, and its walls were vast sweeps of stone. Each of those walls was inset with its own red, blue, and blood-green mosaic images showing off past glories and metal trophies from various interstellar victories. A gleaming silver fragment of Starfleet ship hull embedded in one wall even commemorated one rare but spectacular victory against the Federation.

But no one was bothering with any sightseeing just now. The Romulan Senate was in session, which meant at the best of times an unstable mixture of stoic calm and warrior ferocity.

Right now, Praetor Neral thought, watching the senators in action where they were seated along both sides of the long, dark green stone table, they were shouting back and forth at each other out of grief and shock mixed in with fury. And right now, fury was uppermost.

At least they were all still in their seats, not hurling themselves across the table at each other's throats.

Dralath, Neral remembered suddenly, had once slit a senator's throat at one of these meetings, right there, where stolid Senator Durjik sat now, just to make a point to everyone about loyalty. They'd had to scrub the bloodstains off the stones.

I am not Dralath. And my predecessor never deserved the title of praetor.

His immediate predecessor, Narviat, had been a different matter, suave, charming, and dedicated to the Romulan people. Too good to live. Not that Neral had had anything to do with the "accident." This time, at least, his hands were perfectly clean.

Besides, Neral could thoroughly understand the senators' anger and horror. How could such a massacre have happened to innocent colonist Romulans? Why? His own blood burned as well, just as fiercely as that of the senators, every time he thought of those lying murderers, those utterly foul, totally against all law or honor perversions that called themselves the Watraii—

No. Calm yourself. You cannot afford to lose your self-control.

After these few . . . interesting years as praetor of all the Romulans and a good many more years before that as an ambitious young officer working his way up through the ranks and managing to survive two regime changes, he'd gotten very good at that bit of self-hypnosis. But then, one thing he was, Neral thought wryly, was a survivor. If he'd managed to stay alive during all of the perilous, utterly corrupt reign of Dralath, no one was going to get him now.

Brave words. But there were times—such as right now—when he could almost wish he'd never fought to be praetor.

Yes? And be what instead? A politician and officer who had the misfortune of having outlived his career while still young? A nobody too unimportant to assassinate, policing farmers on some remote colony world? Oh, he hardly thought so! Neral could hardly imagine any worse fate than quiet, powerless stagnation.

Besides, he thought dryly, he did look the part of praetor. Why waste any assets? Neral's face was still strong-featured, although there were premature lines of stress at the corners of his eyes and mouth that had not been there before he'd assumed the rank and streaks of gray in the glossy black hair.

But I still live. Which is more than my predecessor could say.

The shouting had gone on long enough, he thought. It was growing too fierce. Allowing everyone to let off his or her tension in harmless noise was well and good, and truly necessary in this case. But even unarmed Romulans could do each other genuine damage if they grew too angry. Too much blood had already been spilled in this chamber under Dralath's reign.

"They have attacked without provocation—"

"—attacked sovereign Romulan territory—"

"—colony destroyed—"

"—*eradicated*—"

"—murderers—"

"—killing without warning or cause—"

"—monsters!"

"Silence!" Neral shouted. "Enough of this! *Silence!*" Curse it.

That hurt. "Do you not think me as utterly horrified, as utterly outraged as the rest of you? Do you not think that every drop of my blood burns like yours to exterminate that sickening foulness that calls itself Watraii?"

"Yes!"

"Of course!"

"Destroy them!"

"Wait, Senators. *Wait!" I am going to get an amplifier built into this chair, I swear it.* "Whatever we might want to do, we must face reality! I don't have to tell any of you that the Dominion War was long, vicious, and expensive. Difficult though it is to admit, difficult to accept, the hard fact is this: *We cannot afford another war!"*

That only started up the storm anew:

"How can you say—"

"We cannot lose honor—"

"The accusations, lies—"

"I had a cousin on that colony!"

"I had a nephew!"

"I grieve with you," Neral said in a moment of genuine pity. But pity wouldn't help anyone. He gave them a second, then added in a more stentorian voice, "But hear me, all of you. The facts cannot be bent and twisted into becoming whatever we want them to be! And the facts state, whether we like it or not, that *we cannot go to war, not now, not yet!"*

No, curse it, they were off and shouting again.

"Silence!" Neral shouted again.

But this time even his trained voice couldn't penetrate the noise, and by now he was truly tired of having to shout. He was armed, since who was going to have the nerve to search a praetor? So Neral calmly drew his disruptor pistol and fired it directly at the support of one of the overhead lights—one of the smallest ones, and hanging right over the table and not over any chairs since he didn't want to kill anyone.

The light came crashing down onto the table with a most satisfactory amount of noise and a shower of sparks, smoke, and bits of glass. Gasping and swearing, the senators nearest the crash staggered back from their chairs, frantically brushing out sparks, and then meekly sat again.

Into the stunned silence that followed, as the last of the sparks sputtered out against the stone of the table and the senators cautiously regained their chairs, Neral said suavely, "Now that I have your undivided attention, Senators, you *will* hear me out. I said that we could not afford a war, and that fact remains quite true. I did *not* say, however, that we would not defend ourselves! We may not be at our full military strength, Senators, but we are hardly defenseless.

"As of today, I have ordered all available crews to their ships. They are already launching, and by now will be forming an impenetrable guard around the homeworlds. In addition, all ground personnel have been ordered to report to their gun batteries.

"We may not be able to fight a wide scale battle in space, Senators, but let me assure you all that any Watraii who try to attack the homeworlds are in for a deadly surprise."

And let it only be enough, he thought, remembering how easily the Watraii had destroyed that colony. *Let it only be enough.*

The Office of Homeland Peace, as it was deliberately and euphemistically mislabeled, was tucked away into a quiet corner of the Ki Baratan government buildings, as though it were nothing more important than just another room in the Romulan government bureaucracy.

It was actually the head office of Romulan Security.

The room hardly looked like an office, let alone a dangerous place. It was ironically tranquil, with walls painted a soothing pale blue. In addition to a desk and chair of pale golden shera-wood, the room also contained a softly cushioned beige chair of Irlani design, and a finely woven historic tapestry of Estrak and Thuraka that would not have been out of place in a noble lady's mansion. Only the viewscreen and piles of printouts cluttering the desk spoiled the illusion of luxury—that, and the war trophies hanging on one wall.

They were Charvanek's personal trophies, all of them earned by her in battle.

Charvanek herself could never have been called anything as weak as pretty, even when she was still young. By now, though, the years of hardship, stress and grief had burned away any trace of softness, leaving the Romulan woman looking as strong, fierce, and beautiful as a bird-of-prey. And every bit as dangerous.

Until I fade away from disuse, that is, she thought dryly.

It had been quite a varied career so far. Once upon a time, she had been Charvanek the warrior, a noblewoman who was distantly related to Narviat and the Emperor both, and who was also the honorable captain of the *Honor Blade.*

But then a mistake, one moment of ridiculous weakness with the Vulcan Spock of the *Starship Enterprise,* had turned her instead into Charvanek the disgraced, the woman who had been tricked and captured by the Federation and who had needed to be ransomed from them.

She had survived that disgrace by sheer determination, and survived all the perils of Dralath's regime as well, slowly working her way back until she was trusted with *Honor Blade* again.

But when Dralath had treacherously attacked the Klingon

colony of Narendra III—fierce irony there, she thought—Charvanek had been forced by honor to fight against his fleet, and lost the ship and her rank.

She'd survived that, too, with the help of none other than Spock.

For several amazing years, she had then been both Charvanek, consort to Praetor Narviat, and the chief of Romulan Intelligence.

She was still the latter.

Akh, Narviat . . . I warned you that too many reforms too quickly would make too many enemies. You were so sure of the people's love. . . .

And now Neral was the praetor. Neral made a sly and calculating praetor, a true politician and warrior. He was, without a doubt, ambitious and out for himself. But whatever else he had done or might have done, Neral had had nothing to do with her husband's death. Charvanek knew that; she would have been a poor chief of intelligence if she did not. And Neral knew that she knew. The assassination had been a stupid thing launched by a few stupid senators upset by Narviat's reforms and wanting a return to Dralath's way of doing things. They were dead, now, of course, every treacherous last one of them, and Neral had, to his credit, very much approved of their deaths.

Which was why she was still chief of Romulan intelligence. And why Neral was still alive.

Charvanek sighed and ran an impatient hand through her reddish-brown hair. Yes, she still grieved for Narviat. Even though she had never truly loved him, she had been . . . more than fond of him.

And this was a ridiculous way to spend a day. Usually there were, perhaps, one or at worst two reports per day that were a nuisance. Today, though, every file in the latest batch of intelligence files seemed to be a problem. What was even more frustrating, the information in several of them conflicted with the data in others.

And here I'd thought the worst of the data-keeping was over when Narviat and I had finally managed to straighten out the last of the mess Dralath left behind him.

She snorted. That thinking had been naïve of them both. It wasn't easy to run an empire, even when its government *wasn't* corrupt.

So here I sit like some deskbound clerk, going over bits of information about petty criminals who mean little to Romulan security, while out there the Romulan Star Empire is being attacked and I can't do anything about it.

That was at the heart of her discontent. Her agents did all the fieldwork, took all the risks, and all *she* did was just sit here and interpret the data, determine the innocent and have the guilty eliminated.

As for having once been a praetor's consort . . . well, that was a different matter. Charvanck's hand rested on her wrist, where the marriage bracelet had once circled it, for one brief, atypically sentimental moment. Then she shook her head. What had been, had been. And now, like Neral or not, she worked with the new praetor for the greater good of the Romulan people.

Whatever else she was or might become, Charvanek told herself, she was, and intended to remain, utterly loyal to the Romulan people. That in turn meant she would be utterly loyal to Praetor Neral's reign as well, since he was doing the best he could for Romulus. No easy job, that, what with a treasury left half empty by the corrupt Dralath, and then nearly completely emptied by the demands of the Dominion War.

And now, when we can least afford it, comes this sudden, savage, obscene challenge from this new enemy.

The . . . Watraii. Who or what were they? Other than cowards and murderers, that was. She had searched all the databanks, and found absolutely no references to them or to any aliens even remotely related to them. As far as she could tell from the records, as far back as records were available, that was, there was not even the slightest bit of evidence to support their ridiculous claim and horrifying actions.

And what are we going to do about it?

But then Charvanek, with brutal honesty, changed that "we" to "I." No matter what he wished, Neral wouldn't be able to actually do all that much, not after the war had cut so badly into Romulan finances. He'd already told her privately his plans to simply go on the defensive, guard the homeworlds and—

And what? Pray that the enemy ignored the remaining colony worlds?

Prayer alone can't keep them safe.

But there were enough warriors still faithful to her, and enough of the older ships still in working condition . . .

Oh, indeed. Five, maybe seven ships at most. The rest would be already part of Neral's protective guard. Five slightly out-of-date ships. Now, *there* was a fine army to launch against the Watraii.

Charvanek got to her feet, pacing restlessly about the room, thinking and planning, her quick brain linking data as neatly as that of any Vulcan.

The Federation, now . . . the Federation would almost certainly have already seen the tapes of the colony's destruction. The Watraii monstrosities had seemed proud enough of their foul work to want to show it off.

Besides, if they knew anything about the politics of this quadrant—and the odds were great that they did, since the Dominion War had hardly been a secret operation—the Watraii would have wanted the Federation to see this "proof" that the Romulans, not the Watraii, were the monsters.

Then again, the Federation had already proven its collective self to be firmly against genocide and massacres of innocents, regardless of species. After all, there had been that matter of Narendra III, where—unlikely thought—she and the Federation had actually fought on the same side. Not that they'd known it. They would not have thought kindly of the Watraii tape.

But would any of the Federation actually act now?

What, to help Romulans? No, and no again, that was truly unlikely. There would be no official action, at any rate—particularly not after that cursed war had depleted everyone's resources.

And that gives them a perfectly good excuse for not helping us and salving their consciences about genocide at the same time.

Yes, and there was also the notorious Federation fear of offending anybody. The Federation officials now would probably be far too worried about keeping the peace with all the various factions, including the Klingons, to risk doing anything that might upset anyone. Particularly since the Romulan Star Empire and the Federation were, to put it mildly, hardly the firmest of allies.

Neral, you who are my praetor whether I like it or not, you may never forgive me for doing this, for acting without the praetor's knowledge or permission, and if I survive what I plan to do, I may have to fight my way back from disgrace yet again.

Charvanek stared up at the tapestry of Estrak and Thuraka. It had once hung in her family estate, then been shamefully sold during the time when she was in disgrace and no one would help her. She'd managed to ransom it back only this past year. Estrak and Thuraka had never shrunk from doing what must be done. And neither, Charvanek thought, had she.

But what other choice is there for me? For both of us? If you can't do anything more to protect us than ringing round the home-worlds—and I don't really blame you for that, I know what dire straits the homeworlds are in—if you can't do anything but that, and the Federation almost certainly won't do anything at all to help, then there isn't much of a choice for me but to take what action I can.

She sighed sharply.

I will commandeer those leftover warbirds and whatever war-riors will follow me, and see what can be done. You won't be able to stop me; you can hardly afford to order your men to shoot down your own Chief of Intelligence.

I don't think *that you would, at any rate.*

Then Charvanek shrugged. Whatever happened, as the saying went, happened. It would, at any rate, be far better to go out as a defender of Romulus than as a desk clerk!

Then she whirled, pistol drawn—

"Would you assassinate your praetor?" a coolly amused voice asked.

"Neral! Curse it, man, I almost shot you!"

A secret passage linked his office and hers, dating from before the time of Narviat. Since Charvanek knew that she was too valuable to Neral for him to try an assassination, she had never bothered having it sealed up. It was too convenient. There were, after all, still some deeply urgent affairs of state that had to be kept quiet.

This time, though, Neral had, for whatever perverse reason all his own, apparently decided on secrecy without a cause, and had managed to slip into the office with utter silence. It was rare these days for anyone to surprise her. And now, pistol still in hand, Charvanek could have cheerfully felled him for managing to star-tle her.

Neral, blatantly ignoring the weapon, dropped down into the elegant Irlani chair with a sigh, eyebrow raised at her vehemence. "And wouldn't *that* have shaken everyone up? 'Scandal! Political Intrigue! Praetor Shot by Chief of Intelligence?' " He gave her a thin almost-grin, as much humor as he ever showed. "Who knows? It might have even stopped the damned senators from fighting with each other."

Neral could afford to be relatively open and mostly honest with her—and with her alone—since they knew too much about each other's careers and less sanctioned activities for it to be otherwise. And when it came down to it, they both wanted the same thing: Romulan survival.

"I doubt it," Charvanek said. "Not for longer than it took for them to form ambitious thoughts." She returned the pistol to its holster, making sure that he saw her safely fasten the holster's catch again. "My praetor, you didn't steal in here just to almost get shot."

"Of course not." Neral leaned forward earnestly. "You mean to go, don't you?"

This time, Charvanek didn't even tense a muscle. She wasn't at all surprised that he'd figured it out; after all, Neral had not gotten where he was by being either foolish or naïve.

"Yes, I do," Charvanek said. "And if you know me at all, you know that I must."

"Just tell me this: Why?"

"You know why."

"But what do you hope to accomplish? I can't let you have enough ships to do any real damage. You have to know that. Much as I wish that I could find a way to let you blast the Watraii out of existence, the homeworlds' safety comes before our own."

"Of course I know that. And of course I don't expect a big fleet.

Give me as many as you can spare, that's all I ask. Give me the ships, the older ones, even the ones ready to be scrapped, and I will do what I can to find us a way to fight the Watraii."

"But do *you* have to go, you, yourself?" Before Charvanek could wonder if he'd actually just shown concern for another, Neral added dryly, "I would hate to have to train a new chief of intelligence right now."

"I'll try to spare you the inconvenience," she returned, just as dryly. "But who else is there to do this?" Before he could even try to answer that, she followed it up quickly with "Let's not waste words. You don't like me, I don't like you, but we work together perfectly because we both love our homeworld. Who else can you trust? And who else, in this time of war, can you spare?"

For one instant, she wanted him to argue with her. It would be wonderful not to have to do anything more. Hadn't she done enough for Romulus by now? Hadn't she given enough of herself?

That, Charvanek told herself grimly, was not and could not be a consideration.

Neral got to his feet, lean face expressionless. "Were it anyone else, I would be sure that I watched her go to her death. And yes, I would already be training her successor. But you—if ever there was a survivor, it is you, Charvanek. Go. See what you can do."

"It may be more than you expect."

Neral hesitated just a moment, as though about to argue with her. Then he said only, "So be it," and left.

SIX

MEMORY

At dawn, the wind changed direction, blowing in not from the Forge, but from near ShanaiKahr. By the time Karatek and his guests rose and made their way to the Vulcan Space Initiative for the senior staff meeting held every ten days, their badges showed enough radiation exposure that decontamination was a medical necessity—as well as mandatory if he, Surak, and Surak's followers were to be permitted inside.

"Does your logic explain this?" Karatek, who had always found the inoculations painful, snapped at Surak.

"There is no logic in this type of destruction," Surak said. Surprising Karatek, who had decided that Surak was as undemonstrative as he was cold, he reached out to take his hand. "There is no pain," he said.

Astonishingly, the discomfort in Karatek's arms—and elsewhere—subsided.

Karatek nodded thanks. "I am ashamed," he muttered.

"Why? Your discipline is physics, not the science of the mind," Surak said. He swept his cool, uncanny glance over Varen and Skamandros, who had finished their treatment, and reached for his overrobe just as the ground shook.

"This installation is reinforced," Karatek reassured his guests, and led the way from Decontamination to the VSI's main conference room.

And just in case it wasn't, a hardened network of tunnels led to the surface, bringing potential refugees up outside the city.

As they sat down around an immense oval table, aftershocks rattled the room, sending anything not fastened to walls or tables sliding. Heat prickled beneath Karatek's high collar. Unusual: the room's temperature was comfortable, cool, even, and perspiration was inefficient. Was he suffering a reaction from the decontamination procedures?

Like most of the other scientists present, Karatek glanced at the sensor panels. At this point, seismic activity was well below the VSI's tolerance. Its atmosphere was purified: if the radiation increased, there could be no better shelter.

But what of the people outside the VSI, outside ShiKahr?

Let this level of fallout continue, however, and I cannot answer for the health of my grandchildren, Karatek thought. *Assuming any of us on Vulcan live that long.*

It was apprehension that had made Karatek sweat. The mind could write deep in the body, although the adepts and Healers had always striven to control that. Surak, though he had seen more of the war than Karatek, looked as serene as always.

I wonder: Will he be as composed when my colleagues get through with him?

Surak's presence could be no surprise to them: some had even met him at Karatek's house. But now they were staring at him as if they had never seen him before.

Was it logical for them to overplay their curiosity and surprise? Karatek asked himself and knew that for a question he would not have asked before Surak came to stay with him.

He had known for at least one hundred days that it would be his turn to present his most recent findings at this meeting. He had been looking forward to demonstrating the fuel efficiency of his latest engine model. In fact, he had gone without sleep for at least fifteen of those days to prepare.

Yet, here he was, rising to introduce his guest and yielding his long-awaited presentation time to Surak.

Some will say this will affect my performance evaluation, even the course of my entire career. But if I am right, if Surak is right, I will not have a career—or anything else—if we Vulcans continue on our present course.

Karatek and T'Vysse had spent far too much of the strictly limited private time available to them debating the risk to his career of substituting a speech by a notorious radical for a reasoned, even exciting presentation of his own research.

Ultimately, it hadn't been Surak's arguments, his passionate concern (despite his claims of being motivated solely by logic) that something of Vulcan be preserved, but Karatek's own perceptions that motivated him to take the risk.

The risk was acceptable, he told himself. Those were not words that he would have used before he met Surak.

It seemed that Surak had already convinced him that all Vulcan was in peril.

What will he decide to convince me of next? Karatek asked himself, with another prickle of apprehension. Perhaps he would ask this uncomfortable guest of his to show him the meditation techniques that allowed even young Varen to suppress his emotions—at least, most of the time.

In the days since Karatek had claimed Surak and his followers as guest-friends, he had observed them keenly. Varen was all youth and fire. Skamandros? The man who called himself Surak's shadow was still an enigma. Karatek might not trust him, as Surak did, at his own back, but the quiet, sardonic man wasn't just fanatically loyal to Surak, he was stubborn enough to cling to the old ways of not violating guest-friendship.

As for Surak himself, Karatek found him valuable, if arduous, company, about on the level of his *kahs-wan* trial or the hike to Vulcan's much-shrunken Eastern Sea to see the statues of the Ancients of Days, carved and set on the cliffs leading to the strand in days before Vulcan even had recorded history.

And he had this consolation, at least: he would be able to observe Surak's impact on his colleagues.

Again, the installation shuddered. It was considered improper to introduce news feeds into this staff meeting, but Karatek knew everyone in the room was speculating about where the last attack occurred.

"In my opinion, evacuation is not a necessary option," Surak said, before he was acknowledged by *T'Kehr* Torin, seated at the head of the table. "I calculate an 85.67 percent probability that this installation will sustain only minor damage, primarily to its occupants' composure."

Torin raised an eyebrow. As chair of the Vulcan Space Initiative's Research-and-Development team, it was his prerogative to manage its staff. He frequently compared the task to herding *lematya,* but it would be a rash man who tried to wrest it from him. Older than his associates, with a warrior's scars earned in twenty years of fighting enemies ranging from the te-Vikram to the High

Command and a scholar's silvering hair, Torin had as little patience with presumption as he did with shoddy logic. Even scientists who had worked with him for years still called him *T'Kehr.*

"Indeed?" Torin asked coldly. "Clarify."

Surak inclined his head. "In the last 10.3 years, the period since this facility has been in operation, ShiKahr has suffered five seismological perturbations of greater magnitude than the episodes we have encountered today. Because I have heard nothing of damages to this installation in the days I have spent as *T'Kehr* Karatek's guest, I must assume that its fabric is sound. Therefore, it is likely to withstand this incident.

"Furthermore," Surak continued, "given increased levels of contamination in the atmosphere, I would hypothesize that this is one of the safest places in ShiKahr."

T'Raya, seated beside Torin, flinched. She had a son preparing for the *kahs-wan* and a husband who was an agronomist. Even his laboratory was outside.

Her fear sparked Karatek's. Had T'Vysse made it to shelter in the Vulcan Science Academy? His wife was no one's fool, Karatek reminded himself. If radiation traces grew any higher, everyone in ShiKahr would have to go on potassium iodide, at least. Karatek closed his eyes, thinking of the last pilgrims he had seen. If they could make it to Seleya, assuming the Exiles in the Waste and te-Vikram raiders did not pick them off, the shrine's Healers would tend them.

Logic. *Logic,* Karatek reminded himself. Surak clearly had a point. If he could reason through his emotions, he could achieve control.

Was that why their world—their splendid world with its passionate emotions like a rising and ebbing blood-green tide—had gone so wrong?

Torin, wonder of wonders, was inclining his head in approval. "Thank you, *T'Kehr*..."

"Surak will suffice," the man cut in so smoothly that Torin did not register the fact he had been interrupted. "May I continue, sir?"

"I am sure that you will continue to reassure us in your own peculiar way," Torin consented. So, he had been aware of Surak's rhetorical tricks. Been aware, yet permitted them. That permission might actually constitute approval, although Karatek suspected Torin would later have acerbic words for Karatek himself. Surak's presence at the meeting had been prepared for, but nothing could have prepared them for what Surak might choose to say. And Torin had never tolerated surprises at staff meetings before.

But, Karatek rationalized as if he already stood in Torin's private office with the door closed, surprise was a valuable element of warfare. Because Torin had been a warrior, he might accept this analogy. That is, if he were thinking logically.

A fascinating possibility. Surak's logic clearly had potential Karatek had not foreseen.

"Varen," Surak said in an undertone, "will you please operate the viewer our host said we might use?"

Reminding them that he had a right to speak. Clever, Surak, clever.

If Varen had moved any faster, he might have incurred a rebuke for being overeager.

"I am obliged," Surak raised his voice slightly, "to *T'Kehr* Karatek for his invitation to join your staff meeting at the Space Initiative. I hope you are as aware as I am of the illogic of an installation designed to take Vulcans to the stars needing to cower beneath rock and soil."

Now, he acknowledged his obligation, albeit in a manner calculated to annoy everyone, Karatek thought. His decision had been made. It was pointless to second-guess himself. Illogical, even. Karatek suppressed a sigh.

Varen projected an image of a star field.

"Would you not call 'cowering' an emotionally laden term?" Torin asked, as if stepping out on the sand to challenge an adversary to single combat.

Surak swept his glance about the gleaming room, with its heavy rock tables, the computers set into them, and the men and women leaning forward attentively in tubular metal chairs. He flicked it over the seismograph, the radiation detector, and the communications gear, then over the scientists, whose glances seemed fixed upon these links with the outer world rather than on the screen on which Varen flashed a series of (declassified) prototypes of ships built from VSI designs.

"I consider 'cowering' an accurate description, not an exaggeration or insult," Surak said.

No "I regret to say" or "it seems to me." Surak might be logical, but he was blunt almost to the point of discourtesy. And no one could call him modest. But then, no zealot ever was.

"What is, is," he added. "Expressing regret that is illogical to feel not only compounds the illogic, but wastes your valuable time. During my travels, I became aware of the ships that you have been building for the Northeastern Alliance. I have come here to propose that you repurpose these vessels. As it stands, they face a variety of uses, all undesirable. They might be subject to sabotage by agents of the te-Vikram; or the High Command might decide that the time for deterrence has passed."

"We have agreements of neutrality with the Southern Hegemony as well as the te-Vikram," T'Raya pointed out. "Including the right to pass over the Forge unmolested not just for religious pilgrims, but for trading convoys."

"Have you indeed?" Surak half-bowed. "The lady T'Vysse, consort to my host, is an historian of some note. She could tell you better than I how often in Vulcan's history such agreements have been broken. As matters currently stand, I calculate a one in 93.56 chance that neutrality will become an untenable position, even here in ShiKahr. While your city's position as a trade center has enabled it to maintain neutrality while cities around it have fallen into war, history has shown us there invariably comes a time when enemies become stronger and seek to renegotiate agreements. Either in the council chamber or in blood."

"In other words . . ." Torin broke in, impatient as a student who deserved a reprimand.

"In other words, I think the VSI will face a choice within 10.9 years: to become either a combatant or a target. And because of the expertise here, your entry into hostilities . . ."

Lights flared on the communications panel. *"May we have your attention? Security has received reports of missiles detonating north of us. Initial threat assessment is that they will explode harmlessly over the Sea. Meteorological reports indicate that radiation levels should rise 0.003 percent. Please remain inside and stay calm."*

T'Raya leapt from her chair, then, with a great effort, seated herself. Her son's teacher would lead the survival class to shelter in one of the caves outside the city. Her husband would take shelter. What would be would be, and she would have to endure it.

But what of the others? What of their entire world? Karatek closed his eyes on his memory of Vulcan's one sea, which he had visited once on pilgrimage. Now he saw it transformed, its shallow tides replaced by an image of a hideous, irradiated wall of water, rushing toward the shore, obliterating all it touched. . . .

No. What was, was. He looked down.

Varekat stirred in his chair. Of middle height and age, but great personal assurance, Varekat was their arms expert. Most of the VSI kept silent on his research, but the Womb of Fire beyond the Forge was mute testament to the efficacy of the research of his colleagues from prior generations.

When confronted by the evidence of history, Varekat had always retorted that Vulcan had survived those wars. It had rebuilt, using what technology and what scientists remained as a base. In fact, it had rebuilt stronger than before. This time, however . . . Just because Vulcan had always survived did not mean that one quantum leap of technology might prevent them from surviving the next war.

Now, Varekat too looked down and to the side, as if Surak had spoken of the blood fever to a celibate of Gol.

He rose and bowed. "I apologize," he said.

"For showing emotion?" Surak asked. "For shame? Or for the type of research you have made your lifework?"

"I cannot say," Varekat muttered. "But my resignation will be on *T'Kehr* Torin's console after this meeting."

"Superfluous," said Surak. "You jump to conclusions. Your learning is valuable. Listen to what I propose. From our earliest days in exploring our system, we have faced the possibility that, one day, we might meet another race even more violent than ourselves. That is, however, no reason to . . . cower here on Vulcan and wait for our own wars to destroy us."

"Do you really think that's going to happen?" asked T'Raya.

"I calculate odds of three hundred and fifty to one," Surak said. "Unacceptably high when the subject under discussion is the survival of our species and even our world. As a result, I have been speaking to every Vulcan who will listen. My goal is to wage peace as aggressively as the warring clans have waged war as far back as our history runs. But, should that fail, I think we must consider the possibility of sending some critical remnant of the population to journey far, far offworld.

"In other words," he said, gesturing at Varen to flash images of ships reconfigured as colony vessels, augmented life-support systems that included vast green areas of gardens and hydroponic tanks, "it would be logical to turn your warships into generation ships. Send out those who are willing to go, who are weary of the constant battle, the poisoned air, the desolate ground."

Karatek glanced around the room. Torin's brow was knitted in deep thought. T'Raya stared intently at the images of the sorts of hydroponic engineering that generation ships would require before her eyes lit with hope. Varekat glanced away, and covered his face, while others brightened at Surak's phrase "those who are willing to go." Like Zerin, who always had been more politicized than the rest of them, more prone to advocating the sorts of general theories that would sweep hundreds of thousands of Vulcans into action.

"Should total war erupt," Surak said, "should the weapons created by the Varekats—if you will forgive me, sir—of this Mother World all be used, it may be that these people become all that might remain—anywhere in the universe."

Karatek heard himself gasp. He was not alone.

"Madness," shouted T'Arvot, a much older woman whose work on navigation had so preoccupied her in the sixty years since she had finished her training that Karatek suspected she didn't know the names of their allies, much less their enemies. For her, the stars programmed into her guidance models had become a replacement family.

"That I am mad is a possibility you must factor into your risk assessment," Surak said gently. "But will you run the risk that our lives, our culture, our world itself be destroyed because you find the thought unpleasant? Or"—he eyed her shrewdly before sweeping his gaze across the room—"will you rise to a technological and scientific challenge greater than any your discipline has ever confronted?"

T'Arvot chuckled. "You are shrewd, stranger. I would have given much to see you persuade Karatek to yield his presentation time to you. Ordinarily, we cannot keep him quiet. And now?" She fixed a glance like a laser on Karatek. "What have you to say for *yourself,* young man?"

Karatek rose from his chair. "Let me have that thing," he muttered to Varen as he replaced him at the viewer's controls. "I am a propulsion engineer, a competent one, I hope, but I became an engineer because the High Command told me there were not sufficient jobs for pure physicists."

He raised a hand. "Regret is, as our guest would say, illogical. Inevitably, the study of propulsion leads me to engines, to quantum mechanics, and then it brings me up against a barrier: the speed of light itself. Now, it might be logical"—he inclined his head sardonically at Surak—"to assume that we are bound by that number. However, history points out that we are not a species that accepts bounds readily. Nevertheless, thus far, we have found no way, no funding, to conduct the research to try to exceed that velocity."

"The High Command has said that the speed of light cannot be exceeded," Zerin reminded him. He was probably sending his patron on the Council a message right now. His computer beeped, and he gave it a betrayed, hostile look, then glanced at Torin, whose face had darkened at his discourtesy.

" 'Cannot' is not a word to be used to princes," Torin quoted. "Some of our ancestors died to prove that axiom untrue. But 'cannot' is a word that should be forbidden to scientists. Proceed, Karatek."

"If," Karatek found himself almost stammering as he fought to bring out thoughts that he had only half-formulated, "if . . . we headed out to the stars, it might be that that isolation would force us to concentrate upon the problem. Freed of the constraints of justifying our funding and adapting our best designs for war, we might . . . I cannot calculate the odds as quickly as my guest, but . . ."

Surak bowed, but did not supply a number.

Karatek flashed through the presentation he had hoped to make, of how their current propulsion systems could be boosted to eighty-five percent of the speed of light.

"And if these generation ships of yours ran out of resources?"

"We have suits," Varen cried. "There are star systems along the way. We do not need *Minshara*-class worlds to mine for metals or tap for gases. And catalytic chemistry . . ."

"*Kroykah!*" Torin commanded. "We are getting off the main subject, which is our guest's overall plan. Have you anything else to add?" *Anything else outrageous,* his tone indicated. As he swept his gaze around the room of tense, excited scientists, Torin's gaze was as expressionless as Surak's own.

"If my host will allow me, I do have one more thing to say," Surak said. "Karatek raises the question of how propulsion systems might be augmented to break the barrier now imposed by the speed of light. As you may know, when I laid aside my research into computer science, I went to Seleya and, thence, to Gol. Are you aware that the work that the adepts do there is more than religious? They can manipulate minds, true. Time spent working with a Seleyan Healer can coax the sick at heart toward renewed purpose. I have spoken to the adepts and the Healers, and I am

74

convinced they work not just with thoughts and minds, but with the very energy that minds produce. Like the rest of us, they are touch telepaths, although they have developed their skills to a degree the rest of us have not. But some of them are equally adept in moving matter and hearing at distances: telekinetics and clairaudience. So, without offending anyone's faith, I would consider it logical and desirable to see if they were willing to offer solutions drawn from their own expertise."

"And if they're not?"

"Then we should attempt to persuade them. Logically, and persistently." Surak inclined his head.

"In short," said Torin, "you require more information. How much more?"

Now it was Surak's turn to look down, almost abashed.

"I ask pardon. I do not know," he admitted.

"So," asked Torin, "you do just not wheedle your way in here, the latest mad prophet from off the Forge, demanding we change our way of life or the world will end. Your message is much the same, but your method . . ."

He ran his hand over the left side of his face, where a scar slashed down one cheek and continued past where the high neck of his sandsuit and laboratory coat concealed it. Karatek had once asked him why he had not had the scar removed and had never forgotten Torin's answer. *"When I got these injuries, I was sent to Seleya to be healed. They left me this mark. At first, I cursed them. Now, I see that they wished me to remember and to learn from my memories."*

"I confess, I am intrigued by your suggestions," Torin said. "Oh, don't look so horrified, Zerin. Yes, I would be tempted to hire our guest as a consultant, but I know we don't have the budget for it. So, instead, I will do the next best thing. I am sending Karatek on a fact-finding mission—no, he is not going on administrative or personal leave, but as a fully accredited representative of the VSI and at full pay. Surak, if he wishes, may accompany him. I gather he travels light: Karatek may find himself wanting to upgrade his survival skills," he added wryly.

With an effort, Karatek kept a rueful grin off his face. Torin had managed, simultaneously, to discipline him and hand him the freedom of research he had always wanted.

"We will do everything we can to help our host!" offered Varen.

Skamandros, sitting in the shadows, raised an eyebrow at the younger man, silencing him. Then he saluted Torin with his water flask and drained it, accepting the chairman's instructions.

Torin turned back to Karatek. "Karatek, here is your assignment: Accompany Surak. Listen to what he says, to what people you can respect say to him. Learn what he learns. If you can find us no answers, at least, find us some better questions than the ones we've been dealing with since the last war."

Again, the ground shuddered. Harder this time than the earlier quake. A wall panel buckled, and the table jumped. Torin held up his hand, keeping his people in place.

Threat assessment must have been wrong. Either that, or a missile had triggered a landslide that activated a fault.

"You'd think you never felt a quake before," said T'Arvot. "And you are the people who want to go to the stars."

"Correction," said Torin. "*You* wish to go. I suspect Karatek wishes to go. And I think T'Raya might persuade her husband that he wishes to go.

"Still, I would deny no others their vision—and would gain their knowledge."

Again, he cocked his head, as if he listened to words no one else could hear.

76

Possibly a bone implant, linking him to High Command, Karatek thought. *Would I allow such a thing? I would not. But at least, it means that whatever I do is sanctioned, at least until yet another New Order replaces the current one.*

"When the all-clear sounds, depart in peace. And return," Torin told Karatek, "assured of my welcome and your position back—with whatever information you find."

Karatek rose and held up his hand, showing palm and split fingers in the most formal greeting.

"Live long and prosper," he wished Torin and his fellow scientists.

He did not see how they could wish him peace and long life in return. Nor did they try.

As Karatek might have expected, Torin managed the last word. "May your life be interesting," he wished.

"That," said Surak, "is self-evident."

Now that Surak had obtained precisely the concessions that Karatek realized he had wanted all along, he rose and bowed deeply to Torin. Then he swept from the underground conference room, closely followed by Varen and Skamandros.

I'm damned if I'm going to scramble after him, Karatek thought. Surak, Varen, and Skamandros, though they wore security badges, would have to remain in the VSI's underground complex until the alert passed. So Karatek rose with as much composure as his guest-friend, bowed with slightly less formality, and turned to escort his guests to the nearest dining room.

"A moment," said Torin. "I wish a word with you."

Even though Karatek had expected just that, he sighed.

If the desert, the *le-matya*s, war, Surak's many enemies, or Torin himself didn't kill him, T'Vysse would.

SEVEN

MEMORY

Karatek trudged behind Varen across Vulcan's Forge, Varen padding behind them. Skamandros was walking point. If danger lay ahead, he would warn them. Seleya's spires loomed to their right, casting an immense shadow across their path, darkness without true shade.

I am the metal being beaten out upon this Forge, Karatek thought.

Adding to the discomfort of the Forge, he was running a light fever, his usual reaction to anti-radiation medication. But there was no point in stopping to rest now. When the sun reached zenith, they would have no choice. Meanwhile, it was logical to cover as much ground as they could.

According to the maps Karatek carried, if they rested only briefly at noon, they stood a fair chance of reaching a medical research facility that had taken over one of the old way stations by sunset.

If they did not reach it, however, they faced undesirable alternatives. They could either venture on by starlight, avoiding the leaf-traps that uncoiled their tendrils in the dark, the sandpits with their patient, hungry inhabitants, or rock outcroppings that could slash their feet to the bone. Or they could hole up in any cave they found and calculate the odds that wild *sehlat*s or *le-matya*s hadn't found it first. They could either hope they found enough vegetation to build a fire, or risk using up the power charges on the torches they carried.

So, tired as Karatek knew himself to be, he knew it was best not to stop. And to drink only at noon.

In the agonizing first three days of his journey across the Forge, his companions had repaid every bit of their obligation to him as their host. Now he was in their debt. Torin had been right. If Karatek were undergoing the *kahs-wan* now, he never would have survived.

Sand stung his face, as hot as sparks flying from a crucible. At first, the glare from ground and side had all but blinded him. Surak had advised against the use of protective lenses, "for, if you lose them, you have no endurance, whereas, traveling with us, you can adapt in safety."

Such safety as there was, here on the Forge. They were but four: too many, perhaps, for even a hungry *le-matya* to attack, but not enough to fight off a pack of wild *sehlat*s or Vulcans turned raider.

The weapons Torin had given him, knife and blaster, were weights beneath Karatek's cloak that he forbade himself to call comforting. He was no dealer in arms.

Deliberately, he broke stride lest the rhythm of his footsteps lull him into a dangerous trance.

When Torin had asked Karatek to remain after the staff meeting at the VSI, Karatek had expected a rebuke or, at best, a "your strategy worked, but don't try it again." Instead, Torin had offered a dinner invitation, not just to Karatek, but to his household. It had been an evening to remember. Torin lived almost on the edge of the Forge in a house so old that, until Torin took it over, even ShiKahr's Preservation Society had thought to pull it down. Torin had intervened and reconstructed the ancient place as it must have been in its prime, during the Last Migration, when a splendor of tapestries, rugs, and bronze vessels reflected the wealth of no-mads who had finally settled in what was now ShiKahr.

Torin's first wife and eldest daughter had died in a biocide at the Gates of AraKahr. Bonded now to the fiber artist Mitrani, Torin greeted Karatek's household with ancient courtesy. He met them at his gates, even slashing his hand in token of a host's obligation to defend his guests to the death, before leading them to the inner courts, where they knelt as Mitrani offered them fire and water.

Mitrani and T'Vysse might be artist and historian, not scien-tists. If anything, that gave them a greater appreciation of why Karatek had to accompany Surak.

After dinner, they sat in the courtyard while Torin poured them each a glass of firewine so old that it was almost syrup. Surak, Karatek knew, did not drink alcohol, but "this is not a depressant but a work of art," he said, and drained it to the health of his hosts.

For a while, Torin and his guests sat quietly, staring up at the night sky whose starlight, so far away, mocked their firepits as petty and ephemeral. Then Torin beckoned Karatek aside.

"I need to talk to you," he said.

Not "with," Karatek noted.

He bowed assent, a grace he hadn't used for years, but one that seemed natural in this curiously anachronistic household.

"You're all on fire to be gone," said Torin. "Well, I can't blame you. This Surak calls himself a man of peace, but look how he speaks of it. *Waging* peace. He doesn't so much bring peace, but a sword," he told Karatek, as T'Vysse nodded.

"You will walk in company that would defend you to the death, but never forget: These are dangerous men. They cause people to talk sides. You saw how Zerin couldn't wait to report in to the High Council, while Varekat was prepared to see Surak as absolution, and I think T'Raya's probably starting to pack. So you stay on your guard."

Reaching within his robe, Torin withdrew an old knife and well-worn blaster. "My gift to you," he said. "The blaster's power cell won't show up on scans, a little workaround a few of us who survived an ambush . . . well, that's another story. Don't let Surak talk you out of carrying them."

"Sir," Karatek stammered. "I can't accept these. Not your service weapons."

"Now, come on! It isn't as if I'm giving you my House's swords! Now, let me see you put those weapons away. Good! Surak will not like the fact I've armed you; but I do not particularly care what he likes any more than he cared when he came in and robbed me of one of my finest researchers.

"I will tell you why I want you to leave as soon as you can. By now, the messages are flying back and forth. I will be held accountable. In case my decision is overruled, I want you on your way, so far into the deep desert that you cannot be recalled. Leave your com gear at home, too. I won't run the risk that you could be traced. Now, I pried a rough idea of your line of march out of Surak, told him he owed me—and I've sent messages to installations along the way. You'll find a list waiting for you on your secured terminal at home. Most of the people who run these sites are old friends of mine. Old companions. They may hate me in the morning, but they'll take you in. And they'll listen, for a number of reasons beyond old loyalties. If you know anything about me, you know I wouldn't trade on them—at least not past a certain point. VSI isn't the only place that's suffered funding cuts, and I'm not the only one to worry about the direction we're headed."

In the darkness, Karatek flushed with gratitude and apprehension. Torin was pouring a lifetime of contacts, of his immense personal and professional credibility, into his hands.

"I'll try not to let you down, sir," he said, managing not to stammer.

"You'd be letting down a lot more people than just me," Torin snapped. "So don't do it! And when you get back, next time you get some idea out of the epics about claiming a troublemaker as your guest-friend, think again!"

They both laughed. But Torin's eyes flashed so hotly in the darkness that Karatek grew bold enough to say, "I wonder, sir, that you don't come with us."

"Me, you young hothead?" He laughed, and Karatek, the father of three, flushed deeply at being relegated to the ranks of untried youths. "You're not the first person who had that idea. Surak already asked me to join him, both on this journey and on the exile from the Mother World that he preaches like the mad prophet he is. Provided, he adds, that I can control my illogical tendencies to want to fight, not reason, my way out of difficulties."

Karatek didn't even try to suppress a grin. "I wish I had heard him!"

Torin laughed, then shook his head. "I will tell you what I told him," he said, and Karatek knew that he would get the older man's exact words. "I said, 'I am bone of this world's bone, blood of its blood, soul of its soul; and my blood and body will remain a part of my Mother World's rocks and sand long after my *katra* has fled the Halls of Ancient Thought.' "

Karatek started to kneel to the older man, as if before a priest, but Torin's outthrust hands stopped him.

Stopped him and upheld him. Sustained him.

"Karatek!"

The voice was Surak's, not Torin's. Karatek blinked, not at the firelight of Torin's courtyard, but at the blazing sun of midday on the Forge.

"You were drifting," said Surak. "If you had been alone, you would have fallen. You very well might have died."

"I ask forgiveness," Karatek muttered.

They marched on.

EIGHT

NOW

STARFLEET HEADQUARTERS

As the small viewscreen in her private office went dark, Admiral Uhura sat back in her dark brown partha-leather chair, her fingers steepled and her eyes troubled.

The office about her was a comfortable space furnished in warm golds and browns. A Vulcan calligraphic scroll, tranquil in its brushstrokes, hung on one wall, and a Ghanaian kente cloth in an intricate geometric design of brown and sand hung on another. It did not look like the office of anyone in power.

The reason was simple: She wanted nothing obtrusive. As far as Uhura was concerned, nothing flashier was needed for or wanted by the head of intelligence for Starfleet Command.

Uhura had let her hair go completely silver over the years and now it formed a bright halo about her head. Time and trouble had weathered the dark, strong, elegant face. But she had never lost that quick wit—or that keen concern for others—that kept her at the peak of her game.

Uhura leaned forward once more, hands going to the viewscreen's controls. But then she shook her head, and forced herself to sit back again. She'd already viewed the tape about twenty times, at every possible speed, resolution, magnification, and frequency, and like it or not, there were no more clues to be gained from it.

No matter how many times she viewed the thing, though, it never lost its urgency and horror. Whoever the alien enemy . . . the Watraii . . . might be, those ships of theirs were damned powerful, and completely outside anything in Starfleet or Federation databases. Unfortunately, there hadn't been sufficient data to let the experts analyze the weapons the Watraii had used.

Clever Watraii.

But the aliens had not merely attacked that Romulan colony, they had eradicated it in a way that made Narendra III look like a picnic. There was a definite irony, Uhura thought, in the fact that she and most of those with whom she worked had spent most of their careers regarding the Romulan Star Empire as a major threat to the Federation. But that didn't mean that she hated the Romulan people. Good lord, no. They were just that: people. And the people on that colony hadn't stood a chance.

Yes, she thought grimly, but bad though that might be, things were clearly going to get much worse. All of Uhura's sources indicated the same danger. Judging from the attackers' course, they had every intention of next threatening Romulus itself.

Serves me right for thinking things were too peaceful, Uhura told herself, and passed the information along to the Federation Council. *For what good it will do.*

Then she accessed the various available databases again, trying an assortment of cross-linkings such as "Romulan" and "blood feud": thirty listings there, and all between various Romulan Houses, all of whom would have been astonished to learn she even knew of their existence. "Romulus" and "indigenous inhabitants" brought up no entries at all. And a cross-linking of "Romulus" and "ancient enemies" brought up nothing but references to Romulan and Vulcan mythology.

Uhura gave a quick grin to see the name "Ruanek" appended to one of those entries. Well now, wasn't that interesting? Very few people outside Vulcan knew that the lecturer at the Vulcan Science Academy and martial-arts expert—as well as Spock's friend—had actually been born a Romulan, on Romulus

I'll be questioning Ruanek, I believe, just to see if he knows anything useful about his homeworld's past history. Tactfully questioning, that was, since there was no reason to cause trouble for someone who was one of the "good guys" and happily married to a Vulcan.

She tried a new search, then waited . . . waited . . .

Well now, look at this. Not exactly pay dirt, but at least Memory Alpha had finally found a match. Not much of one. There was only one sketchy record of the Watraii, posted by . . .

Uhura nearly laughed aloud in her surprise, and said, "Posted by Admiral Pavel Chekov! All right, Pavel, I guess Watraii are easier to find than 'nuclear wessels.' "

Unfortunately, the record that he'd left was several years out of date. And it was exceedingly vague. But, Uhura thought wryly, it was better than no record at all. And vague or not, even so, it was probably going to make Chekov their only expert on the Watraii.

And isn't he going to love that?

She sent off a new message to the Federation Council, including Chekov's brief report. Again, for what it was worth.

Sure enough, none of the serving Federation Council members could add to the report. One thing on which they all agreed, from Terrans to Tellarites, was that the aliens looked disconcertingly formidable.

Well, yes, gentlebeings, Uhura thought with great restraint, *we already have proof of that: an eradicated colony, remember?*

A career spent on starships and in Starfleet intelligence hadn't hardened Uhura, nor had it destroyed her sense of irony, she who once tried to help Klingons defend themselves against Romulan treachery. But it hadn't made her a dreamer, either. She wasn't at all surprised at the next message she received (through the properly secure channels).

Uhura dipped her head in courtesy as the image formed on the screen. "Mr. President."

It was, indeed, the blue visage of Min Zife, the current president of the Federation. He had never looked exactly carefree, Uhura though. Now, though, after an administration that had included every conceivable type of problem, a horrifying interstellar war, cases of enemy infiltration, and treachery of many sorts by various personnel, he appeared to have aged considerably since he first took office.

I never could understand why anyone would want the job of president in the first place! It's so much more . . . comfortable and productive to stay behind the scenes.

"Admiral Uhura. I fear you already know what I am about to say. And believe me, I like this no more than do you."

"Please, continue, Mr. President."

He hesitated, clearly reluctant, and possibly a bit embarrassed. "While the Federation—or at least, to be honest, parts of it—would like to provide assistance to the Romulan Star Empire, we must consider what might happen if things went wrong. We know next to nothing about the Watraii and the validity or lack of validity of their claim. It would be dangerous to make any sudden decisions, because if we make a mistake, if we back the wrong side, the Federation could find itself in a three-way war."

"Yes, Mr. President, but surely there is a far greater risk in just sitting back and doing nothing."

"Is there? Admiral, we both know that the Romulans are already mobilizing for a war."

"For their own survival."

"Oh, I agree. But they would definitely regard any Federation ships crossing the Neutral Zone as an attack. Yes, and if the Klingons find out that the Federation is aiding the Romulans, we have jeopardized the alliance that was only solidified after so much effort after Narendra III."

"And if the Federation is seen to be openly siding with the Klingons by not acting to aid the Romulans—Mr. President, do you truly think that is a better situation?"

He sighed. "Off the record, do you think I like this mess, either? But the timing is truly terrible."

"I suspect that the Watraii knew it."

"Perhaps. But the cold, hard fact is that we have just fought what was possibly the most terrible war in Federation history. We're still picking up the pieces and assessing the costs. And we're not exactly at peace right now. Many members of the Federation are still keeping a wary eye on the Breen, as am I."

So am I, Uhura thought but did not say.

The president leaned forward, face grim. "In short, Admiral: This is no time to start a war."

In other words, Uhura thought, *the Romulans voluntarily withdrew into their own territory almost seventy years ago, so let them fight their own battles. Oh yes, I know how much can be said and not said.*

Her well-schooled face didn't show the slightest trace of what she was thinking. "I had no intention of starting one, Mr. President. Thank you for your time."

The viewscreen went dark. Uhura didn't even bother with a sigh of impatience.

Then, almost at once, she received a familiar code. Tapping in the acknowledgment, she watched a new image form on the screen.

"Admiral Uhura."

Uhura didn't bother with surprise, or waste time asking him how he'd bypassed security. He was one of the masters at figuring out codes. She merely raised a brow in a way she'd long ago learned from him.

"Hello, Spock. I had a feeling that I was going to be hearing from you before very long. You're here on Earth for the ceremonies, I take it?"

"Yes."

"And I assume that you saw the same transmission I did, and that you'd like to see me."

"Indeed."

It wasn't at all surprising that he'd contacted her this quickly. He would surely have come to all the same conclusions as she, and probably, being a Vulcan, come to those conclusions much faster.

Spock didn't insult her by asking if she knew what he wanted. "We have work to do" was all he said.

Together, they began notifying . . . certain people, the people they both knew and trusted.

The people who would get things done.

NINE

MEMORY

"There." Karatek pointed at the black spires that jutted up from the Forge like the fossilized claws of some immense primordial beast. The rocks cast long shadows that he would have turned into an exercise in navigation if the day spent on Vulcan's Forge by its fierce sun hadn't hammered the strength from him. He reached for his water bottle. Then, seeing that no one else drank, he restored the bottle to its hook at his belt.

Days before, Karatek had seen the first dark splotch that, as they drew closer, resolved itself into a vast rock that seemed to be an unreachable distance away in the thin, shimmering air.

"What kind of installation lies beneath the rocks?" asked Varen.

"According to *T'Kehr* Torin, it is a medical research facility," Karatek said. Now he could see what he thought would resolve into squat domes and massive retaining walls once they drew closer.

"Fascinating," Surak observed. "Anyone lacking this information might see only another of the trading posts scattered on the trading routes across the Forge."

Karatek stretched, careful not to share his suspicions about precisely what sort of research a medical facility this isolated might carry on. "It's as if we traveled back in time," he commented.

"Te-Vikram there, too," muttered Skamandros.

Suspicion, Karatek supposed, was only logical at this stage of the march.

"I see no signs of activity. If the installation is camouflaged as a trading post, you would at least expect to see pilgrims or their pack animals." Surak tensed, listening. "Given the direction of the wind, we should have been able to hear—or smell—it by now."

He gestured, and Skamandros moved forward, subtle and swift as a shadow at twilight.

Karatek waited till Surak turned over a rock and sat down, then seated himself with equal caution. He pressed scratched fingers to his temples. The sun's oppressive light was fading, and he welcomed the respite. Soon, Skamandros would return and Karatek would have to force himself back onto his feet. But, once they reached the installation, his trip would begin to prove itself worthwhile. He would find a welcome among fellow scientists. He would be able to drink as much water as he could safely hold, bathe in the hot springs that were one of the chief amenities of the outposts along the pilgrims' routes, and then rest in safety. Tomorrow, he could set once again about the inquiry that had been his reason for venturing into the deep desert.

The crimson light was subsiding like a dying coal when Skamandros returned. Karatek had not even heard his footsteps on the gritty sand of the Forge.

Surak raised an eyebrow at him.

Skamandros held out his hand. In it was the heavily chased hilt of a dagger. A faceted bloodstone set into its pommel caught the last light of the sun. All that remained of the blade was a jagged shard, crusted with a blackish green.

Skamandros looked as if he wanted to fling it to the ground, but instead brought it to Surak.

"Te-Vikram work," Surak observed.

"Self-evident," Skamandros confirmed. He sank down beside his leader and allowed himself a sip of water.

"Does anything remain of the installation?" asked Surak.

"I saw blood on the sand," Skamandros reported. "But no bodies."

"The te-Vikram consider the use of energy weapons in close combat dishonorable," Surak said.

"No civilized people would sell them blasters," snarled Varen.

Surak raised an eyebrow at his younger disciple, who glanced down in unspoken apology.

Karatek took a deep breath. "Did you find any survivors?"

Skamandros rinsed his mouth again. He spat in a way that would have expressed frustration and grief in anyone else, then shook his head. "You know te-Vikram. They're probably rendering the bodies for their water right now."

If they didn't save a captive or two alive for a sacrifice.

"Do we go around?" Varen said. "Skip it and go to the next one?"

Karatek met Surak's eyes. "No," he said.

"Man, you've made no secret of the fact that today's march exhausted you," Skamandros snapped. "What kind of welcome do you think you're going to get there? That installation is a ruin. The blood on the sand will lure every *le-matya* from here to Seleya. To say nothing of te-Vikram or other scavengers. I saw no signs of scouts, but I would assign a 20.5 percent probability to the fact that I was observed."

93

"Would the te-Vikram have taken the installation's records?" Karatek said. "If they didn't destroy its computers, perhaps there are records that a skilled computer scientist could recover. There might even be survivors," he added, raising his voice and hurling it against the polite attention of his companions. "Maybe they hid from you," he said to Skamandros.

Skamandros bowed his head. "It is . . . possible," he admitted.

Varen was on his feet, shouldering his pack, eager to be on the move before Surak said "stay" or "go."

"You're thinking I could recover these data?" Surak asked Karatek. "You realize that any light, any activity in the ruins could draw the te-Vikram down upon us?"

"I'd wager that at least one part of that installation was hardened sufficiently to withstand the attack," Karatek said. "If we found it, we'd have shelter for the night. As you say, if there's that much blood out there, it'll draw every carrion-eater in this part of the Forge. Some of them might smell us out here, too. So I'd say, in any event, we ought to get under cover before nightfall."

Surak raised himself to his feet. "Your premise may be completely emotional, but you reason well from it. I too agree that if life remains in that installation, we must seek to preserve it."

He waved Skamandros forward. The man seemed not tireless, but efficient in the way he conserved his energy to lead them.

Enough light was left for Karatek to see how the te-Vikram had defaced the rock spire, almost fifty meters high, that had served as a guard post since Vulcans had begun passing this way three dynasties ago. Some of the houses, and at least three-quarters of the wall, remained standing.

Varen and Skamandros kindled torches as Karatek, Surak at his side, sought for the hidden emergency entrances. He found a row of buttons hidden in a crevice in a rock and pressed them. What looked like a crystal inclusion in the rock glowed. Karatek laid his palm against it, hoping that it was set to identify him. If Torin had contacted this installation before the attack, the ruin would give them shelter against the wild beasts and wilder Vulcans—to say nothing of the information that was almost, but not quite, worth the sacrifice of the people here.

Surak narrowed his eyes and raised an eyebrow. He tilted his head at Varen. A moment later, he had drawn his hood up, concealing his eyes, and vanished into the rocks.

"No!" Karatek heard, followed by the sound of a brief scuffle. He plunged his hand into his pocket and felt the metal from Torin's blaster. The power cell was hot against his hand. Full charge. He hoped he would not have to draw it or, if he did, that he would find the resolve to use it.

Instants later, Surak emerged from the shadows. A body lay across his shoulder, and he grasped a struggling boy's arm in such a way that he could reach up and subdue him with a pinch to the nerve plexus between neck and shoulders. As Karatek rushed forward to ease the body Surak carried down onto the sand, Varen reached over and took custody of the boy.

The hood of the sandsuit fell forward, and a long braid swung free.

"You were quite right about survivors," said Surak. "I regret that I had to subdue the young woman."

"Regrettable?" spat the boy. He was very young, possibly too young to have even undergone the *kahs-wan.* "We watch them attack our home, we hide, and just when we thought it was safe, you attack my sister! What do you want? Didn't you kill enough of us?"

"Your assumptions are mistaken," said Surak. "We are not te-Vikram. Look, this is *T'Kehr* Karatek from the Vulcan Space Initiative. We came here to meet with your parents."

"Then why couldn't you have come earlier?" the boy demanded. He broke into racking sobs.

"Those tears only waste your body's moisture," Surak observed. "Answering our questions might be more beneficial to all of us."

"He's not one of your followers to prize logic above the lives of everyone he knows!" Karatek snapped. "Give him a minute!" He knelt beside the boy, who could not have been much more than ten years younger than Varen, and held him close, as he had the night before his elder son's *kahs-wan.* "There is no shame in fear or grief," he murmured. "Only if they prevent you from doing what you must. We will all be safer if you tell us what you know."

"I got the shelter open," he told Surak over the boy's matted hair. "We should find food, spare clothing, sleeping mats inside. Is the girl badly injured?"

Surak shrugged. "Neck pinch only," he assured Karatek.

"What is your name?" Karatek asked the boy. He pulled away as if embarrassed by his momentary collapse, straightening to courteous attention in the presence of elders.

"I am Kovar, son of Soral and T'Liri, and this is my lady sister," he said. "I welcome you to my house. There are fire and water . . . and . . ."

His lips trembled on the words of ritual hospitality, and he gave up the effort before he wept again.

"Tu'Pari said she would have slain herself before she was made wife to one of those savages," the boy said. He drew deep ragged breaths as he fought for control. "She had her knife out, and then she remembered I had not passed my *kahs-wan* and dragged me away to hide. We saw *him.*" He pointed at Skamandros. "She did not trust the look of him."

Surak edged into the shelter Karatek had found. He peered down the shaft where a ladder was carved out of the rock itself.

"Highly satisfactory," he observed.

The desert wind was chill, but Karatek felt a glow of satisfaction. "Let's get inside."

As Skamandros bent to pick up Tu'Pari, Kovar protested hotly.

Karatek sighed. The longer they stayed out here, and the louder they were, the likelier they were to be overheard.

"Young sir," said Surak. "Can you carry your sister? No? Has she parent or bondmate to aid her? Then, you will accept what must be," he said.

"They will not harm her," Karatek whispered into the boy's ear. "Now, permit us to enter your home." He aided the boy down the rough rungs of the stone ladder.

Kovar and a revived Tu'Pari scurried about, finding emergency stores: food, sleeping mats, a firebrick that, when struck, produced heat and light.

"I found it!" Kovar's high-pitched voice echoed in the underground shelter. He backed out of a supply alcove, lugging an immense bottle of water whose greenish glass shone in the chemical torchlight, and dragged it over to where Tu'Pari now sat, leaning against the rock wall.

At the sight of the water, the girl reached out and took possession of the drinking cups Varen had unpacked. Unsealing the water flagon, she filled each cup, then drew herself up and waited. Karatek stifled a smile.

Surak was first to go to one knee, greeting her as he had T'Vysse when Karatek had brought him home. The girl responded with the manners of a princess, and Karatek felt his heart twinge in his side. He would have liked to have met the parents who raised such offspring.

A whisper and a push from Tu'Pari sent Kovar scampering for

additional supplies, including incense, flatbread, and even a small firepot: everything that she could do to turn this shelter into a semblance of the home that had been stolen from her.

Karatek watched Surak and his followers exchange grave nods of approval at the children's conduct. They spoke no words beyond the proper granting and accepting of hospitality until all had eaten, and Tu'Pari sent her brother off to an alcove with a sleeping mat.

"My mother, T'Liri, was medical administrator here," Tu'Pari said. "My father, Sovar, maintained the facility, including security. Three nights ago, he failed to return from a routine patrol, and my mother said . . ."

Slanted dark eyes sparkled with tears that she repressed firmly. "I heard her say that there had been a call from ShiKahr. Someone, she told me, had to survive to greet our guests. She told Sivanon, my betrothed, to hide us away, but he . . ." She looked down.

"The attack came, and he held off fighters long enough for you to get away?" Karatek asked. Tu'Pari's "betrothed" was probably an agemate, fostered with her since the moment of their bonding. The girl bent her head so low that he could see the pallor of her skin where she had parted her long hair and rebraided it neatly in a few moments snatched from serving her "guests," as she insisted on calling Karatek, Surak, Varen, and Skamandros.

"I grieve with thee," Karatek said. He was not looking forward to the moment when this brother and sister came to the end of their endurance and collapsed. Surak nodded. "And I. There is much to do," he said, "if your parents are to be honored."

Tu'Pari looked up. "There was no time to pass on all that they were. And now they . . . the raiders have taken them."

Surak shook his head. "Their work. Their records," he said.

"And"—his voice warmed—"their heirs, whose conduct honors them. Has thee thought what shall become of thee? Has thee kin?"

Tu'Pari imitated his gesture. "Why, you're Surak!" she said. "My father said you were a dangerous radical, but my mother was glad you were coming. She said you'd been a fine computer scientist before . . . before you went into the desert. . . ."

And lost your mind, Karatek bet the woman would have added.

"She had questions to ask you. It was the only thing she and my father disagreed on. She wanted to change our names, take S-names, but he said time enough when we were fully grown."

Tu'Pari drew herself up. It would be hard for this self-possessed girl, the emotions frozen out of her by her grief, to go back to being a child. "We have kin," she said. "In ShanaiKahr. It is not logical for us to expect you to turn back and take us there. The next facility is at the hot springs some seven days' journey from here. You could leave us there, but I have heard they are short of food, resources, funding"—she looked down, and Karatek had a distinct vision of a mischievous, eavesdropping child—"because they are always complaining. So I think it is best that we accompany you to Mount Seleya."

Varen almost choked on his water. Skamandros scowled, then caught himself. The two of them exchanged fast mutters of what Karatek was sure was protest.

Surak inclined his head. "You have thought logically under harsh circumstances. I find your conduct satisfactory," he said.

Tu'Pari looked away and down, clearly abashed but trying not to betray emotion.

"We will discuss this tomorrow. You may be Head of House now, but you still need your rest. Please join your brother, and we will discuss what is best to be done."

*   *   *

Kovar stood like a tiny guard before his sister as she knelt on the sand.

"There is no logic in taking rocks on a journey across the Forge," Skamandros hissed.

Carefully, Tu'Pari chose two shards of rock: a chunk of obsidian, patterned with white, for her brother; for herself, a rock perhaps the size of her thumb, encrusted with rough crystals.

"We will use them when we build our new hearth," she told the men. "They are not large. They will not be heavy, and we will not complain," she said. "We have already burdened you sufficiently. We will try not to slow you. And my father taught me to fight."

She put a hand out to silence her brother's protests that he would protect his sister.

Karatek bent. Surreptitiously, he pocketed two striated stones as well as a cabochon ruby, hacked perhaps from a te-Vikram weapon, in memory of the girl's parents and her betrothed.

Then, shouldering their packs, they set off for the Hot Springs weapons installation.

TEN

MEMORY

Heads proudly raised, Kovar and Tu'Pari walked at Karatek's side as Surak led the way out of Hot Springs. At the two tall columns that hid the gates' sonic generators, Skamandros turned to block their path.

"Reconsider," he said. It was not a suggestion.

Karatek considered the blaster and knife that he now wore openly. He was fitter, leaner, and more alert than he had been in ShiKahr. Skamandros's desert skills no longer intimidated him.

"You consider your own observations," he replied. "There was no place for these children in Hot Springs. No welcome."

From the moment they had reached the installation at which Kovar and Tu'Pari had expected refuge, Karatek's sense that he had journeyed not just across the Forge but back in Vulcan's history had intensified. The guards who stopped them outside the gates had all been male. They had all been unbonded and therefore expendable. Although they had conceded that Karatek fit the

101

description that Torin had sent and allowed them into the compound, Surak, Skamandros, and Varen had been required to accede to genetic testing before they were all escorted to Aravik, a weathered man, more veteran than scientist, whose wariness reminded Karatek of Torin. Aravik's official title might be director of research and development, but Karatek heard him addressed as *T'Kehr* and even "my lord."

Eyeing Surak narrowly (and Skamandros more narrowly still), he had told Karatek, "your life secures their conduct."

"They are my guest-friends," he had agreed, bowing like something out of one of T'Vysse's lectures on First Dynasty Vulcan history. Once he had been a scientist and a civilized man. Now Aravik, a department head, swaggered like a lord and looked at him like a junior captain whose warriors were unruly!

Anachronistic behavior aside, Aravik had acknowledged his old ties with Torin, Karatek's claim on his hospitality, and regret at the children's loss, but deferred all conversation until after the newcomers had visited the compound's shrine.

Paying ritual respects might be appropriate for a Second Dynasty village, but for a scientific installation? Bowing over the throbbing of the drums and gongs, Karatek withheld judgment. But, during the days and nights that followed, he saw more reason to wonder if Hot Springs remained solely a scientific installation or whether the scientists, workers, and students who guarded it had been turned by the times into a clan that regarded strangers with suspicion, a clan that behaved as if it were one generation removed from the nomads who had once ranged through the Forge. And to think that the Vulcan Space Initiative had been preparing to go to the stars!

If he survived to return to T'Vysse, he would have to tell her that history had changed. Throughout Vulcan's history, strangers had always been honored guests. It was one's neighbors who could prove to be enemies. And Kovar and Tu'Pari were neighbors. There would be a place made there. Kovar would soon be of age, and Hot Springs had many unmated males who watched Tu'Pari, young as she was. But Karatek could not help but think the children's parents had hoped for more than this installation could offer.

True, they were offered food and water and fire, but only fire seemed in plentiful supply, and when Karatek asked to call ShiKahr, he was informed that his call would be timed: Hot Springs was conserving power.

Monitored, too, Karatek thought, and determined to guard his words, expecting Torin to be equally discreet.

Torin's news had proved ominous. Treaty violations on the South Continent. Te-Vikram presence in the Assemblies. Protests outside the VSI itself.

"Tell Surak I am initiating my contingency plans," Torin had ordered.

Karatek had wanted to demand an explanation, but tremors shook the ground, the generator flickered, and his call was cut off.

In the days that had followed, Aravik had spoken with him often: clan lord, he realized, to ambassador. "It is quiet here," he admitted to Karatek, "but safe."

Tu'Pari passed by, carrying bowls, with three other unbonded girls. Tu'Pari's home should have been safe. Karatek raised a skeptical eyebrow.

"Lesson learned," Aravik growled. "You already know we can't rely on our generators. We'll replace the gates with stone and desert glass and tunnel ourselves a retreat into the hill caves. What happened at one station will not happen here."

Karatek inclined his head as if he really were an ambassador, not a propulsion expert. Some ambassador! Aravik had agreed to hear Surak, who had done his persuasive best. But had it been enough?

Karatek couldn't tell. And since when, he asked himself, had he begun to care?

Perhaps, he thought, since they had found two children in the ruined installation.

When the subject of Kovar's and Tu'Pari's futures had come up, "Their lives are mine," Karatek had told Aravik. He didn't know what he'd have done if the older man had challenged his claim.

Now, Skamandros did contest it. Karatek glared at him. He had not let Aravik stop him from doing what was right. He would not let this follower of Surak—what was the man, a converted terrorist?—stop him either.

"Skamandros!" Surak called back. "Yield to the logic of the situation."

Tu'Pari's eyes filled with relief—yes, and admiration of Surak. Karatek would give much to have that look turned on him, he realized. He would adopt these children, he decided. Once the initial grief passed, T'Vysse would be glad.

"*T'Kehr?*" Tu'Pari edged closer to him.

"There is no reason to fear," he told her. "You will join my House."

She walked in silence as the sun rose in the sky. "If I am to have a new House," she said at length, "I should have a new name, as Kovar will once he passes *kahs-wan.*"

"So, you have given thought to this, daughter?" he asked.

She shrugged under her pack. "When you refused to let us remain in Hot Springs, it seemed logical you might take us in."

Karatek chuckled. Tu'Pari did not.

"I have selected my name," she told him. "Let the girl Tu'Pari die with her parents and betrothed. I am Sarissa."

"Heard and witnessed!" cried Varen. His eyes glinted, and Karatek recalled that Surak's younger disciple had often glowered at the unbonded males who followed Tu'Pari—no, Sarissa—with their eyes.

"We will consecrate that name at Mount Seleya," said Surak.

"Is that where we go next?" Karatek asked. Shielding his eyes, he glanced across the Forge, estimating distances, longing for one of the flyers that had been grounded as too-easy targets.

"Seleya will be the last stop on our pilgrimage on Vulcan," Surak said.

Meaning, Karatek thought, that Surak was convinced their next stop had to be the stars.

The installation turned village at Hot Springs seemed to herald the reception Karatek and his companion received in every other installation along their line of march. As little as the scientists liked it, Surak's arguments struck a chord within them. They didn't trust the technocrats who used funding as a way of controlling them and who were injecting observers and managers to constrain free research. And they were appalled by the warring clans and priests who rejected the advances made by science and the quest for all castes, clans, and people to get along.

As the days passed, Karatek saw what Surak intended him to see: Scientists like him were very much in the cross fire. They, their Initiatives, and their families and clans could all be held hostage as long as they possessed a resource that everyone wanted: access to the Great Ships.

Karatek had seen the models. He had worked on the drives. Now he found himself acting not just as a fact-finder but as

Torin's ambassador. The man had smoothed the way in a manner Karatek would never have expected, spending a lifetime of trust and honor as if he poured water out onto the Forge. All along the Forge, from base to research site to security installation to weapons emplacement.

"You said nothing about your conversation with Torin," Sarek observed to Karatek one evening. Koval and Tu'Pari—no, Sarissa—had been sent to the children's quarters in the safest place the community possessed, and he and his companions had been quartered together—no doubt for greater security.

They might feel like specimens under observation. Ostensibly, they were guesting at a research station devoted to desert agronomy that had recently accepted a group of ship architects into its community. Hydroponics, Karatek thought. He could see T'Raya forming a valuable membership of this tribe, assuming she could be persuaded to leave the Vulcan Space Initiative. Assuming the Vulcan Space Initiative survived.

Karatek looked down and aside, a sign that his communication with Torin was too personal to discuss in detail.

"I ask forgiveness," Surak said.

"There is no offense," Karatek replied instantly. "It requires no logic to know that many of my . . . my former associates in the VSI have become increasingly concerned. The priest-kings have stepped up their raids. Three days ago, they struck within sight of the East Gate of ShiKahr, leaving ten dead and tracks that led all the way back to the Womb of Fire."

Ignoring Sarek's disapproving lift of the eyebrow, Karatek made the ancient, propitiatory gesture about the Womb, a region more desolate even than the Forge. It was possible to cross the Forge and live. To enter the Womb of Fire and emerge alive required more than preparation: it required the cooperation of the te-Vikram Brotherhoods, whose chief shrine lay within, ruled by the Old Mother of Fire, or perhaps her son, if the whispers that she'd gone into the desert to die were true. In that case, the whispers ran, the Womb would be doubly accursed.

It was not a place that Karatek wished to go. And yet it lay perilously near the borders of the Forge where they must pass if they hoped to reach Seleya.

"Our work here is done," Surak said. "We should leave for Seleya at dawn."

Rock formations, striated blood green and a deep red, rose out of the ruddy sand. Their outcroppings were roughly symmetrical, reminding Karatek of ShiKahr's East Gate or the menhirs at Great Houses' sanctuaries of *Koon-ut-kal-iffee*.

Sarissa raised her head, sniffing the air.

Varen nodded at her. "Water," he said.

Kovar tensed, visibly controlling his impulse to dash forward and walk between those jagged pillars.

"Where there is water there is the potential for war," Surak murmured. He dropped into a crouch, stretching out on the sand.

"Beasts would wait until nightfall to drink," Varen said.

"Not if we disturbed them in their lairs. Certainly not, if we disturbed a *le-matya* and her kittens or a dormant *vai-sehlat*," Skamandros replied.

Tu'Pari—no, Sarissa—put her hand on her brother's shoulder, forestalling a protest of "I *knew* that!"

"Do you wish me to scout?" she asked Karatek. But her eyes followed Surak worshipfully.

He shook his head. He and Surak could not be risked, as hard a dose as that was to swallow. Kovar was too young. Sarissa? There were reasons why she was the worst possible choice. It would have to be Varen or Skamandros, and Karatek didn't wholly trust Skamandros.

"We will all go," Surak said. "That way, it cannot be said that we are spies."

They rose. Hands well away from their weapons, they approached the rocks. The desert floor sloped up. From here they could be seen for at least a hundred *k'vahr.*

"Halt, water thieves."

The voice was the coldest thing Karatek had ever heard on the Forge.

"It is illogical to accuse us of breaking water truce," Surak said. "We have not even approached your well. But we would purchase water if you would sell."

"Water is life," the voice retorted. "We do not sell our water—but we would sell our lives dearly."

Sarissa shot an outraged look at Karatek. He nodded minutely at her. Just because these people probably were te-Vikram didn't mean they would automatically kill this time.

"Stand or die!"

Six te-Vikram left the security of the rock with an assurance that told Karatek that more remained hidden. They moved so that the sun was in Karatek's eyes and he longed for the lenses he had left behind. Veils flickered across his sight. All he could see was tall figures, dark in the sunlight, except for where it glinted off drawn blades.

Of course! The te-Vikram would not use blasters on strangers whose bodies' water they hoped to reclaim. Karatek thought of the blaster at his waist, thought of how quickly one of the men confronting him could throw his knife, factored into the equation the fact that he had never killed that he knew of, and sighed.

Surak stepped forward.

"We are children of the same Mother," he began, his rich voice echoing off the rocks. "Lay down your weapons, and let us reason together. There is no logic in fighting and none in dying of thirst when all may drink."

"Eminence!" a shout rang out. "This is the outcast our brothers tracked across the Forge!"

In his last call, Torin had warned Karatek that the te-Vikram had taken oath to destroy Surak and all his works—along with the VSI.

A seventh figure, not as tall as . . . *his guards* and not nearly as young, emerged from between the rock spires. Light glinted off the gems in his belt, in his dagger, and trimming his sandsuit.

"Sir," said Surak. "We come in peace." He continued to move forward. Varen and Skamandros started to flank him, but he gestured and, obedient, they stayed where they were.

Surak moved nearer, talking, always talking, but not raising his voice above the tone he might use at a dinner symposium. "I am not one of your disciples," said Surak. "But that is no cause for hostility. I have learned that infinite diversity exists in infinite combinations and it is logical to accept that. I come to serve. How may I serve thee?"

"You can die!" the te-Vikram priest snarled.

Drawing his jagged ritual knife, he lunged forward, determined to silence Surak through death if he could not do so by logical argument.

The priest was fast, very fast.

At this distance, Karatek could not outrun him. His hand darted to the blaster at his belt.

But Varen was faster.

"*T'Kehr* Surak!" he shouted. Ardent, impulsive, and profoundly loyal, he dashed forward. And flung himself between

Surak and the te-Vikram priest, whose hooked blade sank into Varen's chest. The reek of copper gushed out with the young man's blood, and he sank onto the sand. One hand struggled up, as Varen attempted, even in his death throes, to defend his teacher.

Surak reached out and caught Varen's bloody hand without looking away from the te-Vikram priest. For a moment, his eyes blazed as if the Fires raged in his blood. Then, they subsided.

"It is illogical to end life without need," he stated. His voice did not even falter.

The te-Vikram ripped his knife free. More blood gouted onto the ruddy sand, dying it dark.

Again, Surak gestured to restrain Skamandros. "Must I tell you twice?" he asked.

Again, the priest raised his blade.

Skamandros would never be able to intervene, even if he obeyed his master.

The time is *now,* Karatek told himself. Recovering the ability to move, he dropped his hand to his belt, drew Torin's blaster, and fired. He was furious at the loss of life, furious at the waste, the stupid, self-righteous waste of the priest-kings and their anachronistic, backward hatred. He was furious at Surak, too, with his childish trust that he could wage peace when others dealt only death. And he was furious that his children had to see this atrocity after they had already endured so much.

His blaster shrieked as energy turned into flame and flesh turned into ash, then into nothing at all. Along with the last of the warriors, his anger disappeared. They had not, he realized, been that difficult to kill after all. Torin would say they had gotten slack, preying on the old, the infirm, and the occasional pilgrim on spirit quest.

Then there were no more te-Vikram to kill. Karatek put the

blaster away. Now, he found it hard to meet Surak's eyes, much harder than it had been to kill the te-Vikram. It was too easy to kill. He had never understood that until now. For a moment, he thought his knees would give way.

"Thy logic failed," Surak observed. Slowly, he knelt beside his dying student.

Karatek's moment of revulsion passed. Too rapidly, Surak might say. If Surak did not talk so much, Varen might not be dying!

"Better my logic than my blaster," snarled Karatek. He too dropped to his knees beside Varen.

"Stay back!" Sarissa snapped at her brother. Kovar listened to her not at all. Both raced forward to fling themselves down up on the sand. Sarissa reached out to clasp Varen's free hand, where it pressed against his death wound.

"Give him water!" she told Kovar.

"No," Varen gasped. "Don't waste . . ."

"We can replenish our supply from the well," Surak assured him.

He gasped as the water dribbled down onto his slack lips. A thread of deep green blood escaped from the corner of his mouth.

"Sir," he gasped. "I ask forgiveness for my loss of control."

Surak laid his free hand on Varen's head. Shutting his eyes just as Varen's eyes rolled back into his head, he slid his fingers over to Varen's temple. He knelt there, utterly still, as if listening to a voice only he could hear. Then he bent forward, closing the young man's eyes and smoothing his black hair, making it sleek once more.

"It is well that we are bound for Seleya," Surak observed. "I can place Varen's *katra* in the Hall of Ancient Thought on Seleya because, truly, it is not ready for release."

His voice was completely level. Only for an instant did his face twist as he fought and mastered a surge of the same hate for the te-Vikram that had enabled Karatek to kill for the first time.

Then, pressing Varen's limp hand against his other, blood-stained one, he rose.

"I ask pardon for my loss of control," he said, bowing to Skamandros.

"The cause was great," the other man replied.

He bent over Varen, stripped the body of gear, then covered it with sand.

Slowly, Karatek sheathed his blaster, then wiped his hand on his sandsuit. How strange: he felt as if it should be coated with blood, and yet it was clean. Clean as the desert.

Kovar and Sarissa walked over to him, looking up into his face, not as if they expected him to make everything right, but as if they wanted to see what he would do next.

Reaching into his pouch, he pulled out the scarred cabochon he had pulled from the ground near their shattered home. He had taken it in memory of Sarissa's betrothed, slaughtered there. It would serve now to mark where Varen lay.

"Would it have been so bad?" he shouted at the sky, quivering with heat. Then, he mastered himself.

"Here," he said gently to Sarissa, who fought not to weep. "Give this to him."

Sarissa edged forward and placed the glinting gem on the shallow mound that was all they could see of Varen. Skamandros was already storing his gear about his person.

"I grieve for thee," Sarissa told both men.

Surak, tucking those of Varen's belongings Skamandros had not already packed, inclined his head. "At least," he told her, "all that he was will be preserved at Mount Seleya."

Karatek turned to look at the shallow mound that covered a young man he wished he had had the chance to know better.

"Karatek!" Surak did not even trouble to raise his voice.

Karatek turned to follow Surak, who carried everything of Varen that mattered now.

ELEVEN

NOW

STARFLEET HEADQUARTERS

Chekov—that was Admiral Pavel Chekov, thank you very much—managed to put the padd down without hurling it against his office's wall. He'd already put a dent in that wall once, hurling a paperweight, and that had been awkward enough to explain. He had a *nice* office after all, a *pleasant* office of smooth wood and thickly padded leather chairs, a gentleman's office.

But thinking of that didn't help reduce his frustration at all. He had never wanted to be a gentleman. "And I vas *not* meant to be a bureaucrat!"

Even after more than a century in Starfleet, he had never quite lost his Russian accent. Or maybe, Chekov admitted wryly, he was deliberately hanging on to it as a last link with the past. The way-back past. The last time he'd been in Moskva, he'd barely recognized the place.

Nara, the young Bolian woman who was his aide, hadn't even flinched at his outburst. "No, sir."

He swiveled about in his too-comfortable chair to face her, accidentally sweeping a pile of printouts off his desk. "But did I not already duly fill out Form 24.15, and in triplicate? Did I not transmit it myself? I didn't ewen question the fact that Form 24.15 seems to deal vith farm animals, not starships. Nara, do you have any idea vhy ve are still using Form 24.15?"

"I don't know, sir." She bent and gathered up the printouts. "Maybe someone at Starfleet Headquarters thinks pigs can fly?"

Chekov started to reply, stopped, and stared at Nara. "*Wery* good!"

In her spare time, Nara was studying twentieth-century American English. She beamed. "Proper old English idiom?"

"Perfect tventieth century." But then Chekov shook his head and sat back in his too-comfortable chair. "Ridiculous thing for an admiral to be doing, isn't it? Before the var, I at least could train Starfleet captains. Now, I spend my days playing vord games and filling out archaic forms."

"I know, sir. It must be so frustrating. Especially when . . ." She stopped awkwardly.

"Go on, Nara. I vill not bite." At her blink, he added hastily, "Another Earth idiom, not a literal varning!"

"Oh." Nara was an excellent aide, but she did tend to blush easily. Right now, she was rapidly turning a charming deep sapphire. "Well, I, it must have been so, so splendid, sir, soaring through the galaxy like that, I mean, working alongside Captain Kirk on the original *Enterprise* and seeing all those new worlds and—"

Chekov snorted. "You make me sound like an antique, young voman. I'm not *that* old."

By now, she was nearly cobalt. "Oh no, sir, I didn't mean that!"

"Never mind, Nara."

It's true, though. I do feel like an antique. Taken out of active use and put on display to be admired. Or is that pitied?

Dammit, though, it's true: I'm not that old. There are active Starfleet personnel in the field who have decades on me.

Well, years, at any rate.

But me, oh no, I—I had to go and accept the honors.

Idiot. I should have done what Captain Kirk did, get the title demoted right back down again to captain.

I could still do it. . . .

Do what? The Dominion War was over, which was why they all had so much of that cursed paperwork, and right now everyone in the Federation was busy just picking up the pieces.

Not much romance in that. No one needs any more five-year missions and boldly going anywhere, not just now.

But, damn. What I wouldn't give for one more adventure.

At least he had actually managed to play a useful role during the Dominion War. . . .

2373

At least, Chekov thought, *I can still be useful even now, with the war almost at our figurative front door.*

He'd given up active command decades ago, tired of being as-signed nothing but routine patrols. *Ah yes, Starfleet's tactful way of telling me to take a desk job,* Chekov told himself. *Sorry, gentlebeings, but ever since that little adventure with Khan Noonien Singh I've been a tiny bit, shall we say, hard of hearing.*

Even if he wasn't commanding a ship, Chekov had avoided that desk job all that decade and made a new name for himself as a quick, efficient, and, yes, merciful trainer of young Starfleet

officers. He looked about the holosuite that right now was a perfect mockup of an Oberth-class ship's bridge, down to the sheen
on the railings and a scuff mark on a panel. It perfectly hid the
fact that it was really just part of a Starfleet facility on Garaita IV,
and Chekov had to hide his grin before one of the youngsters who
were sitting at the different control panels asked if something was
wrong. A really good holoprogram, such as this one, which he'd
helped design, got those using it completely lost in the illusion of
flying a starship to the point that they'd be sweating and swearing
before he let them go.

But they would remember the lessons learned. And he didn't
have to risk a starship or its crew—or, for that matter, his own
life—to teach them.

Without warning, Chekov snapped, "A spatial anomaly has suddenly appeared, starboard, coordinates 21.52 by 623.5." The words
cued the holoprogram to instantly produce one. "At your current
speed, you will intersect it in one minute. What do you do?"

He watched the crew scramble to it, pleased to see that the
"captain," a dark-skinned human with her long hair caught up in a
coronet of braids, correctly ordered "Science," a white-furred
Tariik, to report and at the same time ordered "Helm," another
human who reminded Chekov of a young Hikaru Sulu, to take
evasive action. "Helm" reacted properly, too: On a real ship, she
would have used just enough power to turn them away to safety.

You don't get out of this that easy!

Chekov snapped, "But engineering just reported an explosion!"
The holodeck, cued in, obligingly provided the special effect,
shaking the "crew" violently. "Sabotage? An accident? There's
little time—you have just lost most of your warp capability."

The "captain" was in instant communication with "engineering," a part of the holoprogram.

Good girl. Asking all the right questions. There's hope for you after all, and maybe for Helm and Science as well.

He gave the "crew" a slight breather before he hit them with the "hostile alien encounter" scenario as well. A good starship crew had to be ready to handle two or even three crises at the same time, and maybe even deal with a first-contact situation as well.

So, now, maybe this wasn't the same as some heroic "five-year mission of exploration" as it was in the days aboard the *Enterprise,* but it was good to know he was keeping today's young hotshots from getting themselves or their crews killed, or from starting a war.

Even if the youngsters did tend to treat him like living history. Or maybe that was as a living antique.

You did what you could with what you had. Besides, the youngsters did show promise. And at least he did get to go out into space aboard starships later in the training process. Besides, no matter what the youngsters thought of him, he had yet to lose one of his students.

"What's that?" he snapped.

They picked up on the cue perfectly. "Captain! An alien ship is approaching, warp six . . . uh . . . seven—"

Half-point deduction for that stumble.

The "captain" uttered the words Chekov had heard so many times in his career: "Open hailing frequencies."

"No answer, Captain."

Now what are you going to do, eh, youngsters? No warp capability, an explosion in engineering, a singularity alarmingly close, and a rude alien approaching.

But without warning, the projection wavered, then faded, leaving them back in the plain, black-walled, wire-lined holosuite.

The students, now looking more like ordinary human and Tariik young men and women than an elite starship crew, murmured and blinked in surprise.

"Program malfunction," Chekov said. "Stay vere you are. Your lesson is not over."

Before Chekov could say anything else, though, his combadge beeped. With a grunt of annoyance at the new interruption, he slapped at it. "Chekov here. Vhat do you—"

But before he could get any further, the voice at the other end murmured a code phrase: Information for his ears only.

Now what?

"You'll have to excuse me," Chekov said. "But don't go anywhere. As I varn, the lesson isn't over yet."

With that, Chekov left the holosuite.

"This way, sir," an aide murmured, and led him to a private office.

No window. No furnishings other than a chair and a desk with a viewscreen. Purely utilitarian—and, Chekov knew from prior experiences, secure.

He sat at the console and keyed in his own private code, and then leaned back, waiting with a touch of impatience as the viewscreen went through the various Starfleet security screens, then finally came to full life.

Then Chekov straightened, frowning, as he recognized the image of a tall, lean, pale-skinned man.

"Thomas? Vhat's wrong?"

Admiral Thomas John Randall said shortly, "Sorry to drag you out of a lesson."

Chekov waved that off. "They'll survive. Suspense is good for the young. Not for me. Vhat do you vant to tell me?" He paused uneasily, studying the man's face. "Bad news, I take it."

Randall sighed and nodded. "I thought that you'd want to hear it before it goes public."

"Never mind the drama, Thomas. Vhat happened?"

"The details are just starting to come in. It's begun. Deep Space 9 is under Dominion attack."

Chekov stared at him in a second of sheer disbelief. "*Bozhya moi,*" he said at last. "My God."

"It's official, Pavel: We're at war."

I knew it was coming, Chekov thought grimly. *I knew it as soon as I heard that we were mining the Bajoran wormhole. No way in all the hells that the Dominion was going to give them a chance to finish the job. And of course Starfleet couldn't get help to them in time.*

"Vhat about Sisko and his people?" he asked. "Are they all right?"

"As far as I know, yes. All Starfleet personnel evacuated the station. Unofficial word has it that almost all of them are safe." The man shook his head. "As safe as they can be under the circumstances. But the Bajorans are facing a second occupation."

"Vhat does Starfleet vant of me, Thomas?"

"To put it bluntly, Pavel: With a war on its hands, Starfleet has suddenly found itself needing all the trained starship personnel it can get, and needing them fast."

"Ah."

"You're not surprised."

"Vell, I had hardly expected to be sent into battle. Ve both know damned vell that captaining a starship in combat is a younger person's game. So, let me guess. You vant me to go right on training the youngsters—but you vant me to speed things up, and to cut out anything but the military side of the training."

Randall held out a helpless hand. "Official Starfleet orders. Get them ready as fast as you can."

"Vone, two, three, shove them out into space and hope that some of them surwive."

"Do you think I like it? It's not the best way to do things, every-one knows it, and it hurts like hell to think of how many we're going to lose, but dammit, Pavel, what else is there for us to do?" Randall suddenly pretended to be very busy studying a padd. "You have just been issued passage aboard the *U.S.S. Arcturus,* which will be headed back to Earth in three hours."

"Three, eh? You don't give a man much time, do you? Some one had better go tell the students the lesson is over. I left them vaiting for me on the holodeck. How did Starfleet vord it? 'Neces-sary but not essential personnel' or vas it 'baggage, human, aging'?"

"It wasn't—"

Chekov sighed. "Don't bother answering that, Thomas. And don't vorry, I'm not going to throw a childish fit. I knew this day vas going to come. It's just that knowing it doesn't make it any less of a shock."

"To both of us, I assure you."

Chekov shook his head. "That doesn't change the way things are. So. Tell me, who is the captain of this *U.S.S. Arcturus?*"

"Captain Alan Roberts."

Chekov snorted.

"What?"

"I trained him." *Young Alan Roberts already a captain. Young? Bah, any younger, and he wouldn't even need to shave!*

But seeing everyone else as young was supposed to be another one of those cursed warning signs of age everyone insisted on quoting to him, so Chekov merely gave Randall a wry grin.

"Vell, let's just hope the young man has learned his lessons and learned them vell."

2377

"Sir? The news feed just came in and it's marked urgent."

Chekov, jarred abruptly back to the present, groaned. "Oh hell, now vhat?"

It was beautifully ironic that as soon as he'd stepped back onto Earth again, he'd been rewarded for his time in the war effort with the very thing he'd been fighting so long to avoid: a damned desk job. He could still see the bright and shiny officials in their spotless uniforms and their charming smiles, meeting him in the spaceport where they knew he wouldn't make a scene, offering him the nice, shiny lure of the admiralty—and the strings that came with the title.

I fell for it. And no one ever said that life was fair.

Chekhov switched on the news feed, and as the image formed, dimly heard Nara's soft, stunned "Oh," and himself swearing in horrified Russian.

After that, Chekhov and Nara watched in utter silence as the delayed broadcast played across his vidscreen. They both saw the destruction of the Romulan colony and the savage claim by the . . . the Watraii.

The Watraii? Chekhov frowned slightly, prodding his memory. Something about that name . . . a vague recollection of . . .

Yes. Same name, same mask, same species.

So much for picking up the pieces.

Chekhov didn't doubt that the news feed wasn't giving him all the facts—but he knew where to get them.

"Nara, get me Admiral Uhura—no, never mind, don't bother, I'll do it myself."

As he waved her out, Chekov entered the proper code with the proper automatic scrambling. Almost at once he saw the image of a familiar face with a halo of silver hair.

"Pavel," she said. "How nice to hear from you."

"Uhura, vhat the hell is going on?"

"Just what I was going to tell you." Uhura smiled slightly, charming as ever, but with the steel beneath the smile. "I don't have to ask if your office is secure, do I?"

"Secure as the best communications officer in Starfleet could make it," he retorted. "For which I thank her."

She gave him a true grin at that, no subterfuge or hidden meanings. But almost at once the coolness returned to her face. "Pavel, listen to me. I have a little . . . vacation for you."

He straightened. Uhura in her role as chief of intelligence never contacted anyone about leisure activities. Considering what he had just viewed, there didn't seem to be much doubt about why she'd contacted him.

Chekov shrugged. "One of the perks of being an admiral," he said, "is that I can take leave vhenever I vant, and pretty much no one of any lower rank than another admiral is going to challenge me. Hello, other admiral." He paused. "Ve're talking about that destroyed Romulan colony, aren't ve?"

Nothing changed in that elegant mahogany face. Uhura only answered obliquely, "Come see me, Pavel. We need to arrange a few details."

Her very careful, casual wording gave him the clue: Yes, it was about the colony—and no, this wasn't going to be a Starfleet mission that she was proposing. Not surprising, Chekov thought quickly. Starfleet wasn't going to want to get caught up in Romulan affairs, not right after a war, and not with alliances still so new and shaky.

Chekov surprised himself by suddenly grinning like a kid—no, like the green young ensign he'd once been.

"Yes sir, Captain Kirk!"

You idiot. The mission is going to be something covert and dangerous, and it's probably going to get you busted back to ensign, assuming that you even survive it. Whatever it is.

But even so, he still couldn't stop grinning.

TWELVE

MEMORY

The sun hammered down as Surak led them toward Mount Seleya in a file as ragged as their sandsuits, stumbling down the last dunes to stagger as they reached flat ground once more. Beneath his hood, Karatek felt the very intensity of the light trying to crush him into the sand. If he fell, he might not be able to summon the strength to fight the sun and rise. Then he would die, gazing up at the blazing sky until his eyes dried long before death came.

Avert, Karatek wished it. His scratched fingers moved in a gesture that had been old even in the First Dynasty. Nor did he mind that Surak had seen him indulge in superstition.

In another life, Karatek reminded himself, he had been an engineer. He had sat, comfortably alert, at a workstation in a climate-controlled room and sipped tea. For him, the rigors of the *kahs-wan,* of reclamation work, or rebuilding were memories of service done and long since delegated to others. Now, those

125

ordeals seemed like so much play. He was no longer privileged, softened by city living. And he had children to protect.

Day after day on the Forge, Karatek learned how to fight against breaking into the dreamy, rhythmic stride that would make him drift out of time and awareness into a doze that could tumble him down a slope to smash into hidden rocks with edges like knives. They could shatter bone, those rocks, or slash so deep the blood would not stop flowing. Or, even if he kept his footing, an unwary slide into just the wrong place on a dune could start a sandfall, alert any stray te-Vikram, or even wake the creatures that, legend whispered, swam beneath the sand as if it were one of Vulcan's shrunken seas.

Left foot. Right foot. Pause. Drag. And onward until each muscle ached and beyond.

After days of this slow walking in which he was agonizingly aware of each sound and each muscle, he became sure it would be easier to climb up a rock face. Climbing, Karatek reminded himself, was what they would do soon, if all went well. Mount Seleya never seemed to get any closer.

Karatek's lips cracked and blackened with thirst. Often now, he bent over the children who slouched at his side, Sarissa trying to ease her brother's path as if she were mother, not sister. Surak, by contrast, seemed to move as effortlessly as if he walked within the walled gardens that Karatek could scarcely believe belonged to him in what now felt like another life. Karatek shot a furious glance at him and brought himself up sharply before the two of them collided.

"You must drink your water yourself, not give it away," the philosopher rebuked him. "There is no logic in giving your children your water if you die of thirst and leave them unprotected when they have come to trust you."

Such a weight of trickery in those words! And to think, he had tried to be sparing in his use of water, to deny himself!

Karatek let his eyes blaze, then lowered his head. Anger—any emotion here on the Forge—was simply not worth the energy it consumed.

Surak could not know. He had no children. He could not know how a father might abandon pretense of pride in the daily struggle to endure, to create even a hint of shade for his children, to give them the last drops of water in his flask.

Even if Surak said it was illogical. As Karatek met his eyes, he saw the man's face go gentle for an instant.

Was it true that Surak did not understand a father's love? Karatek asked himself. Again, he saw Varen, bleeding, dying in Surak's arms. Surak's face had changed: his fight to control himself had been a visible, frightening thing. Perhaps that was why he insisted now on making the pilgrimage to Seleya bearing Varen's *katra* when the purity of the desert might have been, even logically speaking, funeral enough.

And perhaps he had other reasons altogether.

Sarissa's face, beneath the hood of her suit, was unreadable. She had allowed Varen to aid her over rocky ground once or twice, had thanked him in a low, sweet voice—and would that have been so bad? Karatek thought. Varen had been a fine, clean young man with a spirit of fire. His whole life had stretched out before him, and now what was he? A disembodied *katra* floating about in Surak's mind. His logic would be as cool as fresh water: a relief for poor Varen.

Under Surak's dispassionate gaze, Karatek felt his rage finally dissipate to a level he could bear. He unhooked his water flask and drank.

*　　*　　*

The last stars paled in the sky when the wind finally changed. Kovar's head went up, and he sniffed the air.

"Water." The boy's bleeding lips shaped the blessed word without sound.

The subtle fragrance of water lured them forward, thin figures in sandsuits that hung in shabby folds on them; sharp eyes whose sockets they had stained against the glare. On other days, they had always sought refuge before dawn against the fury of sunlight on the Forge. Now the scent of water drew them onward. They allowed themselves to step up the pace, but kept wary: where there was water, there were predators—and prey.

As the sky brightened around them, the air cooled, then darkened as they entered the shadow of Seleya's majestic bulk. Karatek squandered a moment to gaze longingly up at the astonishing snow that shrouded the peak behind the sanctuary. The idea of walking in that whiteness seemed like the hallucination of a man dying of thirst in the deep desert.

A rippling glare at their feet dazzled them. They stopped short before they stumbled into the ablutions pools at Seleya's foot. Skamandros turned his head, unobtrusively pointing out the guard post, hollowed out of a giant boulder. Karatek couldn't remember a guard post from the only other time he had been to Seleya. Kovar tumbled to his knees. Sarissa's eyes flashed from Karatek to Surak, observing. Then she knelt in time with Surak and Karatek, bending toward the water as gracefully as a flower.

Slipping off his boots, Karatek scooped water over his feet. Not even the blessedness of that relief altered Surak's expression. *Kylin'the* plants grew by the pool, their spiked leaves forming a crown of deep green and amber. Remembering his old training, Karatek whispered thanks and a blessing before he snapped off a leaf. As his children watched, he used the sap beading the broken edge to coat the worst of his blisters: *kylin'the* balm brought relief from pain and quick healing. He nodded at them to break off leaves and tend their own hurts.

The last rags of his self-respect restrained Karatek from measuring his length in the pool and letting the water refresh his entire body. He contented himself with a drink that was long, but not as much as he wanted, before he sprinkled water on his face and hands. Suppressing a sigh, he rubbed his feet before beginning the ritual purifications.

"Put your boots back on," Sarissa ordered her younger brother. "Thee remains in my charge until thee passes *kahs-wan.*"

Karatek suppressed a skeptical chuckle: the crossing they had just survived had made his own trial feel like a stroll in a garden. Now, they faced another ordeal: the pilgrimage up the thousand steps of Mount Seleya was customarily made barefoot.

"What about you?" Kovar whispered furiously, wriggling away from her as she sought to refasten his boots.

"Sarissa will yield to the logic of the situation," Surak cut in smoothly. "You must all protect your feet. If you cannot mount the stairs before nightfall, we shall have to camp down here."

She glanced imploringly at Karatek. "Father?" she asked.

Why, that clever little *le-matya* kit! Karatek had wondered when she would call him father, had longed for it. What if she never did? What if he could not bear it? Now, she had done so, and he wanted to laugh out loud at his new daughter's guile.

"Listen to wisdom, not pride, my child," Karatek told her. He refastened his boots. "*T'Kehr* Surak asks wise questions. So I will listen to him myself."

After Seleya, they would have to face the return march to ShiKahr. Surak and Skamandros might be hardened to it through long practice, but the others could not make it on feet that were abraded and bleeding.

Skamandros raised an eyebrow, then shrugged. Removing his boots, he followed Surak up the spiraling stairs of Mount Seleya. The stone was hot, but neither he nor Surak as much as flinched. And neither man's feet left dark green smears upon the stones, worn smooth and hollow by generations of pilgrims to this shrine, ancient even for Vulcan.

Karatek gestured Sarissa and Kovar to follow the other men and brought up the rear of their party, guarding his children's backs. It would, after all, have been illogical to dispute his right. And Surak was never that, now, was he?

Father. Sarissa's word did not replace or heal his daughter's death. But the scars that had seemed to replace his heart seemed to ease and his breath came the easier.

Already high above the beasts, the indwellers, and the raiders to be found in the desert, Karatek mounted stair after stair and indulged himself in the discomfort of his thoughts.

Surak wanted the best minds and hearts on Vulcan to exile themselves, to seek out the stars before ships were ready, before they could reach them within a Vulcan's normal life span.

But he knew his people. They would be afraid to go. *He* was afraid. Wasn't it only logical to fear the unknown?

Gradually Surak's logic replaced blind fear and rationalization: like his former—no, his colleagues at the Vulcan Space Initiative, Surak wanted what was best for their world. And if the needs of the many outweighed, as Surak said, the needs of the few and required them to leave their home, perhaps they would have to consider it.

But what of the needs of the few? Karatek protested to himself. After all, they loved their world, too. But the evidence was mounting up that, for the Mother World's sake, some of them dared not stay. War was coming. It might be that those who left would postpone the Mother World's ability to invent weapons that could destroy it once and for all.

And if not, then surely, as Surak said, it was logical for there to be a saving remnant who could look back at the shards that had once been their homeworld and remember it.

And prevent that from ever happening again! Perhaps, next time, Surak's logic would prevent the grief from destroying them as they had destroyed their home.

Hail Surak, bringer of a second chance! Karatek's irony cut as sharply as the stone.

Up the steps of Mount Seleya Karatek climbed. A thousand steps, the rituals said. It felt like far, far more.

The steps narrowed, slanted. The pilgrims passed beneath tilted, cracked arches cut into the ruddy stone that granted them blessed flickers of shade.

And then the ground leveled. They stood on a plateau beneath the snow-topped peak. An immense building, like a truncated cone, stood to one side: the adepts and their disciples lived and worked there. Rumor had it that they had tunneled deep into the rock. If Vulcan burned, they alone might well survive—but for what?

Not thirty yards away, the plateau dropped off into a chasm crossed only by a narrow rock span. No handholds, and even an infinitesimal arch at its center. But beyond that bridge lay the Halls of Ancient Thought.

"Drink your water," Karatek urged Kovar and Sarissa.

Surak, Skamandros padding at his heels, had already crossed.

"Quickly, before the night wind rises!" Skamandros called. An adept might cross the bridge in the wind, but anyone else would surely be knocked into the abyss. As it was, they would have to sleep in the shrine—or make their visit a brief one.

The air was thin. Karatek's back, eyes, and head ached. Lava lay below: he could not see it for the steam that created clouds far, far below the bridge.

"Go," he said. And because they were his children and, already, he loved them, "it is no disgrace to crawl across the span," he said.

Their heads came up. Clearly, he had offered his children not comfort but a challenge. Walking slowly, not looking down, but across the chasm to the sanctuary, they made it to the other side. True, Kovar sank onto the ground for a moment, breathing hard, but Sarissa stood at Surak's side.

"Come, Father," she said in a sweet, steady voice. She held out her hand. Worn as he was, Karatek felt as if he could leap across the bridge.

He crossed, his back as straight, his step as steady as if he were Surak himself. And when he had reached the other side, he stayed on his feet and even managed to keep from grinning in triumph. Skamandros nodded in grudging approval.

Surak led the way past the amphitheatre into the sanctuary. It was the oldest working shrine on Vulcan: two squared towers carved of rough stone that, thousands of years ago, priests and worshippers had quarried, then cut and carried up the slope on patient, muscular backs.

The terrible impact of Vulcan's sun dissipated as they entered the shrine, but not its light. Its rays slashed through lancets carved out of the thick golden stone, glinting with veins of precious copper, flecked with crystals, that rose many times the height of a tall Vulcan. Though the sun was sinking, the light still seemed almost solid: where it met the massive pillars and walls, it seemed to war with them, creating deep shadows.

Immense pillars of greenish bronze metal, their bases wrought in the form of water plants, held light that cast a smell as sweet as the incense that rose from braziers wrought in the form of savage beasts, smoke rising from between their fangs, light glinting in their eyes. Sunlight and flame made the alcoves between columns seem even darker and more mysterious, whispering with the wind and the dancing grains of sand that it blew into the Hall.

In the coolness of those alcoves reposed the urns of memory. Each rested in its own niche, niche upon niche from the worn paving stones to the coffered ceiling, inlaid with priceless wood. Each urn held a *katra*. Some glowed faintly as powerful minds sought to comprehend the world they had known and walked as living beings. Others were dark.

One urn was empty. Its stopper, wrought in the form of a *kylin'the*, crystal dew beading its crest, lay to one side on the hollowed paving, as if the adepts of the mountain had already divined the reason for their coming.

At the end of the hall was a raised platform, illuminated by torches at each corner and blazing with light from a triangular window carved high overhead. Standing on the platform was an immense gong, wrought of the same bloodmetal as the torch holders.

Without hesitation, Surak walked over to the dais and struck the gong. It throbbed until the rock itself seemed to quiver. Kovar swayed as if dizzy, and Karatek put out a hand to steady him, grateful for the reassurance of flesh against flesh.

The light seemed to dazzle him. When it subsided, Karatek saw that adepts had joined them: a priestess in the red and white of Seleya, wearing a gemstone at her brow, set in the form of a *shavokh*. At her side was a priest who wore the dusty white robe with

133

the padded hem and cabochon gems that indicated his rank in the hierarchy of Gol.

Although Skamandros knelt, Surak paid no homage beyond the polite bow he would have accorded any elder. Behind the priestess, an acolyte hissed, then fell silent.

From behind them, across the bridge, throbbed another gong and the beat of immense hollow drums. A double line of priestesses entered the shrine, chanting as they walked. They were graceful, swaying in their white shifts. Their glossy black hair poured down their backs like water in the wilderness, barely ruffled although Karatek could hear the winds begin to rise outside. These were the Unbonded whose unselfish care saved many Vulcans from dying when their blood burned and they had no mate.

"Get behind me," Karatek whispered to Sarissa. As an unbonded girl of no family, she might be of special, specific value to the adepts here. But Karatek had not rescued the girl only to give her to Seleya. Sarissa had already sacrificed enough in her short life.

He raised his chin, challenging the priestess to object. She said nothing. Instead, she pointed to the empty urn.

Surak walked to the urn and stroked it with long, sensitive fingers. Despite his physical and mental control, he shivered as he released Varen's *katra* from his consciousness.

A faint glow kindled in the center of the urn. Surak's face lightened, and he laid his fingers on its side as he might have touched the living Varen's shoulder in approval.

"Sorrow?" Karatek could not resist asking.

"I take satisfaction in the fact that this *katra* has found a home. So many others have died like water spilled upon the barren rock, or blood poured into the sand. Varen will have time to think, to remember, and to realize—" The flicker of Surak's eyelids would have been a wail of pain from anyone else.

His face gentled. "Become wise before thee journeys onward," he told the light within the vessel. A long, long pause. Karatek thought Surak had finished speaking and almost broke in. "My son," Surak finished.

Karatek remembered. Surak wasn't just a noted computer scientist or a rebel philosopher: he was a poet. When the first volume of his *Analects* had been published, it had sparked three riots and won two literary awards.

The Gol priest bowed to Surak. Karatek recalled that the *Analects* had inspired the adepts at Gol to devote themselves to logic with a fervor that would have been fanatic—if fanaticism were not itself illogical.

"Have you come finally to stay with us or to dispute further?" asked the priest from Gol.

"The winds are rising. We request hospitality for the night," Surak replied. "Will the high priestess debate me?"

"She will not!" Gol's adept cut in, to be rewarded by a fierce look from the priestess.

"Hear me, heed me," Surak began what Karatek knew was the long skein of persuasions that had worked on so many scientists.

Priestess and adept listened for a time, the Unbonded clustered at their backs.

"*Kroykah!*" cried the priestess. "Thee may not stay. Thee disturbs every place thee touches."

"I will not ask forgiveness for being myself, walking where I walk, or thinking what I think. You yourself taught me: The mind is sacrosanct. But I will beg pardon for disturbing thy meditations," Surak said. "I admit I came again to debate with thee. But more than that, I came to grant release to a youth who had become like a son."

The priestess's face softened.

"Vulcan thanks thee for the gift of a precious *katra,* a soul," she said. "What thanks would thee ask in return?"

"One does not thank logic," Surak said. "Varen entrusted his *katra* to me. Logic required that I bring it to its long home."

Predictable enough, thought Karatek. He made himself suppress a smile.

"We cannot grant thee the thanks thee wishes of listening, then assenting to thy plans," she said, "when we do not, cannot agree."

"You know my reasoning," Surak began.

"We have read your work!" she cut through his smooth, practiced arguments. "We wish no part of a pilgrimage away from the Mother World. We are bone of her bone, heart of her heart, soul of her very soul."

"And if it comes to war, will thee fight?" Surak demanded. "For I tell you: I will not."

"Nor will we," said the priestess. "At the worst, rather than destroy our fellows, we will stop our own hearts. So, thee will leave this place. But, before thee departs or the world we have known ends, may I present thee with a gift? It was taken from thine enemy, a product of the arts of their hands and their mind. To us, it restrains the mind from its final destiny and is therefore abomination."

"But *I* may wish to study it?" Surak lifted both his slanted eyebrows. "And, incidentally, serve thee by removing blasphemy from thy presence? What can I do but obey? Indeed, I wish to see this artifact. More to the point, if thee wishes to give me a gift, what can I do but accept with thanks?" Surak asked. He bowed again, his earlier resistance gone.

The priestess nodded. One of the Unbonded approached. In her joined hands, she bore something a crown much like the one the high priestess wore, except it was far more splendid, dazzling with a profusion of green gems wound with bloodmetal.

The adept of Gol regarded it with profound disgust. "Do you know what that thing is?" he demanded of Surak.

"How should I?" Surak replied. "Logic would require me to examine it before forming a hypothesis."

The young priestess approached Surak. He bowed at her approach. Looking away, avoiding all but the most necessary contact with his fingertips, she handed him the crown. Karatek and Skamandros edged in at his shoulders.

Surak traced the bloodmetal wires—circuitry, Karatek thought—that encircled the crown. He caught Surak's eye.

"You are the engineer. Tell me what you think," Surak demanded.

"That wiring looks functional, not ornamental." Karatek made himself laugh shortly, although his mouth was dry from tension as well as the long climb.

"The ornamentation is te-Vikram. But the wiring? It looks like some sort of generator to me. Crystals, wires . . . what does that remind me of? Ah!" He thought back to the days when he had begun his study of the history of engineering. "The pattern resembles a transmitter!"

"My compliments on your companion's reasoning," said the high priestess.

"What good is a transmitter without receivers?" Skamandros demanded.

Karatek was tracing the wiring. No, this was no intricate ornamentation: it was circuitry.

"I think it can receive as well as transmit," Karatek replied. But what signal?

Surak nodded toward the high priestess and the crown she wore, with its gem, like the beak of a *shavokh,* jutting from the plain metal band that circled her brow.

Swiftly, Surak placed the crown on his head, stiffened, and fell. Skamandros's shout of "no!" resounded through the Hall of Ancient Thought, shattering its holy silence.

THIRTEEN

MEMORY

"This is your fault!" Skamandros shouted at the high priestess. He flung himself forward until he crouched beside Surak like his shadow. "If my master dies . . ."

"You will extract my *katra* from this crown and bring it, if you can, to the Halls of Ancient Thought," came Surak's level voice. "For now, however, you will apologize to this worthy priestess for your lack of control."

Surak rose to his feet, the crown glowing on his head.

Not even a "thee." Skamandros's face went dark. "I ask pardon," said Surak's shadow.

The Unbonded clustered around the high priestess, clearly prepared to defend her. Most of them, Karatek remembered, were Healers-in-training. Who better to know a man's vulnerabilities than those who knew best how to preserve life?

"Thee had great provocation." The high priestess inclined

her head, accepting Skamandros's apology despite its patent insincerity.

Karatek reached out to take the crown from Surak's brow, then let his hands fall.

"I didn't think such a thing was possible," he whispered. "It's a telepathic recorder, isn't it? Night and day, I would not have thought the te-Vikram were far enough advanced to develop such a thing!"

Everyone knew that the adepts of Seleya and Gol could touch one's thoughts—and more. But for that skill, for an intimacy that profound and secret to reside in the gems and wires of a *machine* . . .

The adept of Gol, who had long forgotten his own name, cleared his throat in what Karatek, to his amazement, recognized as disgust.

"Thy wonder is ill advised," he rebuked Karatek and Surak. "Consider what this . . . this instrument cost. Not in gems, but in the total number of minds the te-Vikram violated in creating it."

Karatek flinched at the thought. In his passage through the desert, he had seen enough of te-Vikram violence by conventional means. All he wanted now was to survive the trek home to ShiKahr and take up his old life. He had not needed Surak's calculations to know how improbable that second ambition was, especially now.

"An interesting moral point," the high priestess cut across his chill voice. "Sacrifice was inflicted on many Vulcans to produce this device, which records thoughts, memories, and even emotions—although *T'Kehr* Surak here"—her voice went ironic—"would claim we should suppress them. I myself am reluctant to destroy what is a work of great craft and, potentially, much use, for good or ill."

"It should be smashed beyond the ability to reconstruct!" snarled the adept.

"Why?" asked Surak. "If, out of a sense of moral outrage, you destroy it, you pay no tribute to the sacrifice forced upon the men and women whose minds were violated in creating this coronet. If you use it, however, in the enhancement of science or philosophy, it would seem to me that you create a memorial."

"I do not doubt," said the high priestess, "that this is a fascinating new ethical speculation. I can think of no one better equipped to pursue it than Surak of Vulcan. It can be the subject for thy *Second Analects,*" she added with a bleak smile. "I shall look forward to them. Take the coronet, then. Remove it from our presence. Create a record. And then, if it seems *logical* to thee, return the device.

"I grow weary now," she added after a pause in which even Surak's control was tested as he thanked her. "This audience is ended. Thee has leave to remain here for the night. My daughters will bring thee food, fire, and water."

As ordered, they departed in the morning after the dawn chants. The sky had already begun to redden toward full day. As the winds subsided, they filed over the narrow bridge, trying not to waver.

Once again, Karatek crossed last. As he touched down onto the plain by the stairs, he looked out across the plain and saw, circling below him, a sundweller. It gleamed in the sun, banked, and took wing toward ShiKahr.

FOURTEEN

NOW

VULCAN

The lecture hall, like all the halls that lay within the buildings of the Vulcan Science Academy, was a tranquil room. There were no ornaments, no statuary, nothing that could distract the eye or mind from the lecturer, and yet the very purity of the room's clean lines was soothing.

The walls were made out of huge blocks of smooth gray volcanic stone. In the practical Vulcan style, the outer wall was thicker than the others to keep out the intense desert heat, and had a row of high-set windows that allowed the easy flow of air and kept the hall comfortable in all but the hottest of summer days. The careful, gradual slope of the floor from the speaker's stand up to the rows of students allowed all who were in attendance to clearly see the speaker, and at the same time the natural acoustics ensured that no amplified speech was necessary.

Convenient, that last feature, Ruanek thought, especially for someone like himself, who'd had two lectures to deliver this day. And who was just now coming to the end of the second of them.

". . . and so," Ruanek continued to his all-Vulcan audience, "it can logically be concluded that the phrase *'T'kal ni narak alat N'garkar Ack,'* or, in modern colloquial Vulcan, 'Midday sun, Soul Eater come,' can be directly traced back through modern Romulan to archaic Vulcan and to the folk beliefs of the pre-Surak era."

He put down his data scrolls and stepped back from the podium, signaling in Vulcan fashion that he was done, and stood looking about the stoic faces and sharply alive eyes of his audience, waiting. Of course there was no applause or any other relatively emotional outward sign of approval; that was not a Vulcan custom. But Ruanek knew by their very stillness that they were giving him a sign of their appreciation, waiting a few moments before asking their questions out of respect for his scholarship. Since several professors of linguistics and folk belief were in the audience, that was high praise indeed.

Flattering, Ruanek admitted.

That there would be questions was without doubt. Vulcans, emotion-controlled though they were, were still every bit as curious as Earth cats. It was one of the traits, Ruanek thought with an inner smile, that he and they shared in common.

Ah yes, here came the questions.

"Have you ever heard *'ni narak'* pronounced *'ni nurak'* as it is in the Kora Scrolls?"

"That is a regional pronunciation from Romulus's Parak Province, yes," Ruanek answered. "They also tend to slur their vowels, *'ni'nrak.'* "

"Is the belief in the Eater of Souls strictly a rural phenomenon or is it also prevalent in cities such as Ki Baratan?"

The Eater of Souls was an archetypal figure in ancient Vulcan mythology, a demon that ate the soul of anyone foolish enough to be out in the midday heat.

"Ki Baratan had about twelve million citizens when I . . . left," Ruanek said carefully. "Logically, I could not speak for them all. I have never heard any codified folktales about the Eater of Souls the way there are some here on Vulcan. But I have, indeed, seen and heard mothers in Ki Baratan scold their children with 'Behave, or the Eater of Souls will get you.'

"On Romulus, with its lack of any sizable desert regions, the demon has been softened into merely a figure with which to frighten children into behaving. However, it has not completely lost its power among adults, since there are even some protective amulets against the Eater of Souls sold in the poorer sections. For reasons that should be obvious," he added, "I do not have any of those amulets to show you."

For a moment, Ruanek was caught off-guard by an unexpected stab of memory, overcome by a rush of nostalgia so bittersweet and strong that he could almost see the maze of streets in the market quarter of Ki Baratan, hear the noise of ordinary people living ordinary lives, and smell the hot, slightly bitter scent of brewing khavas. . . .

No matter how you might wish it otherwise, the past was just that. You couldn't go back to what had been, Ruanek reminded himself sternly. And the hard and bluntly honest truth was that life hadn't been so wonderful back then. He was far happier here.

But his background was, of course, one of the reasons for the questions; he was, after all, the only one on Vulcan with a working knowledge of the most current Romulan idioms and dialects. It was an open secret on Vulcan that he had not actually been born on Vulcan, but was . . . or had been . . . a Romulan. He had not defected, *akkh,* never that. He had come here perforce while working to save Spock's life—and then, by Romulan law, been unable to return home.

But Vulcan had given him refuge, Vulcan, where he no longer had to kill or worry about guarding his back. Vulcan, where he'd found the peace of the desert that he'd so badly needed. And where he had first met T'Selis . . . lovely wife of his heart and soul. . . .

"If there are no more questions, gentlefolk . . . ?"

As he and they filed out of the hall, Ruanek had to admit that he was rather amused at himself. Or was that, perhaps, bemused? Born into a Romulan House Minor, he'd been trained only to be a warrior, since that was the only career allowed for someone like himself. Yet here he was now, a scholar and a linguist as well, someone who had actually come to enjoy intellectual sparring as much as the martial arts.

What would the noble ancestors have thought?

Hah. The noble ancestors probably would have disowned me on the spot. Or maybe just tried to have drowned me like an unwanted arark.

He stopped short at the sight of a small, familiar figure in the brown robes of a Healer, and felt a surge of sheer delight rush through him at the sight of his wife. But her work as a Healer usually kept her busy at this time of day. "T'Selis! What are you doing here?"

She looked up at him with a Vulcan's tranquil face, but her eyes were shadowed. "My husband, there is news that you must know. It seemed only logical that I be the one to tell you."

"Wife? What's wrong?"

"The news . . . concerns your birth world. Come home with me now and you can view it for yourself." With a Healer's gentleness, she added, "I will stay with you while you watch it."

*   *   *

Much later, after he had watched the tape of destruction over and over again in utter silence, Ruanek had rushed from their house, still without a word. T'Selis, understanding, left him alone for a time.

But as the day began to darken into twilight, T'Selis sighed soundlessly. *He has had more than enough time for solitude,* she thought. *It would not be healthy for him to begin to brood.*

Slipping back into her hooded brown cloak, since the evening chill came on swiftly in the desert, T'Selis went looking for her husband. She found him where logic told her he would be. Ruanek found a greater peace in the desert than did many Vulcans.

Husband and wife stood together in silence in the reddish blue light of the fading day, not quite touching, looking out over the vast tranquil sweep of red sand and gray rock, the only sound the thin whisper of the evening breeze rustling grains of sand.

"When I first arrived on Vulcan," Ruanek said suddenly, "I couldn't get over the wonder of realizing that this, all this, actually existed. Living on a world like Romulus, a warrior in the barracks of Ki Baratan, I'd thought I'd merely dreamed it: a beautiful, wild, free place, one where nothing terrible had ever happened, nothing ever would."

"There are predators," T'Selis reminded him.

"Natural ones. Animals doing what they must do to live. They do not kill on orders, or for pleasure, or to exterminate a colony of defenseless people. T'Selis, I must leave."

"To join Spock."

"Yes."

"And are you truly the only expert on Romulan affairs that Starfleet can find?"

"This . . . will not be a Starfleet mission."

No, she realized after a moment of logical consideration, it would not be. It could not be. "Ruanek, tell me this: What do you expect to achieve?"

"The truth. Honor. Justice."

Only Ruanek, T'Selis thought, could say that without sounding sanctimonious or false.

And you, my husband, are still, deep in your heart, a Romulan. But then, she corrected herself silently, those goals were not, after all, so very far from Vulcan ideals.

It would be illogical for her to mention any danger. Ruanek would know there would be danger. It would be even more illogical for her to mention that he was risking their life together—and his own, should he once again set foot on Romulan soil: He might have left Romulus only to save Spock, but that act still made him a condemned traitor in the eyes of Romulan law. But he would know all that, too.

T'Selis was not a human to say emotionally, Come back to me. Of course he would come back, were he able.

"I do not approve," she said at last.

"I know. But—"

"But you are a free and"—with the ever so slight hint of a smile—"*mostly* logical being who is able to make your own decisions. Do what you must, husband. I shall wait."

FIFTEEN

MEMORY

As they descended from the shrine beneath Mount Seleya's peak, the Forge shivered. Rocks toppled down from the high plateau at Seleya's base, ringing in the silence. Karatek shrank against the rock wall, sheltering Kovar and Sarissa with his body. When the tremor ceased, Surak picked up the pace once more.

Karatek met his eyes with complete understanding. That had been no natural tremor. Who had attacked, and where?

Though it was perilous to take a descent too fast, they made what speed they could down to the basin's floor. With each step, Karatek felt as if he were changing identities once again. In ShiKahr, he had been an engineer, a father, a husband, a house-holder. Then, on the Forge, he had become something else: an explorer, a member of a small, endangered tribe, even, for one terrible moment, a warrior who stood in a holy place and shivered as his chieftain dealt with matters he did not wish to comprehend. Now Karatek shivered despite the heat as his old identity slipped

148

back onto his shoulders like a familiar cloak. Once more, he was husband, father, householder, and scientist, oppressed by the thousand tiny but overwhelming questions of *T'Kehr* Karatek's daily life.

How would T'Vysse accept the children he had brought her? How would their surviving two adapt? He fumbled in a pouch for the radiation badges he had carried out of ShiKahr but not worn on the Forge. As they returned to the city, such things became important once again.

"Put these on," he instructed Kovar and Sarissa. His voice was harsh enough that they did not try to protest or question. A new anxiety possessed him as he watched the badges darken . . . no, their exposure was well within the limits a healthy Vulcan could tolerate. Though he could breathe again, reassured for now, his fosterlings would need full medical examinations, perhaps treatment to help them adapt to the lowlands. He only hoped they did not become ill after all they had endured. He had not rescued them only to lose them to radiation poisoning or biocide.

No pilgrims trudged along the sand track to or from Seleya, and that was strange. Skamandros, scouting ahead, loped back in the shimmering haze and pointed. Dust clouds puffed up at the horizon, wavering in the heat.

"What is it?" Kovar asked, speaking up in the presence of his elders as he had not dared while on the Forge.

"Ground vehicles," Skamandros said, taking a sip of water. "Heavy personnel carriers. I would assume they carry armor."

Even before the First Dynasty, when Seleya's shrine had been no more than rocks thrown up on the heights, pilgrims had always taken this road unarmed!

Karatek's outrage must have showed in his eyes.

"It is illogical to assume that times will not change," Surak said. "I am no foreseer, but I suspect that we will find ShiKahr much changed. I would suggest you retrieve your identification now, in case we are stopped."

"That is," Skamandros eyed him with his customary irony, "if you are still willing to tolerate us as guest-friends."

If they were stopped by patrols—patrols along the pilgrimage route! Karatek thought with a sense of outrage he would never have expected, as a secular man, a man of science, to feel—he was the one who would have to negotiate their release.

It might have been easier to endure thirst and potential attack on the Forge.

There being nothing to say, Karatek bowed.

Smoke overpowered the tracks of the groundcars as they neared ShiKahr: sullen, dark puffs of it. Kovar pressed against Karatek's side.

"What sort of attack causes that?" Sarissa whispered.

What sort of world produced children who knew to ask questions like that?

Karatek drew her and her brother close. He met Surak's eyes over their heads. As usual, Surak was right. But Karatek knew the answer.

"It looks like an explosion," Karatek said. *Or an implosion,* he added silently.

Skamandros's head came up. "Flyer overhead," he reported.

Kovar's shoulder tensed under Karatek's hand, as the boy prepared to run for cover. Sarissa clasped Karatek's arm.

"As Skamandros reminded us, he and *T'Kehr* Surak are my guest-friends. I am a citizen here, and citizens have certain rights," Karatek told Sarissa. "Even if it is illogical to assume that all things remain the same."

"Besides, they can use sensors keyed to our body readings to track us," Sarissa said, and flushed olive at Surak's nod of approval.

Karatek moved out into the center of the pilgrims' track, his boots scattering sand that clearly had not been disturbed for what looked like days. A few days more, perhaps, and the ancient road would disappear. The idea disturbed him.

The flyer hummed overhead, lowering until it hovered perhaps the height of three men above them.

Abruptly, Karatek gestured at it. "If they're going to keep us under surveillance, why not simply offer us a ride home?" he demanded.

Surak raised an eyebrow. "If we are honest pilgrims, we would not accept it. If we are decoys for a strike force, they will not risk themselves."

Varekat would say the flyer was already vulnerable to a ground-to-air strike, but Varekat was not here, and Surak's irony was getting as oppressive as the heat of the sun. Karatek shrugged and trudged onward. He wanted to wave the flyer down, or run toward his home, demanding to know what was wrong; but he knew better than to waste his strength.

Nevasa, sinking toward the west, made it hard to see the road ahead. Now, though, they could smell the smoke, all the more so as the wind changed. It was a profanation of the clean desert, and Karatek checked his badge again. They would all need injections as soon as they reached ShiKahr.

An hour later, and Nevasa's slanting rays were no longer painful. Through them, he could see first the pillar of smoke Skamandros had discerned from far off, then the Gates.

What barbarians had knocked a flange out of the one to the left? In place since the legendary First Dynasty, it had been buried in the sand for generations, only to be uncovered and restored time and time again. Now, a white gouge marked where the ancient stone had been ripped away from its base. Karatek would rather someone had broken his arm.

Home, he thought. *What in the name of my mother's* katra *has become of my home?*

As they neared, he saw the faint shimmer of a forcefield outside the gate, reinforcing a metal barrier set up outside it. He had never seen so many guards patrolling the Gate—or so many people, some carrying banners, some chanting, contained behind the forcefield. Noisy they might be, but it was an angry noise, not the joyous tumult Karatek remembered from his childhood.

You should see my city as it used to be, he started to tell Kovar and Sarissa, then held his tongue. Illogical to taunt them with what they could not have, with what he could not have. In a sense, Vulcan's wars had rendered them all homeless, refugees from more peaceful lives.

"Stop right there!" Subcommander Ivek's voice, amplified by microphones in his helmet, boomed over the desert. *"Hands on heads. Don't move!"*

Karatek paused instantly. Daring to defy the order, he produced his identification as Surak had suggested. As if summoned to provide reinforcements, the flyer descended. Its engines whipped up the sand until Karatek and his companions could barely see. Sarissa began to raise her hood.

"Stay as you are!" came the order.

Guards poured out from behind the metal barrier and scanned first him, then his companions.

"This is Surak!" a man behind him called to the subcommander just as another guard's scanner lit, and Karatek shut his eyes in despair.

Torin's weapons. Of course.

Karatek held his arms out from his side.

"The blaster is unregistered," he said. "It belongs to *T'Kehr* Torin of the Vulcan Space Initiative." He was hot. He was exhausted. And now he was deeply frightened. Where fear walked, Surak had said in his *Analects,* anger was its companion. Surak was right.

"Night and day, Ivek," Karatek complained. "You know I report to Torin at the VSI. Call him."

"I'm going to have to," the subcommander said. "I'm afraid I'll have to ask you to wait in the holding area."

He gestured. "You still answering for these two troublemakers? Where's their friend?"

Immensely tired, Karatek sighed. "We lost Varen to a te-Vikram ambush. How many does that make this year? We're back from Seleya."

Ivek dipped his head. "I grieve with thee," he said, with a conspicuous lack of sincerity. "What about the two young ones?"

"Refugees. I'm taking them in charge. They need medical attention."

"All in good time."

"May I at least call my consort?" Karatek asked. The Ivek he knew had been quick to make a joke, with a lively sense of irony at his own expense. This was a more somber man, almost intimidating in his efficiency.

"She's been called," Ivek said. "If Lady T'Vysse speaks for you, it might do you a lot more good with the High Command than Torin, for that matter. They've already said they want to see you."

"Night and day, Ivek, what's been happening?" Karatek demanded. He felt Surak's and Skamandros's presence at his back, reassurance and curiosity combined. "What was that explosion?"

"You had a colleague named Varekat? Arms expert?" Ivek waved his guards back.

"All right, move it out, you men!" he shouted.

Men. No women in the Guard now. When had that happened? So, here too, they returned to the ancient ways.

"Varekat, yes," Karatek said. "But he resigned."

"Apparently, he didn't," Ivek said. "At least, not immediately. What I heard was that *T'Kehr* Torin told him to take some time, think about it."

Karatek shut his eyes. He could see where this was going.

"The VSI's been working with the Northerners, haven't you?" Ivek's voice changed.

He is interrogating me, Karatek realized. Ivek had always been pleasantly wry, self-deprecating, not grim. He had never assumed this type of authority before. It became important to find his old schoolmate again. He had to be concealed somewhere within this angry, driven man.

"Building ships for them," Karatek admitted.

"Well, the Southern Hegemony took extreme exception to that."

"Why? We had agreements of neutrality with them!"

"Sir!" a trooper shouted to Ivek. "This one—it's Surak himself!"

"Yes, I know," Ivek yelled back, removing his helmet so his voice was no longer amplified. The cheekpieces left dark marks on his face, which was no longer agreeably rounded, but haggard with many sleepless nights, even for a Vulcan. "Run him through scan!"

"I did, sir! And look at this!"

As his fellows closed in on Surak and Skamandros tensed, awaiting a command to attack that Karatek prayed would never come, the trooper jogged up to his commander bearing the coronet Surak had taken from Mount Seleya. Ivek took it in both hands and began unwrapping it.

"You would be wise not to tamper with that," Surak said. "It was a gift to me from the high priestess at Mount Seleya. You may report it as 'experimental equipment.' "

"It'll have to be checked, sir," Ivek said.

"Who will you trust to check it, Ivek?" Karatek demanded. "Torin? You've already implied he's under a cloud."

"You should have seen the clouds around here, Karatek," Ivek told him. "Wasn't bad enough we had a te-Vikram raid. Those sonless wonders took out a chunk of the Gate. And here I thought they'd proscribed technology."

Karatek sighed. "They do use blasters. And you don't need to use firepower to break something."

"They didn't. They had some sort of engine. Threw rocks at it. Right through the force shields. That was when we tripled the guard.

"Meanwhile, the Northeastern Alliance declared war on the Southern Hegemony, and the High Command had to choose which one to stay allied to. And if that wasn't bad enough, a new party started getting votes in the High Command. It canceled your ship contracts with the Northeasterners and pressed for weapons buildup. Something about warships: that would sound *logical*, wouldn't it?"

There was a world of bitterness in the way Ivek said "logical."

Karatek sighed. "I designed the engines for those ships," he admitted. "Even the engines could serve as weapons."

He could see it now. They would want to mount Varekat's most secret projects on those ships, press him to manufacture larger and larger— His blood chilled, and his heart raced until it was a thrum in his side. Karatek pressed his hand against it.

"What did Varekat do?"

"That's right, you knew the man," Ivek said. For the first time, his voice softened. Only a trifle, but it was a start.

Knew. So Varekat had died.

Night and day, how many others had died with him?

"Torin told him to think over leaving the Initiative. Well, Varekat thought it over, all right. He and his assistants. Apparently they destroyed their records, at least, that's what they said in their announcement. Then, they blew their lab. None of them survived."

Karatek bowed his head, thankful for the pressure of Sarissa's head against his shoulder, Kovar's weight against his side. Skamandros came up behind him, his shadow falling protectively across the sunlight to ease him.

In a civilized world, Karatek thought. How was this possible in a civilized world?

"I grieve for thee," said Surak.

"Isn't grief an emotion?" Ivek asked.

"It is an assessment of fact," Surak said. "And of threat. There will be more to come."

Ivek shrugged. "They say you're wise. So, tell me something I didn't know. I'm going to save my grief for the people who don't have the luxury to preach subversion and leave their posts. Those of us who will defend their homes to the last."

Being wise, Surak kept silent in his turn.

"My husband!" T'Vysse's voice in Karatek's ears felt like water after a long desert crossing. He held out his hand to touch her fingers. How coarse and dark his hand had become compared with hers. Life pulsed through her hand like pale green shoots in Vulcan's brief spring.

"Please, Subcommander, let my companion through," T'Vysse

was saying to Ivek. He gestured, and Torin came up, shouldering through the guards with respect, but no trace of fear.

To Karatek's surprise, his old supervisor turned first to Surak, who inclined his head.

"T'Kehr Torin, I have returned your man to you."

Now Torin rounded on Karatek, looking him up and down before he clapped him on the shoulder.

"Well done!" he said to both of them. Karatek shook his head. Torin acted as if he were a commander—were still a commander—who had dispatched a young, promising officer to hard duty, so that he would do or die.

Surak, Karatek saw now, had received him in the same spirit. Warriors were ruthless. Intellectuals, he understood, were even more so.

"How much trouble did Varekat let you in for?" Karatek asked.

Torin shrugged. "Good thing your lady here came to pick me up. I doubt they'd have let me through the lines. Smartest thing you ever did, bonding to her."

Karatek breathed a faint laugh. "It seemed the logical thing to do."

T'Vysse had moved from his side to the children. Without a word, she seemed to understand who they were and what Karatek had done. Reassurance resonated in the bond between them as she knelt and took their hands in hers.

"Could be worse," Torin said, drawing Karatek's attention. "Varekat's prototypes could have survived. Not to mention his notes. So we can't replicate his results. At least we won't have that on our consciences."

"Never mind that!" T'Vysse interrupted them. "Besides, these children need medical care. They need their beds, too. Husband, help me get them home. And our guest-friends too! You and Torin can go back to work tomorrow."

She flashed a glare at Torin, who drew himself up.

"Lady Mitrani says you have been away for three days, and asked me to ask you if it is your will that she forget the sound of your voice?"

As Torin threw up a hand in surrender, T'Vysse's smile seemed lovelier than a sundweller riding a fair dawn wind.

Discreetly, Surak lowered his eyes. Ivek shook his head as if dazzled. He even saluted as T'Vysse led her captives away.

SIXTEEN

MEMORY

Karatek pounded his fist against the ancient, hardened clay of the passages beneath ShiKahr's Old Town, trying to visualize the map he had consulted. The sun-blasted things were a veritable maze, and he was no eidetic. The wretched tunnels were remnants of the days, five hundred years past, when the occasional cloudburst would cascade from the Forge across hardened ground to flood the city. Those floods hadn't happened often, but when they did, damage and loss of life had been immense before the tunnels were hacked into the rocky ground and hardened, in the days before lasers, by building fires within them.

Should he turn here, double back, or take the right fork in the tunnel? It was hard to remember.

Had his time in the desert dried his brains?

Bad enough he had been fool enough to leave his house about the same time each day. But today, of all days, when he was to speak at the VSI's symposium on repurposing ships of war for long-range space travel, what madness had made him decide to avoid the day's high pollution index? Cutting through ShiKahr's Old Town with its unruly crowds, complicated now by security checkpoints, would have been bad enough, but taking the covered ways left him isolated, and that was worse.

Fool! One moment, Karatek had been hurrying along, rehearsing the arguments he was going to use to convince the VSI to turn warships into generation ships. The next, as he paused to make a note, he heard the pad-pad-pad of feet. Several pair. A friend would have called out a greeting, at least for the pleasure of hearing the echoes distort his voices. But no one had spoken. Therefore, Karatek decided, he would have to conclude that whoever was following him could not be his friend.

His conclusion might be logical, but it chilled Karatek's blood and made him break out in a rare sweat of fear.

Night and day, were T'Vysse and the children safe?

He stumbled over a chunk of hardened soil and grit, lying on the tunnel's floor. This whole wretched place was collapsing. In a century or so, it might even be time to repair it, assuming ShiKahr survived as anything but a ruin, contaminated by the war that ended not just all war, but all life on Vulcan.

Picking up the masonry, he pressed back against the curved wall of the tunnel and waited, patient as a *le-matya* waiting by one of the Forge's rare water holes. Karatek had kept himself in full training since his desert trek with Surak: perhaps he had lost his wits, but at least he could protect himself.

As his first stalker passed him, Karatek slammed the debris he held over his head and brought the man down, following the blow with a hard kick to his belly. Karatek's personal time seemed to slow, giving him the chance to steady himself, then whirl on his second attacker before he could fire the weapon he held. Kicking

160

again, Karatek heard a cry before the second man toppled. He had been aiming for the belly, but hadn't kicked as high as he had planned. He managed not to flinch in reluctant, incongruous sympathy before he brought his joined fists down on the man's head. That hurt! After all, he wasn't really a warrior even if he had been training with *T'Kehr* Torin ever since he had returned from the desert. His assailants had been overconfident, expecting a timid, sedentary engineer. And Karatek had been lucky.

As he paused for a moment, panting, a third man, who had cleverly hung back, jumped out at him. He was expecting Karatek to recoil. Instead, he lunged forward and grabbed his attacker, pulling away first his cloak, then a strip of fabric from his tunic.

Evidence, he realized as the third . . . assassin lunged at him again.

Fool, don't ever put your head down! Torin's voice echoed in Karatek's memory.

He did not want to kill. He had hated killing those te-Vikram on the Forge, and Torin had long since reclaimed his blaster. But *talshaya* was a method that would let Karatek kill quickly, efficiently, and mercifully. He struck out as he had been taught, and the man's neck snapped. The sound turned Karatek sick and weak. His knees buckled.

Conquering the nausea that threatened to overpower him where the assassins had failed, Karatek dragged the man he had killed to lie against the curved tunnel wall. He might have killed, might still be in danger of his life, but he was still a civilized man, and there were still certain decencies. . . .

A power cell attached to an ancient torch holder cast subtle light on the dead man's face. Why, Karatek remembered him! He was one of the political officers sent from the High Command to observe when the seminar on how to reconfigure the VSI's ships was first announced. Metallic embroidered sigils on the fabric strip he held confirmed it: this was an agent of the High Command.

In that case, Karatek was as dead as he. It was just a matter of time. He turned to the others. Not dead, but unconscious and— Karatek peeled back eyelids—probably concussed. They would need medical attention. Hating himself for the petty thefts, he ransacked their pouches and came away with a gemmed dagger, a light, sedatives in an injector, and a small blaster. No stun setting.

Karatek shivered, not from the shade in the tunnels. The idea of finding himself subject to the coercive mental technology of the te-Vikram or the drugs he knew his own people could concoct made him as dizzy as if he had spent too long staring up into the sun. But the High Command *hated* the te-Vikram. At least, Karatek thought it did. Why had it leagued itself with them?

Only one thing was certain. Karatek had to get out of here.

He ran down the corridor, searching for a skylight, a ramp, any means of exit. There was no telling how quickly reinforcements could be sent.

Light poured down through a jagged opening one hundred meters away. Karatek sprinted toward it, building up enough momentum to let him leap, catch the jagged edge in both hands, and hoist himself up onto the surface of the old waterway. Mother Sun beat down on him, but he was used to the pressure, and, even if the day's air quality would probably earn him yet another injection against radiation, the light glittering off the desert floor was clean.

He glanced at his badge. Well within acceptable levels. Well, readings could be faked. Badges could be damaged. That was always a signal for people conscientious about their health to go to the health center and be tested. Karatek wiped his bloody palms against the inside of his cloak, pulled up his hood, and, drawing on all the control he had learned from Surak, slowed his pace.

Now he appeared to be just another pedestrian conserving his energy under the sun's assault as he walked to his place of work.

Lifelong habit as a good citizen made his conscience assail him: the men in the tunnel needed assistance. He should call Ivek and get his security teams in there.

But he knew how hard he had hit. Those men would not wake for hours, assuming they ever waked again. They were evidence that someone was willing to kill or at least abduct him to prevent him from attending the VSI's conference.

How many others of the senior scientific staff would be missing?

Unobtrusively picking up his pace, Karatek even arrived at the VSI's underground installation early enough to be monitored, receive a fresh badge and attention for the cuts on his hands. The result of a fall, he explained. Yes, he would be more careful in the future, thank you so much; he was sorry to cause concern and extra work now, of all times.

He slipped into the VSI's largest conference room with a murmured apology and a courteous nod to the audience before he took his place at the table set on a dais. If he could not rush home and make sure his family was safe, as he really wanted, he longed just to sink into his seat and bury his head in his hands. But he would not do either. Not when he had a presentation to make and deadly new evidence—in the form of three assassins—to present.

He made himself glance at the screens set into the conference table. T'Raya's "Reconfiguring Cargo Bays for Hydroponics." His own "Adapting Propulsion Systems for Protracted Deep-Space Flight." Torin's "Funding Generation Ships through Spin-off Technologies," and many other presentations that might determine the survival of Vulcan as a race, if not a world.

Monitors set up around the room showed scenes from across

the Mother World. A crater in the Southern Hegemony whose fused sand sent up radiation that meant no Vulcan dared walk there for a thousand years.

A crack in the land, from which steam rose as it did from the lava river beneath Mount Seleya.

A slagged installation, fortunately very far to the north of ShanaiKahr, the result of a portable bomb smuggled in among trade goods.

Demonstrators in the Old Town pleading for the High Command to join in a worldwide consortium to preserve Vulcan's one shrunken ocean from further pollution by runoff from chemical factories erected in the Waste.

Long shots of the corrosion on the faces of the immense, ancient statues fronting Vulcan's last shrunken, polluted sea.

As the audience filled, two chairs on the dais remained empty. Karatek closed his eyes, wondering what would become of the man and woman to whom they belonged. Then, with deliberate contempt, he met the eyes of the political officers who sat as unobtrusively as they could in a corner. High Command had taken pains to send men and women with scientific training, but they were still outsiders. Karatek let his eyes fall from their faces, on which no trace of awareness showed, to their arms. To the badges on their sleeves, which matched the badge he had taken from an assassin.

Torin rapped on the table, a sign that his patience, always a scarce resource, was exhausted. "Although two speakers are late, I think we must start."

He raised his voice over the buzz of last-minute conversation, checking of personal messages, and late arrivals.

"May we begin, please?" he asked with deceptive mildness. "In the interests of time, I will omit official welcoming remarks. We all know one another far too well, or at least, we think we do. And, with the exception of our two guests"—he inclined his head with insultingly elaborate deference to the political officers—"we all know why we are here: to gather information, to give it, and to make the best decisions we can in a hard time. Now that the High Command has severed diplomatic relations with the Northeastern Alliance, we must decide whether to repurpose the ships we had been building for them for long-range travel, abandon the project entirely, or complete them as ships of war for the High Command's use. *T'Kehr* T'Raya has agreed to speak first. She will present a feasibility study about how cargo or weapons bays could be converted to agricultural use, potentially extending the length of these ships' potential voyages indefinitely. T'Raya?" Torin inclined his head to her with sincere respect.

Karatek could not have had a better cue.

"Sir," he rose from his chair. "May I speak?"

Torin snorted annoyance, but suppressed the explosion Karatek might have expected. He pulled out the badge he had taken from the dead political officer and laid it on the table. Next to it, he set the blaster, the te-Vikram blade, and the drugs he had taken from the other two assassins.

Finally, he held up his hands. They were bandaged. He had refused regeneration "so I can make it to the conference before *T'Kehr* Torin goes thermonuclear," he had lied.

Now, he unwrapped the bandages and let the livid abrasions show.

"This morning, I took the qanat through the Old City. I was attacked along the way. Because I have been training with *T'Kehr* Torin, I was able to defend myself."

A ripple of amusement at the idea of Torin as a martial-arts instructor subsided, to be replaced by murmurs of sincere anxiety.

"I killed one man. In the fight, I tore this from his tunic. You will see it matches the insignia on our *guests'* tunics. I accuse them of attempted murder and violation of the laws of hospitality. That was one man. Two others lie in the tunnel. At least, I think they're still there; I hit them pretty hard. But they should not be hard to track, and they need medical attention if they're ever to be fit to interrogate. *T'Kehr,* if you would give orders that Subcommander Ivek be called? He has served us well in the past."

Torin whispered to an assistant, who left the room fast. "Seal the room," he ordered. "You're not going anywhere," he told to the political officers. "I don't want to hear a single word out of you.

"Karatek, if you would, slide that blaster down the table."

Taking it, Torin propped his arms on the table and covered the two men.

"My host, will you yield the floor to me?" asked a clear voice from the audience. After they had parted at the Gates of ShiKahr, Karatek had never expected to hear that voice again.

Keeping one eye on the political officers, Torin rose. "If you were not a dangerous rebel," he told Surak, "you would have made a fine actor. Talk. Talk as if all our lives depend on it."

Torin sounded furious, but Karatek suspected he was vastly amused.

Skamandros rose and leaned against the wall, as if keeping the dais under surveillance. He moved rather stiffly, and a deep bruise shadowed one temple. What had happened to Surak's shadow?

Surak bowed with a deep irony. When he rose, he raised an eyebrow at Karatek.

"*T'Kehr* Torin," Surak began, "even before your colleague

has given his scheduled talk, he has made an excellent presentation of new evidence, flawlessly argued. The conclusion is inescapable. If we extrapolate from the danger in which he found himself, we can logically conclude that you are all in grave danger."

"You make it sound as if we have returned to the days of the warring dukes between the First and Second Dynasties," Torin remarked. "Would you care to elaborate?"

"Nothing so civilized confronts us," Surak replied. "The ancient dukes who endowed Mount Seleya and put up their statues by the sea preserved an honor code. Instead, we confront only politics.

"The high priestess at Mount Seleya told me that she would stop her own heart before she permitted that to happen to her. What will you do? And what will you do if your permission is usurped?

"What if agents who wish you harm come for you, as they did for Karatek here? You may not be as fortunate, or as well trained as he. The high priestess, I grant, posits an extreme case. You are reasonable men and women, and reasonable men and women do not wish to suicide. But what if they kill you? What if they hold your families? You could all be turned into weapons worse than those Varekat and his associates destroyed two years ago."

Whispers buzzed in the hall. Two people seated at the table flinched visibly.

"You do not want to go," Surak told them. "That is understandable. But can you dare to stay?" Surak stretched out one hand to the audience, then at the monitors, which showed only disaster.

Two or three people rose, heading for the corner where the political officers sat with determined looks on their faces. They lunged for the exits. Torin rose. Holding his old blaster in two hands, he took meticulous aim.

"Let them go," Surak called. "Kill them, and who knows when it may be expedient to kill you? Beginnings are important. What we begin here will alter the face of our world. And, if all goes well, possibly others."

SEVENTEEN

NOW

STARLEET HEADQUARTERS

Uhura, seated in her tranquil office on Earth, smiled warmly up at Chekov as he entered, as though no time at all had passed since they'd last served together. She rose from behind the desk to take his hands in hers. "Pavel. It's good to see you again."

"Uhura. *Bozhya moi,* voman, you look more beautiful than ever."

"Flatterer."

"You are deserving flattery." He started to kiss her hand in full Russian chivalry, but then stopped in mid-bend. "Oops, but ve are not alone, I see." He straightened and let her hands go. "Ambassador Spock! How good to see you again."

"And you, Admiral."

"And yes, here is Captain Saavik, too. Mrs. Spock as vell, yes?"

She nodded, granting him the smallest hint of an almost-smile.

"And, ah, you, sir?" Chekov added. "I'm afraid that I do not know you."

The third Vulcan dipped his head slightly in courtesy. "I am Ruanek."

"Ruanek. Pleased to meet you." Chekov glanced about. "All in this together, are ve? Vhatever 'this' may be."

"Pavel," Uhura said, "you are the only one in Starfleet to have had any contact with the Watraii."

"Contact." Chekov snorted. "I hate to disappoint you, Uhura, but it could barely be called that."

"What, then?"

He sighed. "Back in the days vhen I was still captaining the *U.S.S. Undaunted,* ve encountered von of their ships, and I got a glimpse of those strange masks they seem to like. But, vell, that's about it. Negotiations never got beyond the 'Ve do not vish to contact you, go avay, goodbye,' stage." He glanced about at the four sets of impassive faces. "And that, I take it, that little bit, makes me the von and only Vatraii expert."

"Precisely," Spock said.

"And isn't that nice? Then ve are flying almost completely blind." Chekov turned to Uhura. "And vhat, pray tell, is our mission to be? No, vait, let me guess: Ve are out to confront the Vatraii, even though ve don't know anything about them other than that they like masks, and somehow conwince them to tell us the truth about themselves."

"No more difficult than for a Russian to work his way aboard an American nuclear vessel during the Cold War," Uhura said slyly.

Chekov snorted. "It is not the same thing at all, my dear voman, and you know it." He glanced about at the others. "And vhat a big mission this will be for so few of us."

"It will not be 'so few of us,'" Spock said. "The odds are 89.0005 percent in our favor that we will not be the only ones seeking the truth."

"That high a percentage?" Chekov asked dryly.

"That is the lowest estimate," Spock retorted.

"Vell. That does sound a bit less hopeless."

"You do understand," Uhura began, "that if things go wrong—"

"You never heard of this mission," Ruanek cut in.

"Exactly. But should it go wrong or, for that matter, even if it doesn't, you who are of Starfleet could well be looking at court-martial."

"Vhat, again?" Chekov asked wryly.

Saavik said simply, "I remember when another colony was destroyed, this one most populated by defenseless Klingon women and children. And I remember when one Romulan commander risked everything—life, rank, honor—everything, even turning against her own people in combat in an attempt to defend the innocent." She did not need to mention the name. Spock and Ruanek both knew she meant Charvanek. "I cannot be less brave than she."

"Understood," Spock said gravely.

As always when Spock saw Saavik's ship, the *U.S.S. Alliance,* he found himself thinking how sleek and efficient it looked, an elegantly shaped Excelsior-class vessel. And as always, he had a most illogical but satisfying little thrill of pride in his wife's accomplishments.

What Saavik was thinking as they went on board, however, could not be read by even another Vulcan. She looked like the perfect image of a Starfleet captain in her neat uniform and decorations, her persona calm, cool, and unruffled. But Spock, who knew his wife better than anyone else, suspected that she was pleased to be back on board.

As she entered the bridge of her ship, followed by Spock, Chekov, and Ruanek, the crew stood at attention.

"Welcome, Captain!"

"Welcome aboard, Captain Saavik!"

These were the normal courtesies, Spock thought. He'd heard them often enough on various ships. But her crew, a mixed group of humans, Bolians, and Vulcans, did seem genuinely glad to see Saavik. Quite agreeable to see his wife so appreciated in her work.

The bridge of Saavik's ship had been slightly modified from the standard, since at least half the crew was Vulcan and expected a slightly different design. It was a clean and elegant blend of Starfleet and Vulcan tastes, absolutely logical in its layout, with nothing out of place. Spock suddenly remembered that awkward science station that had been his aboard the *Enterprise*. He nodded his approval of the roomier, more practically arranged design of this ship's version. The Bolian man seated at the station gave him a slightly puzzled glance and politely nodded back.

The smooth curve of the bridge included a central command chair and two slightly subsidiary chairs, one to its left, one to its right. As she took her seat, Saavik invited Spock to the right-hand chair and Chekov to the left. Ruanek, however, perhaps with some latent Romulan warrior instinct roused by being on the bridge of a fighting ship, refused to sit passively, and instead took up a guarding position behind Spock and Saavik.

As though it would be logical that either I or my wife would need a bodyguard aboard her own Starfleet vessel.

But then, more of Ruanek's life had been spent as warrior than as scholar. Judging from the martial-arts lessons he taught on Vulcan, he had kept up all his fighting skills as well.

Vulcan could ask for no more vehement defender. And, Spock added dryly to himself, *T'Selis could have found no more unusual husband.*

"Lieutenant Suhur," Saavik commanded, "open intership communications."

The communications officer, a slender young dark-skinned Vulcan man, said, "Done, Captain."

"This is your captain speaking," Saavik said. "I wish to be certain that all aboard understand what we do. This is *not* a Starfleet-sanctioned mission. Even if we succeed, we will still be in danger of court-martial or other penalties. But you all do know why this mission must be undertaken. If there are any among you who feel you cannot take part, there shall be no punishment. But you must speak out here and now."

She waited, and Spock, watching, knew that though she seemed outwardly calm, the tension was fierce within her.

Then the reports started flooding in:

"Engineering: We stand with you, Captain."

"Sickbay here. We stand with you, Captain."

On through the ship the assurances rang out. All the *Alliance*'s crew stood with their captain.

"I thank you," Saavik said. "Helm, take us out."

Almost before Saavik's ship had reached interstellar space, her chief tactical officer, Lieutenant Abrams, a stern-faced, solidly built human woman, reported, "We're not alone, Captain. There are Vulcan ships joining us . . . ten of them Surak-class and, uh, seven of unknown designations."

The hesitation was understandable. Thanks to the constantly

curious Vulcan scientists and their constantly updated designs, Vulcan ship classes rarely fit neatly into the Federation databases.

Lieutenant Suhur, communications, announced, "Incoming message . . . correction, messages, Captain Saavik."

"Put them on screen, Lieutenant Suhur."

The messages came flooding in, the Vulcan ships' captains' serene, solemn faces appearing on the viewscreen one after another.

"This is the *T'Sarik*."

"This is the *Surani*."

"—the *T'Karis*—"

"—the *M'retin*."

"We greet thee," Saavik replied in Vulcan formal courtesy.

But as soon as they were safely out into interstellar space that was controlled by no one planetary government, the composition of the small fleet changed as other ships of other races joined them. The Vulcan ship names were soon followed by a wide variety of ship names, Cyreli, Bolian, Regara . . . Saavik and her crew were soon hard put to keep up with the tallies and the greetings.

"Better than we expected," Ruanek commented to Spock.

"Expectations—"

"Are not logical. Yes, I know that. But just the same, Spock, you can't deny being just a little bit relieved. And yes, I know, I know: That isn't very logical, either."

He and T'Selis must have . . . a very interesting marriage, Spock thought with a touch of wry humor.

"At least you certainly vere not exaggerating, Spock. Ve have picked up quite a good deal of company after all."

"Would it ever be logical for me to exaggerate?" Spock asked.

Even so, he had to admit that the fleet that was gradually coming together in interstellar space was . . . eclectic, to say the least.

In addition to the Vulcan ships, and the independents such as an Arcturan cruiser and two Zedali battleships, there were now several Federation vessels.

"This is Captain Jack Butterworth of the *U.S.S. Verne.* Hello, Captain Saavik." The image that formed on the screen was of a sturdily built man, no longer young, whose carefully dyed blond hair didn't quite hide his age—not that the clearly normally cheerful fellow would care.

"Captain Butterworth!" Saavik exclaimed, and then forced herself back into proper Vulcan calm. "I did not expect to see you here."

"My crew and I could hardly stand by as families were slaughtered. Besides," he added with a grin, "I wanted to see one more active mission before retirement."

"Ah . . . welcome."

As his image vanished from the screen, Ruanek said, not without a touch of sympathy, "Let me guess: He's the sort who gladly shows holos of his grandchildren to anyone who asks."

Saavik raised an eyebrow. "You seem to understand Earth customs very well."

He gave her the almost-smile that over his years on Vulcan had come to be his compromise between a Romulan grin and Vulcan stoicism. "Thank the time I spent as Sarek's diplomatic aide."

"Earth survived it," Spock commented, absolutely without expression, and heard Ruanek snort.

"Ah, Captain Saavik," Lieutenant Abrams said. "I have two Klingon ships in range, and closing fast."

"Their weapons?" Saavik's voice was Vulcan-calm.

A split-second pause, then: "Off-line, Captain."

Friends, then, Spock thought. Then he corrected that to, *Or at least not enemies.*

"Lieutenant Suhur," Saavik commanded, "open hailing frequencies."

"Hailing frequencies open."

"Very good." Leaning forward slightly in her chair, Saavik said, "I am Captain Saavik of the *Alliance.*"

The first Klingon commander was a huge, muscular warrior who proudly declaimed, "I am he who speaks for the *Demon Justice,* Commander Tor'Ka sutai Triquetra, captain of the *Demon Justice,* ship of the Demon Fleet of the Klingon Assault Group."

"Demon Fleet?" Ruanek murmured in question.

"Privateers," Spock told him, just as softly.

"Pirates," dismissively.

"Privateers. Licensed by the Klingon government, no doubt, though of course not officially acknowledged."

The commander of the second ship, which had been painted a startling white, was an older Klingon warrior, one with the flaming red hair that sometimes appeared in the noble Houses. He said with simple dignity, "I am JuB-Chal, captain of the *Dragon's Wrath.*"

"No offense is meant by this question," Saavik said, "but is a white ship not unusual?"

"It is, yes!" JuB-Chal agreed proudly. "This is a white *Kvort*-class bird-of-prey. Some of our enemies have thought us a hospital ship—but have learned to their dismay that we are not!"

JuB-Chal and his crew burst into gales of laughter at that thought. *Klingon humor,* Spock thought.

Commander Tor'Ka cut in, "And now we, captains and crews together, will come along with you on this mission for honor, glory—and blood."

The viewscreen went dark.

"Now *there* is an interesting mix," Chekov said. "All ve lack are the Romulans."

There was a second, not quite stifled snort from Ruanek. At Chekov's puzzled glance, Spock commented, very carefully, "Even as you, Admiral Chekov, are our one and only expert on the Watraii, so Ruanek is our expert, right now, our one and only expert, on Romulan affairs."

"And let me state here and now," Ruanek commented to no one in particular, "that I am growing very weary of being the one and only expert on Romulan affairs."

"It is the price you pay for being born to the profession," Saavik commented mildly.

"Hah."

Chekov, totally bewildered by now, simply shook his head, muttering, "Vulcans."

But Spock knew that behind the banter, Ruanek was, logically enough, uneasy about having old wounds reopened after years of political exile and rebuilding his life.

He is also, I am sure, keenly aware of the death sentence hanging over his head should he land on Romulan soil. I trust that such a landing will not become necessary. If it does, I will do what I can to shield him.

But how can he, being who and what he is, resist the chance to help his people?

"Captain . . ." Lieutenant Suhur didn't lose his Vulcan calm in the slightest, but he still managed to put a world of wariness into that word. "Starfleet is contacting you."

"I am not surprised. I will take this in my ready room. Gentlemen," to Spock, Chekov, and Ruanek, "will you please accompany me? Lieutentant Abrams, you have the bridge."

EIGHTEEN

MEMORY

The afterglow from the last slide illustrating Torin's closing statement faded. Now the screen filled with a fleet of reconfigured ships that soared out of Vulcan orbit into the long, long night, accompanied by a fanfare of commercially inspiring music.

Thank you for that unbiased presentation, Torin, Karatek thought.

As the ceiling lights glowed once more, a crowd of scientists, lobbyists, and Concerned Individuals made a concerted rush toward the VSI's director of research and development.

Better Torin than I, Karatek decided.

He stepped down from the dais, edging toward the door. As the crowd thinned, he found his way blocked by two more figures. Anyone else would have leaned against the wall. Predictably, these two stood almost at military attention.

"I estimate," said Surak, "an 87.23 percent probability that leadership will shift on the High Command to Technology by the

178

end of Tasmeen. More: There is a 64.31 percent probability that Technology's majority will be slim enough that it will have to ally with the Security Party."

Karatek stopped short. Where had Surak and his shadow hidden themselves? Neat and poised though they looked, Surak's balance was uneven, while Skamandros's cheekbone bore bruises and even what looked like a scar from a knife fight.

"Who do you think they will want to fight first?" asked Skamandros. That was it: He looked like he had been in a fight. Or perhaps several pitched battles.

"After our host Karatek's disclosures this morning," the man continued, "the High Command is likely to be able to choose among its enemies. I can think of at least two governments that will blame them for even a temporary alliance with the te-Vikram."

"Live long and prosper to you too," Karatek interrupted what sounded like an ongoing debate. At that moment, he wished that he, like Surak, was the servant only of logic. It wasn't bad enough that, only this morning, Karatek had fought and fled in fear of his life, and learned that the High Command he had served loyally his entire adult life had allied with a splinter group he had reason to hate. He was battered and exhausted, and now, without a word of greeting, Surak and his shadow emerged from whatever refuge they had found for themselves and promptly started arguing.

Surak inclined his head with the ceremonious manners Karatek remembered.

"Since returning from the desert, I have been otherwise engaged," Surak said.

"I can see you have," Karatek replied. "Just look at you! You look as if you, not I, had been the one facing assassins from the High Command."

179

"And the te-Vikram," Skamandros added. "People who forget the te-Vikram come to regret it."

"I find your sarcasm callous in the extreme," Karatek snapped.

"And I find your emotionalism illogical," Skamandros replied.

Parry and riposte. It was a good thing Karatek was a civilized man, or he would have challenged Skamandros then and there, and never mind the fact that he had called the man guest-friend.

Control, Karatek told himself. *If Skamandros can restrain himself, you can too.*

Surak held up a hand for peace.

"To answer your question," he said, "we were waging peace."

"Interesting methods you have," Karatek remarked.

"Now who is employing sarcasm?" Surak asked. "You accurately imply that we, like you, encountered assassins. Only in our case, the assassins were sent not by political bodies, but by my nephew."

"I thought your family wanted nothing to do with you anymore?" Karatek asked, distracted despite himself into what he knew was improper curiosity.

T'Vysse had told Karatek that Surak had broken with his family, which was one of the most aristocratic in the Confederation.

"Until I die or resign my place in the family," Surak said with a lift of his head, "I am still Head of House. My nephew, who is heir presumptive, hoped to assume his responsibilities somewhat . . . prematurely. The discussion grew somewhat intense until I convinced him of the error of his reasoning."

"Was that how Skamandros got his scar?" Karatek asked. He looked away, as courtesy required when prying past propriety. Within the family, all was silence—but not now.

Skamandros sketched half a bow, acknowledging Karatek's courtesy.

"You know, it is illogical to retain a scar when surgery is available to remove it," Karatek said.

"I retain it to remind myself to move more quickly next time," Skamandros said.

With anyone else, Karatek would have laughed. With Surak and his shadow, he threw up his hand in the gesture he used with Torin when he was outmatched during arms practice. He kept his hand motion restrained, though, modeling it on Surak's own physical control.

"You are still my guest-friends," he told them. "Will you come home with me?"

"No, I thank you. I have agreed to stay with Torin for the present. I suspect he will be followed home by half the audience from today's presentation, and ground remains to be won. Two counselors will be joining him for dinner, and I estimate more than one chance in four that I will be asked to speak with yet others. Besides, now that you have been attacked, I think it would be more prudent to follow through on my plans."

Plans. Just how much of this had Surak orchestrated? How much had he planned with Torin? Scientists and politicians. None of them could agree, much less reach the consensus Surak argued for, but they would argue for the sheer enjoyment—or perversity—of it. Karatek wondered if they were aware yet that Surak wasn't just more logical than they, but more stubborn.

He bowed. "Then I will not detain you. Live long and prosper," he wished them.

Karatek was pleased to learn that Commander Ivek, promoted during the past months' confusion, had detailed two of his City Guards to escort him home. He was less pleased to see them carrying energy weapons—not just blasters, but rifles—through the main streets of ShiKahr.

He would look as if he were under guard for some crime, Karatek thought. Instead of being guarded because he had been attacked. The guards left him at the door in the wall surrounding his home, refused the offer of water, while appreciating the courtesy, and suggested that Karatek lock his gates.

What sort of world has this become?

Two months back, the High Command had imposed a blackout on ShiKahr. Karatek's house was dark, its windows covered to keep in the light from firepits or fixtures. It looked as if it would give only scant welcome, but Karatek knew that, once within, he would be welcomed. Rich cooking smells—not meat because of recent austerity measures, but plentiful and highly spiced—would rise from kitchen and courtyard, and the thermal pool in his bathing chamber would be almost as comforting as T'Vysse's caring, knowledgeable hands.

With a pang of disappointment, quickly suppressed, Karatek remembered that T'Vysse was now studying each night for a medical certification. But he would be met by his children: the two of his begetting who had survived and the two he had adopted. In her parents' absence, Sarissa had even begun to cook dinner. Karatek watched her for a moment he knew he would treasure for the rest of her life as she worked, cutting and measuring with an absurd conscientiousness that made his heart ache with tenderness before he controlled himself.

He had expected to spend the evening tracking news feeds across Vulcan, scanning for the impact of the VSI's conference that day. Instead, when T'Vysse came in, they ate quietly, then sat together as Vulcan's dark night enveloped them as if reluctant to allow the outside world entry.

Finally, Karatek accessed the news feeds. He and T'Vysse watched in silence while Sarissa watched them with more caution and more fear than a girl her age should ever have had to have learned.

A riot in the northeast. A raiding party, apprehended shortly after it left the Womb of Fire and entered the Forge. One government severed diplomatic relations with ShiKahr's High Command, whose leaders resigned in a bloc, to be replaced by a coalition of technologists and militants.

"Surak estimated that the government would fall within a month," Karatek told his wife.

"He did leave a margin for error," she said. She ended transmission during news of the assassination of a tribal king, and rose to go to bed.

That was when the ground rocked.

"Incoming!" screamed Kovar.

Was the child reacting or flashing back to the destruction of his first home? T'Vysse was at his side, raising him in her arms.

"Where is thy control?" Sarissa chided. Her voice barely shook.

"No time for that!" Karatek cried. "All of you! Down to the shelter!"

Not for the first time, he rejoiced—no, that was too emotional a phrase—he was gratified that he had bought a house that had been built only two hundred years ago, when ShiKahr warred with its nearest neighbors and all houses came equipped with underground shelters.

Last to enter the shelter, Karatek activated its scans. He hoped his neighbors all had refuges of their own, that no one wandered the night in danger and needing a place to hide, so that he would not have to go out, find that person, and share limited resources that might be all that stood between his family and painful death. He hated himself for that feeling and suppressed it ruthlessly.

Surak was right: Emotions could prove to be traps. Look at what hatred and fear did, once again, to Vulcan.

With the news feeds playing over the shelter's antiquated systems, he began what he knew would be a nightly task from now on—expanding the shelter, making it more comfortable. Making his family safe.

He only wished he could secure his homeworld the same way. Once again, the ground rocked.

Toward dawn, Kovar cried softly. Again, Sarissa urged him to self-control. "How will thee fare on thy *kahs-wan?*" she asked.

If all went well, Karatek thought, many living now on Vulcan would soon face a different ordeal—not in the desert but in the depths of space.

NINETEEN

MEMORY

ONE YEAR LATER

A veil of reddish sand drifted in the evening wind above the scaffolding that enveloped ShiKahr's ancient gates and concealed the long, long track that led out into the Forge as the citizens of ShiKahr waited for their sons to come home.

Centuries ago, it had not been the same foregone conclusion that it was today that the youths who went out into the desert in the *kahs-wan* ordeal would all return safely. Centuries ago, the boys went out as a class, then straggled back one at a time, or in twos and threes to families who waited behind the security of their walls to see if they had gained adult sons who might further protect them or whether they had need to crop their hair and mourn.

In recent years, however, *kahs-wan* classes had sprung up and become extremely successful. Now it was the custom for the

185

parents and family of boys facing the trial to meet at the Gates and wait for Rovalat to return with the boys.

Rovalat, a grizzled, hardy man, was of *T'Kehr* Torin's age cohort and, in fact, his military unit. For decades, most families in ShiKahr had chosen not to teach their sons in the ways of the desert themselves, but instead to entrust them to Rovalat to be instructed in the ways of survival and the lore of the Forge.

Rovalat had created innovations in customs that were at least a millennium old. It used to be that men would go down to the Gates, wait, and escort the new adult males to a feast where they celebrated their responsibilities and, if they chose, took adult names. But Rovalat marched his charges out through the Gates, prepared for their ordeal. Then he went out into the Forge himself and waited to collect his charges, now successfully adult, so he could march them back into their families' embrace.

Kahs-wan had become a festival. This new custom had become so popular that some daughters were protesting that it wasn't fair that they be denied the praise and gifts bestowed upon their brothers.

This year's celebration had even drawn out *T'Kehr* Torin, even though his last son had completed his ordeal many years ago. The old scientist strode back and forth, as if mounting guard. At times, he stopped to talk to Subcommander Ivek, while at other times, he stared out into the desert.

Sarissa, who had suffered more than any boy who had survived his trial when her family's installation had been destroyed, sat beside her foster parents T'Vysse and Karatek. Hands steepled in her lap, she was practicing her composure with the same care that she brought to her meditation, her martial-arts training, and her other studies.

For most of the young people who waited by the Gates, the

186

kahs-wan ordeal was their first solitary experience with the dangers of the Forge. But Sarissa and her brother Kovar had already lost their parents to attacks of te-Vikram in the deep desert. She had been Tu'Pari then. Now, her S-name, testimony to her veneration for Surak, became something she struggled to live up to as she settled the folds of her cloak about her so that they flowed as elegantly as those of T'Vysse and stared once more at her hands, seeking the calm-within that logic was supposed to provide.

As the evening drew out, and the reddish veils of sand muted and deepened into dusk, soon to be replaced by the deep night, the women and girls sat by the walls, their clever strained faces frozen into masks of composure, the ornaments in their hair tinkling, while the men forced themselves not to pace.

"He is late," T'Vysse mouthed to Karatek over Sarissa's head. Rovalat had trained their first two sons, who had returned to them barely tired out from their isolation in cave and sand. Even now, Karatek remembered how the boys had marched behind their teacher up to the Gates, singing as they came. It had been a solemn and wonderful moment.

Ivek stirred. It was part of his responsibilities to assume the worst. Perhaps a boy had fallen and broken a leg, and required help. Or perhaps Rovalat was simply debriefing his young students. It was clear that the security officer wanted to stride down into the sand, find the *kahs-wan* class, and bring it back, dragging all of them if need be.

The *sehlat* belonging to young Aloran, son of T'Loran and Varek, whuffled in distress, and bayed once, inappropriately, before T'Loran silenced it with firm pats to its broad shoulders. *Sehlat*s always wanted to accompany their masters into the desert and always had to be kept penned up until the boys were safely away. Now the *sehlat* whined with eagerness to have its Vulcan cub safely home.

Sarissa leapt to her feet, faster than the adult decorum that she had been trying on in recent months permitted.

"They're coming!" she cried. "That's *T'Kehr* Rovalat, but—oh, night and day, there are so few of them!"

Karatek had his hand on T'Vysse's shoulder. She reached out to her foster daughter, but the girl shrugged it off. She took a few steps forward, then stopped.

"I see him," she whispered in a soft voice. The Veils flickered once over her eyes. She pulled her hood down over her face, seated herself, and forced decorum on herself once more with the resolve that had been one of the first things Karatek had noticed about her.

Aloran's *sehlat* howled again, a terrible, disconsolate sound. His young master was not part of the straggle of ragged, bleeding, and exhausted boys whom Rovalat aided in their trek back to the Gates and home. His parents sat motionless, too stunned yet to grieve. All around the Gates, the families whose sons had returned pulled away, for fear and decency, from those whose sons had not.

Other *sehlat*s were racing off into the desert: they might return in a day or three, nudging their masters along in the same way they had shepherded them since they were infants.

A boy or two might struggle back even now, Karatek protested silently. Surely, it was too early to despair.

But the numbers were terrible. Of the twenty boys who marched out onto the Forge, heads up, shoulders back, and as well prepared as everyone in ShiKahr could make them, only thirteen had returned. And of that thirteen, Rovalat was carrying one of them, ragged and bleeding.

"There's got to be raiders out there. I'm taking my people out,"

Ivek announced. "They'll find the boys. And if they don't, they'll find the . . ."

Torin put himself in front of the security officer with a speed astonishing in a man of his age.

"That thee will *not* do, Subcommander," he said.

Ivek stiffened before the veteran. "Who's going to stop me?"

"I am," said Torin.

"I can't fight a man your age," Ivek grumbled.

"It would be more accurate to say you can't fight *me,*" said Torin. "Look at it tactically, man. Let's say there are raiders out there. What if they're waiting for our security guards to do precisely what you plan? You leave the city defenseless, and they come in and strike for a second time. And we lose more than we've already lost."

He looked around at the families who had begun to realize that their sons would not return and lowered his voice guiltily.

"I knew it was a mistake to tear down ShiKahr's walls," said Ivek, as if he took personal offense at an event that had occurred three hundred years in the past. "But *T'Kehr,* it goes against the grain to abandon those children."

"We're not going to abandon them. Thee," said Torin, returning to the language of formality, elder to younger, "will return to thy duties guarding this city. I shall lead out the fathers and brothers of the boys who didn't come back, together with their teacher, who desperately needs some occupation. Who has a better reason to go out there and hunt with all their hearts?"

So, Torin felt responsible for the old survival-training specialist? Karatek supposed that was only logical.

The man had done his best! he reminded himself, fighting down a stab of resentment.

Then, as Kovar trudged past the Gates, Karatek's heart lifted.

He studied his son. The boy's sandsuit was ragged, with one sleeve torn and wrapped about his leg as a bandage, stained with blackish green. He was limping, braced by some sort of stick he had found. As he spotted Sarissa and his foster parents, his face brightened, then fell again, as if he was controlling his joy in the presence of other families' anguish.

Kovar saluted his teacher, who kept his face impassive—just barely—then walked over to Karatek.

"Live long and prosper, Father," said the boy. "I have returned." His bare arm was burnt deep by the relentless sun, and he leaned on his improvised crutch. Something about it . . .

"Peace and long life," Karatek said. He could not suppress the smile that spread across his face.

How can you smile when others are weeping? he asked himself.

My *son lives.*

He would mourn the other boys later, but he *would* mourn. To each joy its celebration; to each sorrow, its observance. That was, as Surak said in his *Analects,* only logical.

"Thee is injured," Sarissa said. Already, she had knelt beside her brother. Her hands were patting at him, examining him. Now that Kovar had been reunited with his family, he was wilting, sliding down against his sister, as if only the staff he still clutched held him upright.

"Let's get you home," said T'Vysse.

The feast would be a fast; the festival, a funeral.

Drawing her cloak about her, T'Vysse rose, walking over to speak with the *kahs-wan* instructor. Tears poured down his face, a terrible, illogical waste of water.

"Let's see that staff." Karatek held out a hand to Kovar. "If you don't mind." An adult's weapons were almost sacred.

Kovar leaned against Sarissa. He was almost as tall as she. He held out the staff to Karatek.

He had expected to see some ancient, toughened brush, or a structural support from one of the deserted, half-buried settlements that turned up on the Forge every time there was a strong sandstorm.

What he saw instead, broken in half, was a carefully turned shaft, surmounted by a cruel, pyramidal-shaped metal blade bearing te-Vikram marks.

Karatek felt his blood chill. "Where did thee get this?" he asked softly.

"I took it from the man who carried it, Father," Kovar told him. "Te-Vikram have been moving in, just as they did . . ." He gestured, clearly not wanting to talk about the circumstances in which he had met his new father. "I saw them take Aloran. I don't know if they are looking for new warriors," the boy added. "Or sacrifices."

It was one thing to condemn the te-Vikram as barbarians who sacrificed their own, or their captives. But Karatek now realized that worse could lie ahead of the men of ShiKahr. They could die at the hands of warriors whose faces, once, had been familiar and beloved. Had been family.

The boys, though, were on the threshold of adulthood. They might be too old to change. In that case, Karatek knew, they would die.

Ivek had an arm around Rovalat's shoulders. "Let's get you home," he said. "No, man, I don't blame you. *T'Kehr* here's gotten so many boys through the trials for so long we just forgot how dangerous it really was. It's not your fault," he was saying.

The blame was collective.

"Now we will have to remember," said Rovalat. "But someone else," he added. "I have sent my last charge into the desert to die."

"Get home," T'Vysse was saying. "The boys who have returned need to tell us of their ordeal. And they could use baths, dinner, and bed. The rest of us will fast and meditate. When you have all heard from your sons, let us come back here and find out what happened."

Karatek led his family across the bridge leading to their house wall. It creaked, sending up the traditional warning. Pressing the lock panel, he opened the door and gestured to Kovar to be certain to step over the threshold using his right foot.

That was his son's injured leg, he realized. The boy pressed his lips together, leaned on the staff that had once been a te-Vikram spear, and entered. T'Vysse swept Sarissa off to the kitchens. In ancient times, the women of the house would have cooked a feast: these days, however, the feast had been shared among all of the families rejoicing in their sons' returns.

Karatek suspected they would return in later years to the older custom. He led Kovar into the baths, shutting the door, leaving the womenfolk on the outside while the male adults bathed, allegedly in peace and quiet after their labors. The boy flickered a grin at him before peeling off the rags of his sandsuit.

"Let me see your injury," said Karatek. "What caused it?"

"Energy burn," the boy replied. "Good thing I was fast. He just grazed me, and the injury was cauterized. I used *cholla* root for the pain and wrapped the wound in the pulp of *ches'lintak,* secured by bark. *T'Kehr* taught us the pulp has natural antibiotic properties."

Suppressing an impulse to race out and waylay the first Healer he saw, Karatek examined the burn. As the boy said, it was healing nicely.

"It's not his fault!" Kovar protested about his teacher. "If it hadn't been for what he taught us, I'd have been dead. As it was, he showed me how to braid a cord and secure it to two rocks, and that let me come up behind the te-Vikram and . . ."

Karatek eased his son into the hot water. The boy sighed in relief.

"Better, isn't that?" Karatek asked. "You know, there's some sort of speech I'm supposed to give to the newest warrior of my house, but . . ."

He went to the door and took a pitcher, glistening with condensation, and pungent with the odors of citrus and cinnamon from T'Vysse's hands, and brought it over to where the boy lay in the water, submerged almost to his ears.

"Warrior?" said Kovar. "I fought. I didn't expect to have to, but that's what I'm saying, I could adapt what *T'Kehr* taught me, and that was how I lived when I came back from gathering fruit and found the tc-Vikram . . ."

Karatek heard a protest from outside the bathing chamber. Sarissa, certain she was missing something important, allowed her disapproval to be known.

"Is this the respect you grant returning warriors, young lady?" Karatek called. This *kahs-wan* was hardly a laughing matter, but she had made him smile.

"Not one more word," he ordered. "Your sister's conduct is proof that she and your mother wish to hear this story too. So, finish your bath. Empty that pitcher; you need fluids. I will not hurry you, but you may not talk about this until the family can hear you." He flickered a grin at the boy. "Unless, of course, you prefer to waive the privilege of having escaped the women's quarters and admit them?"

Kovar reached for his cup again. He raised it as if preparing to gulp, then sipped prudently.

*　　*　　*

Dressed in fresh clothing, cut like a man's robe, not a child's, and with House sigils embroidered upon it, Kovar seated himself in his father's place at the table by the firepit. Blue globes of fire floated in a bowl of water, providing centerpiece and light. The boy's eyes brightened at the array of dishes that T'Vysse and Sarissa had managed to improvise. Kovar had to have been ravenous, Karatek remembered from his own *kahs-wan* and those of his older sons, but he controlled himself, raising his soup bowl in time with the rest of the family. With a pang, he remembered Varen, dead in the desert defending Surak.

After what felt like the interminable rituals that followed *kahs-wan,* it finally came time for Kovar to tell his story. He had found himself a small cave in a rock escarpment, clear of feral *sehlat*s or *le-matya,* and made it his. He had dragged brush into it and made himself a bed. He had chipped flakes of stone and used them as plates, tools, and weapons. And he had, he realized now, become entirely too comfortable.

He had been careless, and he had been observed by one of the te-Vikram who had been moving into the part of the Forge nearest ShiKahr for the past year or so. The man had been overconfident, however, thinking Kovar a soft, city-bred boy who could be intimidated if a warrior invaded his campsite. Instead, Kovar had seen a shadow approach his cave and slipped out—not quite fast enough.

The te-Vikram had fired at his shadow and injured his leg.

At this point of the story, T'Vysse bit her lip, while Sarissa simply took her brother's hand.

Kovar had crawled off. He had had a bad couple of nights of it, but had managed to dig himself into shade long enough to bring the pain of the burn down. Once his meditations succeeded, he was able to dress his wound.

"I had been the hunted," said Kovar. "Now I became the hunter, and snared my warrior. Then, I tried to wage peace with him, convincing him what an error it is to prey on boys taking the *kahs-wan*. He said I was weak, but I pointed out that he was the one bound like a *ferravat* for plucking at a harvest festival. We debated for day after day, sharing the food from his pack, because I feared to leave him."

"How did you leave him?" asked T'Vysse. "After all, if you unbound him, he would pursue you. He was a man grown, and you were already injured."

Sarissa drew in her breath sharply.

"No, sister," said Kovar. "I saw no logic in killing him. But it was surely a dilemma. If I left him bound, the *le-matya* would have him. Now, perhaps he deserved to be *le-matya* fodder, but did I wish the responsibility of providing them with a feast? If I freed him, he would come after me and I could not trust his word."

"So what did you do?" asked Karatek.

"Hit him on the head with a rock, loosened his bonds, and stole his spear. I wanted it as a prize of war and a way of easing my path. I had just enough time to meet up with the others of my year—those who made it back," he finished up soberly.

Sarissa's eyes flashed with pride before she subdued it. "It sounds as if you behaved very logically," she said.

"Don't!" cried the boy. "Don't you understand? I tried to wage peace. I failed. My logic didn't work, but my training did, which is why I am alive and my friends—"

Now it comes out. T'Vysse flashed Karatek a look.

All control gone, Kovar flung himself weeping at his elder sister. She caught him and held him, both of them crying as they had not wept the terrible night Kovar had met them.

"I grieve with thee," murmured Karatek.

They were adults now, and they had adults' griefs. And adults' burdens. He walked over and put his arms around his two newest children, who remembered themselves, controlled themselves, and sat up.

"Has thee thought of the name thee will take?" Sarissa asked. She had been Tu'Pari, then chosen an S-name to indicate her attempt to follow Surak's disciplines.

"I did not give my name to the warrior in the desert, though he demanded it as a right. As Kovar, I fought him and escaped. As Kovar I returned to ShiKahr," he said, his head high. "And now I give that name to you, along with the prize I took. And I choose a new name. I am Solor."

"Kovar's name," said Karatek, "will be written on the wall beside your spoils of war, near the other treasures of our House."

Sarissa tensed, hearing the bridge outside the walls creak. "Someone's there," she said, more a shape of her lips than a whisper.

"I shall go," said Karatek.

Rising, he went to the door. A package lay outside, wrapped in layer upon layer of filmy silk, each layer a faintly different shade of red. Attached to the package was a scroll, exquisitely calligraphed.

"Permit me to share your rejoicing."

It bore the sigil of Surak's House. Of Surak himself.

When the silks were unwrapped and carefully put away, Kovar—no, Solor, now—held a beautifully wrought blade the length of his forearm. Its pommel was wrought like a *shavokh*'s head, with its wings, outspread, forming the hilt, and its blade shimmered with the striations, like layer upon layer of silk, of the celebrated ancient smithies found at the lip of the Forge.

"I will wear it always," vowed Solor.

196

TWENTY

NOW

U.S.S. ALLIANCE

The communication from Starfleet began, not surprisingly, considering the circumstances, as a tirade. In fact, almost before the face of Admiral Randall finished winking in on screen, his lean, normally pale face had turned to an angry pink and he was all but shouting, "Captain Saavik, just *what* is going on out there?"

"Sir, it would not be logical for me to attempt to answer for any of the non-Starfleet vessels that may be in the region."

The pink deepened into an angry red. "Don't play logic games with me, Captain Saavik. You know that isn't what I meant. What is the *Alliance* doing with a fleet of, as you just said, non-Starfleet vessels, heading out on an unapproved flight?"

With a surreptitious signal to the others to be silent, Chekov leaned forward. Resting both folded arms on the ready-room

197

desk, he stared into the viewscreen. "Thomas? Thomas John Randall? Is that you?"

"Pavel? Pavel Chekov! Good lord, man, what are *you* doing aboard the *Alliance?*"

"I'm afraid that I can't tell you that, Thomas," Chekov said honestly. "But I vill say this: Neither the *Alliance*'s captain nor its crew are at fault here. Any blame that may be incurred in this expedition, no matter vhat happens, should fall squarely on me."

"What *are* you—"

"And no, Thomas, I vould rather not explain any further. I vill only say that Starfleet and the Federation Council both can consider vhat ve are doing as maneuvers and surveillance, if they like, rather than humanitarian—or Romulan— assistance."

"Oh hell. You're going after the aliens."

"Ve are?"

"You won't make it."

"Ve'll give it a good try."

"Come on, Pavel, you know better than this! If you somehow manage to survive, which is doubtful, they'll court-martial you for this!"

"Let them!" Chekov answered cheerfully. "Chekov out."

With that, he cut off the transmission, and grinned at the others. "I've been vanting to say something like that for years. So, now. That should buy us a little more time. By the time that they decide vhat to do about us, ve vill be vell on our vay."

"Agreed," Spock said. To Saavik, he added, with only the very faintest edge of irony, "I believe it best for us to, as Dr. McCoy might have said it, 'Get the hell out of Dodge.' "

"Dr. McCoy," she replied, "was a wise man, indeed."

*   *   *

Saavik's command sent their improvised fleet zooming toward the Neutral Zone.

"All ships' channels open," she ordered, and the command raced throughout all the fleet. "Captains, if we are to survive this mission, we must all be in agreement on tactics."

"I agree!" said Captain Tor'Ka. "There is no greater danger in battle than an unpredictable ally."

"If we are fortunate, it will not come to battle," Saavik said. "But we must be prepared."

With all the ships' channels open, she and the other captains plotted an intercept course with the Watraii ships in accordance with the coordinates that Uhura had given Saavik. She and the other captains hurriedly plotted strategy for the two possibilities, peaceful or warlike encounters. It was definitely one of the most complicated and intricate group transmissions that Spock had ever thought to help arrange.

The actual plans of action were relatively easy: Since they didn't know how many of the enemy there were, or what firepower they carried—move quickly and keep moving.

It was the cultural and linguistic differences between captains that were causing problems.

"We will keep the code words simple," Saavik said to them all, "since we all know what the heat of battle does to the remembering of elaborate codes even in Vulcans."

"We are used to battle fury," cut in the Klingon captain, JuB-Chal with a harsh laugh. "It does not cloud our minds."

"Congratulations," Captain Butterworth retorted. "It must be nice to have such clear heads."

"Did you call us empty heads?"

"No, Captain JuB-Chal," Saavik said smoothly. "I'm sure you agree with us that the plans must be followed precisely?"

"We understand battle plans!" roared the other Klingon captain, Tor'Ka.

"Then you understand that there must be no 'loose cannons.' "

That silenced everyone until Spock explained, "It is a term dating from Earth's nineteenth century, and meaning someone who is dangerous because of his or her unpredictability. A cannon that had broken loose from its moorings on the deck of a wooden oceanic sailing ship was a danger."

The term seemed to strike both Klingon captains as hilarious, for whatever Klingon reason, and Spock suspected from their enthusiasm and the way that they kept repeating "loose cannon" that he had just added a phrase to the Klingon language.

But even they agreed that it made good battle practice for all the captains to hold their fire until they knew for certain what they were facing. There would, indeed, be no "loose cannons" here, but a unified fleet.

"And," Saavik added, "since there can logically be only one person giving the orders, the orders you follow will be mine. And no, gentlebeings," she continued before there could be any arguments, "I am not trying to grab power or to insult anyone. It is simply the fact that my ship is the only one to carry an expert on the Watraii."

Surprisingly enough, the first to agree with this were the Klingons. "You are the one who first called together this glorious adventure," Tor'Ka said. "As war leader, it is only right and honorable for you to be the one to give the orders."

The Vulcans and Starfleet personnel agreed without argument. One by one, the others grudgingly fell into line.

"They will follow my orders," Saavik muttered to Spock, "until I give one they don't like, that is."

Judging from his wife's suddenly fierce eyes, Spock thought

that Saavik's Romulan side was in perfect agreement with the idea of having taken leadership of the fleet. But at the heart of it, she was a true Vulcan, not someone to let herself be swayed by any emotion, particularly not one as dangerous as pride. No danger of any errors of judgment due to emotion.

"Now that one problem is solved," Spock said to Saavik, "I must try to solve another."

He retreated alone to Saavik's ready room, where he prepared and sent a careful message. The channel he deliberately used was one that was years out of date, since it was a frequency rarely in use now and as a result one less likely to be traced, and the message was scrambled with codes that only Spock and one other knew.

He added one word, a name, to the message to show its authenticity—a secret name, one that had been whispered to him once, back when he was still Spock of the *U.S.S. Enterprise*: Liviana.

Liviana, whose public use name was Charvanek. Charvanek, widow of the Romulan praetor.

Spock had first met Charvanek back when he was still a member of *Enterprise*'s crew and she was the enemy, a Romulan commander . . . a commander whom he had, in the name of Starfleet, seduced so that he could steal what had then been a cutting-edge secret device.

But what had happened between them during that time had not been all utterly cold duty.

Nor had it been all cold duty between them ten years ago on Romulus, when Spock, on a secret mission there, had worked together with Charvanek—with Ruanek's aid—to overthrow the corrupt Praetor Dralath and put the more honorable Narviat in his place.

The Narviat whom Charvanek had wed. And who was now

deceased. Assassinated, which was the usual way for a Romulan praetor—and sometimes even an emperor—to die.

It didn't matter now whether Charvanek was wife or widow. Saavik—ah yes, she was his true mate, she always would be his true mate, and there would never be any doubt at all in his heart or mind about it.

But now Charvanek was both Narviat's widow—and the head of Romulan intelligence.

Would she answer him?

Was she even receiving the message?

She was, indeed, receiving it. The contact was made with such swiftness and clarity that Spock suspected Charvanek was already offworld. It would seem, from what he remembered of her fierce Romulan nature and utter honor and love of her people, that she was already trying to go after the Watraii.

However, she cannot logically have the number of ships for any effective action.

As her image formed on the viewscreen, Spock, even though he was most happily married, even though he knew who and what Charvanek was now, did feel that odd, familiar little twinge of what could almost have been regret shoot through him.

How very ridiculous.

Being of Vulcan stock, she had not changed notably in such a relatively short time, but her strong, handsome face had hardened ever so slightly more than it had when last he'd seen her, which was not a surprising fact considering her current twin occupations.

"Spock," she said, as casually as if they had only recently been having a conversation. "It is . . . quite agreeable to see you again. But I must be brusque: We are very busy here just now."

"It concerns the colony."

"Of course it does! Do you think the Federation is the only force to have received word of that massacre?"

"No, such thinking would hardly be logical."

"Ah, Spock!" Her voice softened the tiniest of bits. "You are still so very much a Vulcan."

"I could hardly be otherwise, Charvanek. And you?"

"I am as I have always been," she said, her tone clearly telling him not to pry into any private aspects of her life. Fair enough. "And yes, before you ask," she continued, "I have indeed been making my own preparations—in addition to those the Empire is performing—to mobilize in defense of my people."

That afterthought about what the Romulan Star Empire was doing could only mean that they were doing very little, or at least less than Charvanek would have liked. "You have already launched, I see," Spock said. "But logically you cannot have many ships."

"Ah? Do you think that my praetor does not trust me?"

"Never that. But Neral would certainly have thought to keep his defenses guarding the homeworlds."

"Logically argued."

He dipped his head slightly, accepting the compliment, and then added, "A united force is stronger."

He saw by her slight start that she knew perfectly well what he meant by that: Her small force would be far more effective if it was united with the fleet that he and Saavik had already assembled.

"Awkward questions might be asked," she countered.

"The Charvanek I knew had no fear of such things."

"The Charvanek you knew wasn't the praetor's Chief of Intelligence!"

"And would it not be better for Praetor Neral and the Romulan image—and economy—if such uncomfortable problems as the

Empire now faces were handled for him by those who are safely outside of the complication of Romulan politics?"

"Oh, clever, Spock! You manipulate people very well."

He raised an eyebrow. "I could not possibly manipulate you, Charvanek, if you were not already halfway in agreement."

She was silent for a long while. Spock waited with Vulcan patience. Then Charvanek's mouth quirked up at one corner in wry approval. "So be it" was all she said, and ended the transmission.

By the time he had returned to the bridge and taken his seat again, Spock wasn't at all surprised to hear Lieutenant Abrams suddenly announce in a voice that was tight with tension, "Captain, there are six Romulan ships, warbirds, heading straight at us, closing fast."

"On screen," Saavik snapped.

Pre-Dominion War design, Spock recognized at once. *Quite understandable that these wouldn't be more modern ships. Charvanek or possibly Neral would have realized that she would not be able to appropriate any of the newer warbirds without too many awkward questions being asked.*

"They are not enemies," Spock said.

That earned him a quick sideways glance from Saavik, who had clearly also recognized the type of warbird and had come to the same conclusions, and a muttered "I don't vant to know how you know that" from Chekov.

Spock in turn thought that he didn't want to know how ruthlessly Charvanek had overpowered any opposition to get here on the edge of the Neutral Zone so swiftly.

It was indeed Charvanek, as she proved by instantly opening communications and letting them see her on the viewscreen: a Charvanek looking as fierce as a bird-of-prey herself. Without any preamble, she said, "Three of you know perfectly well who I am. The rest of you need not know more save that yes, my crews and I are Romulans. Let us merely say we are joining you, because of this."

"She is sending visual data, Captain Saavik," Lieutenant Suhur said.

"On screen," Saavik ordered.

The records that Charvanek sent were of the Romulan colony's destruction. But these tapes contained even more details than the presumably Watraii-edited tapes that had been received by the Federation. As if deliberately composed to terrorize the Romulans, they included horrifying images of helpless people unable to fight the long-range enemy, standing and dying in final defiance or dying while trying in vain to shield their dying children.

Spock heard the non-Vulcans around him gasp or swear softly, and someone even stifled a sob.

No, the Watraii would not have wanted the Federation to see such details.

"The aliens," Charvanek added in a cold fury, "even captured two warbirds before they had time to seek refuge in Final Honor."

But almost before Charvanek had finished speaking, Lieutenant Abrams warned, "More ships. And . . . they are not recognizable kinds this time, Captain Saavik."

"*I* recognize them," Ruanek said shortly.

"As do I," said Spock. "Those are Watraii ships."

Saavik frowned ever so slightly. "Let's see if they will talk with us. Open hailing frequencies, Lieutenant Suhur."

"Hailing frequencies are open, Captain," Lieutenant Suhur replied almost instantly.

"This is Captain Saavik, commander of the Federation starship *Alliance*."

No answer.

"Lieutenant Suhur?"

He looked up from his console. "They do hear us, Captain. They are simply not choosing to reply."

Lieutenant Abrams added grimly, "And they're powering up weapons. Whatever those weapons are," she continued under her breath, her fingers busy at her own console.

"Red alert," Saavik ordered, sending the alarm to the entire fleet. "All ships: Go to red alert."

TWENTY-ONE

MEMORY

TWENTY YEARS LATER

A carrybag containing his limited personal allotment slung over his shoulder, Karatek waited quietly with his family until their names were called over the loudspeaker in the VSI's auditorium. Then, it would be their turn to board a shuttle that would take them to one of the fleet of reconfigured ships that would carry tens of thousands of Vulcans offworld into the long night of deep space.

The shuttle's long, bronzed ramps were fully extended as people filed on. Ivek's security force kept order in a way Surak would have found highly satisfactory. Once the shuttle lifted, its wings would extend, buoying it in Vulcan's thin air until all air vanished and its secondary engines kicked in, taking them to their ship.

He glanced up at the screens showing the ships orbiting Vulcan. They were immense, but even they were dwarfed by the metal blossom that was Vulcan Station, the magnificent compromise that would enable those Vulcans who had chosen not to make the long journey of exile and exploration to take a slower, more cautious way to the stars.

How beautiful they were, he thought. The immense weapons and cargo bays that would have made them formidable ships of war had converted well to sites for hydroponics, manufacturing, laboratories, and living quarters. The layers of decks upon decks looked more crowded than they actually were. Space would be a premium. But they were Vulcans and, most of them, followers of Surak. They no longer needed the desert for isolation: they carried their privacy within themselves.

It occurred to Karatek that the ships had only numbers, not names. There would be time, he supposed, for names to be chosen. After all, there had been time for so many other things he had not expected. He remembered watching the station being built. He remembered how his own first shuttle ride to one of the ships nearly overset the control he had attempted to learn from Surak over the past twenty years. Once he regained his composure, however, he recalled how useful that mastery of his emotions had been as he had examined the ship's propulsion system and performed meticulous internal checks before suiting up, walking its hull, and, for a brief moment in which he succeeded in repressing fear, losing his sense of direction as he looked away from the hull into directions that were neither vertical and horizontal but only far, far off.

Now the day toward which he, the scientists of the Vulcan Space Initiative whom he had managed to persuade, and hosts of Vulcan's citizens had worked had finally arrived.

They were leaving. As if he adjusted an engine, Karatek monitored his breathing and his heart rate until they were appropriate levels. And, while exhilaration at achieving his goal was logical, the emotional response would impair his judgment. Still, he thought that even Surak would consider it illogical not to take satisfaction in Vulcan's accomplishment.

His com buzzed, the bone induction unit relaying Torin's voice. *"Representatives of the High Command are here. Again."* Only someone who knew Torin well would have heard the irritation. And apprehension.

But then, politicians who would not take no for an answer were, logically, grounds for apprehension. Karatek supposed they had a right to make a final plea: when the fleet left, it would take a substantial portion of Vulcan's physical and intellectual capital with it. It was a good thing that Torin was almost as stubborn as Surak.

Beside him, Solor—Kovar's chosen adult name for himself— shifted from foot to foot. Skamandros. Sarissa. And now Solor. As Surak's philosophies took hold, approximately 28.6 percent of Vulcan's population had taken names starting with "S." At this rate, the whole planet would follow suit—Karatek began to perform the calculation, then paused.

"Where *is* Surak?" Sarissa asked.

Surak's whereabouts, and whether he would accompany the fleet into Exile, had been fascinating topics of discussion. So many people had chosen to go whom Karatek would not have expected, while others, like Torin and the high priestess of Seleya, had refused.

"Perhaps he is polishing the last volume of his *Analects,"* said T'Vysse. She had all but memorized the first two, and had been one of the few people Karatek knew who found Surak's long absences from the VSI or the chambers of the High Command promising. It was a pleasurable thought. Karatek liked to think of

Surak, wearing the coronet he had received on Mount Seleya, creating great art as he contemplated the chance he had won for Vulcan to have peace. Never mind his *Analects:* the hope that Vulcan would survive was Surak's greatest achievement.

So many people had taken S-names. How curious it was. Karatek remembered how his own thinking had evolved from skepticism to advocacy—right about the time that two warring parties had united to send assassins after him. Governments had fallen, along with bombs. That was when he had begun his work of persuading a critical mass of the space scientists living and working near the Forge to leave Vulcan.

For all that, however, he had not chosen to forsake the name his parents had given him. Nor had Torin or many others. Perhaps, the diversity was better than the tribute to Surak, whom so many on Vulcan regarded as a philosophical, even a spiritual, master. He suspected Surak would agree.

In the past twenty years, Karatek had become a wearier, warier, and perhaps even a wiser man. He had watched the expansion of the qanats until they could shelter ShiKahr's population underground. He had lobbied for the reconfiguration of the ships and, as a compromise that Surak had helped engineer, committed to help build the station. Vulcan's exiles might be leaving forever, but Vulcan too was going into space. He remembered the first voyages that proved that robots and remotes could mine tritanium and duranium, even small amounts of hyponeutronium, from their system's asteroids: they would have to pause along the way to enable the ships to endure past their projected lifespans.

What was a year or two, if it extended the ships' effectiveness? Vulcans had learned patience in good causes. And their lives *would* be long, now that they had ended the need for war.

The Vulcan Space Initiative's pilgrims had tried to keep the day of their departure a secret. Tried to keep it calm. They had succeeded in building a fleet. They had not succeeded in overpowering Vulcan curiosity. Inevitably, the news feeds learned, perhaps through their contacts among academics, some of whom still wished to "revisit" the entire question of Exile.

And with the news feeds came the politicians. And the soldiers.

Again, the bones near Karatek's ear buzzed. *"They are very insistent,"* Torin told him. *"I need you to help keep order. Keep them calm."*

Karatek stepped out of line, his elder sons with him. How amused Ivek would be to see him assuming the role of security guard, directing the flow of pilgrims on board the shuttle. Ivek was another one who deserved a place on board but had refused it.

"It's the usual argument: What would be the harm in waiting? We could develop more fail-safes. This is pointless!" Torin's voice grew crisper, and Karatek knew he was now addressing the politicians he had reluctantly consented to receive. *"Sirs and Ladies, I am going to the launch site. If you wish to say your farewells, it would be courteous to accompany me."*

Now, that invitation was not the best idea Torin had ever had. The damned politicians must have harassed him past his best judgment.

"Incoming!"

Speakers screamed the threat of attack that all Vulcans had come to dread.

"Move quickly, move along, don't stop to pick that up, quickly now!" people urged all along the line of march.

"Shut the gate!" came a shout from one of Ivek's men, followed by an instant scream of protest from the people about to be left behind.

"They'll have to wait for the next shuttle!" his eldest son shouted.

"Will there *be* a next shuttle?"

There was no time to calculate the probability.

Karatek saw his eldest son, Turak, step out of line. His wife, carrying their daughter, pushed through to join him. Just in time, Karatek reached out to stop T'Vysse from running after them.

Her eyes were terrible.

Now Karatek could hear weapons, screams of rage and pain. "Get the others on board," he told T'Vysse. "I'll join you as soon as I can."

If I can.

He had worked too hard to get those shuttles off the ground, to get those ships out of Vulcan's system. He remembered Surak's great aphorism. "The needs of the many outweigh the needs of the one."

Yes, he deserved better. But he was only one.

He ran toward his son and tripped over a body. His fall saved his life, as an energy beam raved over where he would have stood, and a scream of rage told him that his enemies had broken through.

He saw te-Vikram insignia. He saw the sigils of personal guards as well as ShiKahr's own guards.

He saw Elonat, Ivek's second-in-command, brought down by the butt of a laser rifle, then trampled by agents of the priest-kings. He was not the first of many to die, and he certainly would not be the last.

"Karatek, what are you doing?" Torin's voice roared over the struggle. "You have to lead this wave!"

Karatek saw the old man at the end of the corridor, pressing toward the toppled security barriers. "Get those things back up!" he was ordering the surviving guards.

"Get out of here!" Torin ordered. "We'll hold the line!"

Karatek turned. His eyelids tightened as he fought back unworthy tears. The last he saw of Torin was his old mentor, swaying with the energy of his blaster as he fired methodically into the crowd, chanting the sixth Stave of "Azeraik's Last Stand."

"Listen to your master," came a familiar voice. "The needs of the many outweigh the needs of the one."

Surak!

Karatek whirled and seized the man just as an energy bolt glanced across the carrybag he had somehow retained. He thought to shed it so he could move faster, but it had saved his life and should be retained.

"Where have you been?" he demanded.

Surak raised an eyebrow at him. "Your question is superfluous. I have been waging peace, with, apparently, only limited success, so I will be returning to my duties here on Vulcan. I regret . . ."

An immense explosion rocked the landing field, and the two men clutched each other, fighting to retain their footing.

"We have no time for regrets. I wanted to give you this."

He thrust a package at Karatek. In the tumult, its outer wrappings had been torn, and Karatek saw the precious silk of an inner casing. When he took hold of the thing, he knew what it was.

"The coronet!"

"Take it with you. I want you to keep records," Surak said. "Tell your story, all of it. And one day, bring it home. *Remember!*"

His voice rose to a shout.

"*T'Kehr!* Surak!" Skamandros's voice boomed over the crowd.

A mistake. Half the people left standing took up the chant, while Surak's enemies tried to rush him.

"Go!" Surak ordered, and ran back the way he had come, to wage peace or die trying.

213

It didn't take Surak's logic to know which fate was the more likely.

Skamandros fell, a charred hole in his chest. For a moment, Surak's face twisted. Then, he went over to join Ivek at the barricades. He stood watching, and Karatek knew he was deciding which enemy to speak with first to forestall their last, desperate attempt to prevent the shuttles from lifting off.

Waging peace to the last.

Tears were a waste of water, Karatek chided himself.

"*Karatek!*" T'Vysse's voice in his ear. "I await thee."

Karatek ran back the way he had come, trying not to weep.

A hideous light bloomed in Vulcan's bloody sky, bloodier now, as Vulcan Station exploded.

The sheer enormity of that act stunned friend and enemy alike on the landing field. In the silence, Surak's voice rose, rational, persuasive, aching with compassion.

Karatek found his feet and ran back to his family, weeping as he went.

He was last on board the shuttle, reaching it just as its hatches sealed. Its pilot lifted off before the last arrivals were seated, much less strapped in, and they reeled across the corridors. Karatek fell against a biologist whose laboratory had been three floors down from his in the VSI for the last five years. They steadied each other, but then she all but tripped over a man whose sigils proclaimed him a te-Vikram acolyte. He, in turn, rose to his knees, steadying a small girl-child, whom he restored to her anguished mother before facing off against a guardsman.

The two of them stared at each other, hate in their eyes.

"You can't afford this!" Karatek shouted and thrust himself between them. "We will talk about this later."

Later.

Perhaps they would fight. Or perhaps he had won precious time to wage peace, one of many such skirmishes that the people who had crammed onto the shuttles at the last minute would have to win over the next years.

The years of their exile.

He could hear people crying out for their families as turbulence buffeted the shuttle. He fought his way toward the control room, although, logically speaking, he should have taken his place among the engineers. But Torin had told him to lead this group, and lead he would.

The shuttle rocked, and someone cried out that a surface-to-air missile had taken out the one immediately ahead of them. It rocked again as its pilot began an inspired series of evasive maneuvers.

When they reached the ships—assuming they reached them—he would have to create a roster of the people who had actually survived. He expected there would be some surprises, like the te-Vikram who had been swept up into the rush to get the shuttles off Vulcan. They would have to be dealt with—incorporated into the community. Vulcan-in-Exile would find uses for all of them. It was logical to leave their battles behind on the homeworld.

Perhaps it would be possible to reunite clans and families. He forced himself not to think of his son, his wife, and his grandchild, remaining on Vulcan. They had made their choice. If the Mother World survived, it would be through the efforts of people like them.

TWENTY-TWO

NOW

U.S.S. ALLIANCE

"Formation Alpha!" Saavik shouted over the open channel to the rest of the fleet.

With captains who were, regardless of race, all professionals, the ships instantly zoomed into the agreed-upon formation. They began enclosing the enemy fleet in what would quickly become a three-dimensional trap—

No! Someone of the Watraii fleet had seen the danger just in time. The Watraii ships moved almost as one, forming an arrow of ships that surged out of the trap, turning with alarming speed and fanning out.

They are dangerously well organized, Spock thought. *We must not underestimate their mobility, either.*

"Beta!" Saavik shouted.

The Fleet opened up more room between them, then opened

fire with testing bursts. But as Spock had expected, the Watraii were every bit as swift to react, returning fire on Saavik's fleet. The darkness around them lit up with flashes of blue, red, and eerie green—but in the quickly shifting pattern of ships, no one was struck.

"Gamma!"

Another quick shift of positions created a new attack formation. It was a duel in space with the Watraii, their ships also in motion, each side maneuvering, each side trying to get the other to leave an opening. The Watraii fired first this time, as though tired of the duel, but Saavik's fleet retaliated in an instant and this time gaudy flashes of green and blue showed where ships on both sides had been struck.

"Damage reports!" Saavik ordered.

Quick messages shooting from ship to ship assured everyone that, thanks to the swift maneuverings, there had been only minor damage and no serious injuries to anyone.

"The Watraii?"

Lieutenant Abrams shook her head, not looking up from her console's screen. "Looks like . . . no. No major damage to any of the Watraii ships, either, Captain."

This is what humans call a standoff, Spock thought. *Perhaps now the Watraii will accept the facts and open communications with us.*

The aliens evidently were thinking the same thing. "Captain," Lieutenant Suhur said suddenly, "they are hailing us."

"Looks like they've finally learned some manners," Ruanek murmured. "Or at least some common sense."

"Open hailing frequencies," Saavik ordered. With what only another Vulcan would have recognized as wry humor, she added, "Admiral Chekov, I believe this call is for you."

The figure that appeared on the viewscreen looked vaguely humanoid in its general outline, but its face was completely hidden behind a dark green oval of a mask that was ornamented only with vertical zigzag lines like so many slashes of lightning. All that could be seen of the face behind the mask were hints of pale blue-white skin and dark blue eyes.

"They haven't changed," Chekov said without hesitation. "It's the Watraii."

The Watraii leader—or at least their spokesman (the universal translator picked up a voice that sounded male)—said flatly, "You know our race. Give us yours at once."

"I am of the human—" Chekov began.

"We do not recognize that race." *And we don't care about it* went the unspoken words. "But you must know this warning and believe it: Your race and you are in error. You have made the fatal mistake of allying yourself with the murderer race."

Chekov glanced at Spock, Ruanek, and Saavik. "These people? But—these are Vulcans, not—"

"Would you lie? I see them beside you."

"We are, indeed, Vulcans," Spock said calmly. "Not any other species. We are truly Vulcans, bred to peace, not war."

"You speak soft words, but that does not lessen the lie that hides within them."

"They haven't learned manners after all," Ruanek muttered.

"You are one of the murderer race," the Watraii continued in that flat, deadly voice. "And you, human creature, you are given this one warning: Turn back. Turn back before the Watraii destroy you along with those of the murderer race."

Chekov didn't blink an eye. "Sorry, but ve cannot do that. The laws of the Federation ve serve forbid genocide."

"What nonsense is this? I fail to see why you call it genocide."

The mask hid all emotion, and the translator flattened out the words, but the anger behind the words could not be masked. "We are not criminals. We do what we must do! Eliminating the murderer race is not an act of genocide but the necessary actions of a legitimately sworn feud."

That was too much for the Romulans. Charvanek suddenly shouted, her voice sharp with fury, "I am a Romulan, not some gentle Vulcan. Your fight is with me! And I state this for all to hear: We have sworn no feud with you, you masked coward! We have done no harm to you. And there is not and can never be any justification for what your vile and dishonorable kind has done to innocent, defenseless colonists!"

"They were not innocent!" the Watraii replied savagely. "Those creatures were nothing less than members of your murderer race. There was no such thing as disgrace in the destruction of that nest of monsters."

Angry cries shot up and down the Romulan fleet. Charvanek shouted fiercely, "Silence! In the name of Praetor Neral, I call *silence!*"

Instant quiet fell. Even so, Spock suspected that it was only strict Romulan military discipline that kept them from attacking.

Unmoved by their reaction, the Watraii commander continued in that cold, remorseless voice, "So now, you members of the murderer race. Did you think that would be our only strike against you? Hear me and tremble!

"We openly declare here and now that the Watraii intend to work the same destruction, total and absolute, on Romulus and Remus. We declare nothing less than the total annihilation of the Romulans!"

This time, even the Klingons roared with rage.

"We will attack!" Commander Tor'Ka shouted.

"We will slaughter these masked cowards!" Captain JuB-Chal agreed. "The Romulans may be our sometime foes—but there's no honor in letting someone else kill them!"

"We will not let the Klingons fight our battles!" one Romulan captain shouted back.

"We can fight for ourselves and our honor!"

"No one threatens the homeworlds!"

"No one threatens the Romulans!"

"Silence!" Charvanek shouted. "Take no action!"

"Stand down, all of you!" Saavik ordered. "*Stand down!*"

Spock, ignoring the turmoil around him, said, "It is only logical for us first to be given the details of this 'sworn feud.'"

"The truth is not for you!" the Watraii snapped, and abruptly broke communications.

Saavik sprang to her feet. "Spock, Chekov, Ruanek, to my ready room. We have some quick plans to make."

As Saavik traveled the short route to her ready room, Spock, Chekov, and Ruanek accompanying her, her mind was busily multitasking in true Vulcan fashion. Humans, of course, were only partly able to perform such efficient mental agility, and had, at their first meetings, been rather bemused to learn that Vulcans definitely could think of two things at the same time, and not lose their concentration on either account.

But right now most of Saavik's conscious mind was analyzing the current situation with its lack of clues, puzzling over the Watraii and their claims, and hunting for a logical and—it was to be sincerely hoped—a peaceful way out of what seemed like a truly illogical and potentially warlike situation.

But part of her mind was also suddenly remembering the past, and looking for useful links or data in the strange chain of events that had led her to become who she was and to be where she was now . . .

. . . a flash of memory:

The child, thin and fierce as a wild thing, half-starving and so terribly alone but determined to survive . . . the half-Romulan child that the Romulans had abandoned along with the other half-bloods they had begotten, thinking them of no value . . .

Not useful. Forward in time.

. . . flash of memory . . .

The feral girl, rescued by the young Spock and gently, kindly, civilized by him and by his father . . . Sarek, a moment of genuine grief at the thought of his loss, he who had given her the first home she had ever known . . .

Not useful. Forward in time.

. . . flash of memory . . .

The girl, now known as Saavik, her first true name, gradually liking what she found on Vulcan, gradually liking to be civilized and trying her best to learn Vulcan ways and logic . . .

. . . flash of memory . . .

The young woman, Saavik totally civilized now, a Vulcan of the Vulcans, entering Starfleet and admitting to herself with brutal honesty that she was doing this because of Spock, because she wanted to please him, in a blatant case of what the humans so accurately called "hero worship."

. . . flash of memory . . .

The horrifying information years later that Spock had died, and the amazing realization that he still lived and that she could rescue him . . .

. . . flash of memory . . .

All the events that had led at last to their stunned realization that there was much more than logic to their marriage . . .

Pleasant memories, but not useful now.

Memories of career choices . . . yes. Career choices and changes.

Yes, Saavik told herself, she had truly enjoyed her time serving with Captain Truman Howes aboard the *U.S.S. Armstrong*. He had proven a good and honorable captain, and she had learned much during her time on board about the most practical and logical ways to deal with humans and other races.

But during that time, Saavik had also learned much about herself, gradually coming to terms with her Vulcan as well as her Romulan blood.

And soon after, her adventures with Spock on Romulus during the overthrow of Dralath and the installation of Narviat as praetor had taught her at the end not to be ashamed of either side of her heritage.

And, indeed, she had finally known what she wanted to do and to be. . . .

The suite looked more like part of a private home than a Starfleet office. A comfortable private home, Saavik thought, with cushions on the chairs and handsome photographs of Earth on the walls.

Behind the smooth mahogany desk, Admiral Edward—Ed (not that she would ever call him that)—Clement beamed at her. "Ah, Commander Saavik. Please, come in. Sit down."

"Thank you, sir." *I am willing to gamble like a Romulan that those frames on his desk hold family photos.*

"Would you like anything to drink? To eat?"

"No, sir. That will not be necessary."

Saavik kept her face a mask of Vulcan calm. Admiral Clement had the gentle face of a man who was truly concerned about those in his care. Right now, she knew, he was politely, if illogically, making it seem as if he hadn't ordered her to his office.

But the admiral's gentle face didn't hide the keen intelligence that shone in those deep brown eyes.

"Commander Saavik, we both know you are qualified by now to captain almost any ship in the fleet."

"Yes, sir. I am aware of that."

"Yet you have put in a request simply for a science vessel."

Humans did have a way of stating the obvious. He was holding a printout of her request. "Yes, sir," Saavik repeated patiently.

"Commander, I don't have to tell you there is always a need for qualified Starfleet captains. And you have already shown an ability to work with, ah, some of the more emotional races."

"Yes, sir, I have." *I'm doing it right now.* "Nevertheless, I do request a science vessel."

Admiral Clement leaned forward, hands on desk. *"Why, Saavik?"*

Why, indeed? Saavik mused. *Because I've already seen more than my share of violence for a Vulcan? Because violence is also there in every drop of my Romulan blood and having chosen to be Vulcan I wish to keep the violence under control?*

"Because I wish to add to knowledge," she said at last.

Admiral Clement sat back in his chair as though a bit disappointed in her. "Ah. Well, knowledge is a good thing. I'm not going to argue with you, Commander. The science vessel is yours. But please remember that if you ever change your mind . . ."

"I have no intention of changing my mind."

*   *   *

Saavik truly had had no intention of changing her mind. At the time, it had seemed quite logical to look forward to years of peacefully satisfying scientific exploration, interspaced with equally satisfying time with her husband.

And for some time, she and her crew worked well together, enjoying their journeys and discoveries. Saavik, a little bemused and, were it not illogical to be so, proud, had even had a chance to lecture at the Vulcan Science Academy on a new variety of xerophyte that her away team had found on an otherwise barren planetoid. It had been a . . . fascinating experience. Particularly since Spock had been in the audience.

Yes, but then came the war.

The Dominion War had broken into the ordinary existences of millions of beings with all its horror, shattering lives and civilizations. There was all at once no place for peacetime scientific exploration, only for the cold, hard science of weapon design. All able-bodied captains had been pulled away from their peacetime vessels and reassigned to the war.

Even before she could be commandeered, though, Saavik, fiercely determined to defend Vulcan with a passion that she freely admitted to herself was pure Romulan, had asked for and received a warship.

This ship.

Saavik had, to her immense inner relief and satisfaction—and yes, of course such emotions were illogical—brought the *Alliance* safely through the war, and in the process had lost no more than a handful of her crew (not that the loss of even one crewman or woman or being could be taken lightly). She had taken a wound herself, and spent some time convalescing on Vulcan, but had been back in service soon enough.

But even wars end. And with the end of the Dominion War,

Saavik had even begun to think rather hopefully, though albeit not totally logically, that maybe now in this new time of peace, the *Alliance* could change its ranking, become an explorer, not a destroyer.

Illogic, indeed. Now it would seem that we may be forced to become a fighting ship yet again.

I could hope it were not so.

"Gentlemen," Saavik said as they sat about the table in her ready room, "there's no time to waste. We have to make some difficult decisions, and make them quickly."

"First and most difficult of those decisions," Spock said, "must be the puzzling out of where the truth and the moral course of action lie."

"Oh, I think that's easy enough to see!" Ruanek exclaimed. But then he settled back, aware of Chekov's startled stare. "Your pardon for the illogical outburst. But the fact is that I can hardly be unprejudiced in this affair. In case you didn't know it, sir, I was raised on Romulus."

Which, of course, was true enough. If only part of the truth.

After a moment of startled silence, Chekov retorted dryly, "Vell, not all of us can have so clear-sighted a view. And clearly, the aliens, the Vatraii, feel that they have cause—although vhat cause it might be, I admit, they have not said—to attack the Romulans."

"But there is no logic in a massacre," Spock countered, "and no possible justification for what the Watraii clearly consider nothing less than a war of utter extermination."

"Yes," Ruanek continued, "and quite understandably, the Romulans feel that they are in a battle for their survival."

"Vonderful," Chekov said. "Ve have found ourselves between that prowerbial rock and that uncomfortable hard place."

"There is worse," Spock corrected.

"Oh, there is, is there?"

"Indeed. Not only we, but the Federation itself, have found a situation in which there may be no 'good side.' "

"To fight for?" asked Ruanek.

"With whom to make peace."

"Oh, but—"

"We know very little of the early days of the Sundered. Ruanek, think. You, yourself have admitted to me that the Romulans know very little about the time of arrival on Romulus and Remus. Can you, yourself, tell us more? Can you separate fact from mythology?"

After a moment's hesitation, Ruanek reluctantly shook his head. "So many records were lost over the years."

Spock continued, "Then without facts, there can logically be no clear judgment. And so I must ask this: What choice can be made if both sides are at fault?"

Ruanek glared at Spock at that, clearly wanted to say something that would be very much out of Vulcan character. But then, as if remembering where he was and who he was supposed to be, he . . . only shrugged.

TWENTY-THREE

MEMORY

Alert/danger/takehold whooped from speakers in each corridor of Karatek's shuttle. It lurched to port, then banked so steeply its metal creaked, throwing him against a bulkhead. He crashed into a clump of people huddled together on the deck, unable to find seats or handholds. They shouted in pain, fear, and alarm before he found himself a safety hold and scrambled to his feet, which were getting heavy, heavier . . . but this shuttle design wasn't supposed to subject passengers to the actual sensations of higher gravity forces until it approached its critical tolerance levels.

"We're breaking up!" someone shouted from the people huddling together for comfort.

"We're not going to break up!" he shouted. His response was reflex, not reasoned, but it was what had to be said: Vulcans, especially those who had chosen Exile, might be many things, but they were definitely not cowards. "We're taking on more speed, that's all."

"How in the name of all the hells do you know that?" snarled a man who wore the jeweled lappets of a te-Vikram underpriest.

He was going to be unpleasant company for the rest of the journey, that was for certain.

"I designed this thing!" Karatek said.

It wasn't quite the whole truth. He had worked on the propulsion systems for the shuttles. He knew they were at least as tough as the multigeneration Great Ships themselves because they, unlike the Great Ships, had to be able to break free of planetary gravity and fly in atmosphere.

They were also considerably smaller targets. Right now, that was a great advantage.

(Karatek felt, then suppressed, the horror and grief at the loss of Vulcan Station he knew would mark even his *katra*. All those people. The beauty of that disk in the sunlight. The science. All those people. Dead in an instant.)

Bank, dive, swoop, long, long after you feel as if your stomach were left behind.

Karatek braced himself against the heavier gravity and just endured.

He pressed a hand to his tunic, over where the wrapped coronet lay. He imagined he could hear the great central crystal wrapped in copper and bloodmetal whispering to him.

Record, Surak had ordered him. *Remember.*

Not now.

Now, the imperative was *survive.*

The shuttle quaked, attempting to rock in all directions at once as it was buffeted. . . .

"It's going to tear apart!" someone screamed again.

Karatek clung to a safety hold, as he tried to reach a screen. He had lived with these ships so closely for years. The creaks from the hull weren't the noises a shuttle made as its hull buckled, he comforted himself, albeit with conspicuously little success.

The buffeting came again. Perhaps someone had gotten the Great Ships to fire a warning shot. There had almost been a civil war on the subject, but when the shouting had subsided, the decision had been made: the Great Ships would carry weapons. The decision was perhaps neither the outcome nor the tribute that his late colleague Varekat, who had blown up his laboratories to expiate his guilt in creating war machines, might have wanted, but it was pragmatic—and a concession that had to be made by Surak's disciplines to the Technocrats, who had held up funding until the Great Ships were properly armed.

The pilot eased off until Karatek felt only the vibrations in the deck that indicated steady, growing acceleration.

"We made it!" he cried.

His screen lit. Well within structural tolerances. Not even on the green line between acceptable and unacceptable risk levels.

His screen showed something else too.

The Great Ships had sent out their Stings—small, vicious ships designed to operate in the twin regimes of space and atmosphere. The presence of Stings represented another argument that Surak's disciplines had lost. For that matter, Karatek too had opposed the inclusion of fighter craft, adapted from the types of ships that enabled Vulcans to make war on other Vulcans, on the ships that would take the Exiles out into the infinite night.

He saw now he had been in error.

Karatek ended the dataflow. Being wrong wasn't necessarily illogical: it was a fact that tended to reflect factual error. And it was subject to change. A time might come during their long journey when the weapons and the Stings might turn on their creators. As he turned away, he met a woman's eyes. Even blurred with tears and fear, they held his.

"Your engines held," she said. "Good work!"

"Commissioner T'Partha! What are you doing here?"

The woman who congratulated him was indeed one of the newest appointees to the High Command. Of all the people who had no incentive to leave Vulcan, he would have thought that a newly appointed commissioner ranked very high.

When the explosions and the shooting began, her security forces must have rushed her on board this shuttle. The shuttles were intended to join the Great Ships and would be used, however long from now, to make planetfall when the Exiles arrived at whatever world they chose to be their new home.

The formal trousers-and-tunic combination she wore, of a teal green enough to hint at femininity, was stained and rumpled. As he watched, she adjusted the folds of her bronze silk dress cloak to conceal the worst of the damages. Bloodstains on the cloak: Karatek had to conclude that her security had not survived. Best not ask right now.

He held out a hand to assist the commissioner to rise.

She eyed it, raising an eyebrow and flinching at the bruise on her forehead. Scratched and bloodstained: Karatek's hand was nothing she cared to touch. Instead, she pulled herself up by a safety handle. Then she lifted the hood of her cloak over her head, concealing a greenish bruise on her forehead while signaling that she deeply wished to regain her control. T'Partha had always been as self-contained as any follower of Surak, her thin, taut face revealing little beyond intensity and ambition. But now her long eyes were wide with shock and loss as the realization that her exile was permanent sank in.

She has been used to effortless success, and here she is, con-
fronted with an absolute that she cannot change. If she is not
given an exterior focus, her mind will break, Karatek feared.
Torin told me to lead. Leadership is just applied problem solving.
Here is a problem, Karatek: solve it.

He had been an ambassador once, and had led, had he not? He
had. What else had he done? He had adopted two children. Lost
one friend. Killed several enemies.

And negotiated quite successfully with a number of leaders
who had seen themselves as tribal lords. He could hear Torin's
ironic voice adding, *You'll manage, son.*

But would T'Partha?

In her own way, T'Partha was as much a warrior as old Torin.
She probably would. And where she survived, she would be of
use. Right then, Karatek decided he could probably be pleased
that she had survived. Depending on whether she chose to ally
with him or oppose him.

"So," Karatek said, "now you tell me I did good work. You
were not so complimentary when I came before the High Command to request an increase in funding," he reminded her.

"You were the VSI's most effective lobbyist," the commissioner said. "Do you agree now that I was right about the Stings?"

Concede something.

Karatek made himself laugh. It came out wrong, discordant,
and that made him laugh in truth.

"I have never been more relieved to lose an argument," he told
her. "The Stings and the Great Ships' weapons may well have
saved this ship."

"Are you well?" she asked. "Your family?"

"My eldest son and his family—they were trapped, could not
board . . ." He felt himself losing control of his voice and flinched

231

away from her hand upon his arm. The touch would give away too much.

"And yours? I know you did not choose this," Karatek said.

Her face fell.

"My bondmate brought our children to watch the shuttles. When the attack started . . ." She shook her head.

She doesn't know whether they are alive or dead! They might even be on board this shuttle or another one, Karatek realized.

Give her a task, something to occupy the minutes for now until you can get her scanned for concussion.

"Commissioner?" he asked. "Have you seen my wife? Or my middle son? Young Lovar had an internship with the High Command last year; you might recognize him."

Her eyes flashed at him. "The reason I ask," Karatek went on, "is that I am looking for some sort of passenger roster so we can adapt it. My eldest's family is gone. You are here. Did you see that te-Vikram *and* some of the Technocrats also got swept up?"

"Unlikely shipmates," T'Partha agreed.

"Surak taught me, 'What is, is,' " said Karatek. "I do not say give up hope, but for now, will you accept that what is, is, and give me your aid?"

She inclined her head.

Acceptance, if not consent.

"I shall find your family for you," T'Partha said. "And if anyone has secured a passenger roster and cargo manifest, I shall require it for you."

She bowed to him, then headed down the corridor. On the one hand, she might have thought she was meeting a constituent's needs. On the other, he had sent a member of the Vulcan High Command on an errand for him, and never mind who stood where in which chain of command.

If I do nothing else today, I have made an alliance.

The ship rocked again. More buffeting.

More attacks?

"It's all right," he assured frightened passengers—two te-Vikram, a Technocrat family that had apparently come out to watch the show, and four followers of Surak who looked gravely offended that Karatek would assume they needed reassurance.

And Ancestors forgive him if, in the next moment, an explosion made him out to be a liar. The pilot, clearly, was flying his heart out. He didn't know if the shuttle's crew had bothered to arm its (exceedingly token) weapons; if Karatek had been commander, he would have ordered the crew to reinforce the engines and life-support.

He was not commander, not in the military sense. Torin had ordered him to lead. Surely, Torin had not expected him to be burdened with such a bedraggled and terrified group, but . . .

What was that?

Something was pounding rhythmically on the deck one hatch down. Voices rose, sharpening to the vicious edge Karatek had only heard in mobs.

Never mind the ship's passenger manifest, Karatek told himself. The way they had hurled passengers onto this shuttle at the last, it was likely to be all wrong. He whirled and, bracing against the bulkhead to counteract the ship's acceleration, made his way into a compartment where a man whose white hair and thin shoulders indicated he was well into his second century was pounding another te-Vikram's head against the deck plating.

Karatek leapt over a knot of cheering observers, and pulled the old man off his victim. How'd he get the drop on the te-Vikram anyhow? He was easily one hundred years younger than he.

Rovalat! Torin had refused the Journey, but Rovalat, his agemate, had not. While the old survival teacher had restrained himself from walking onto the Forge alone in penance for the boys lost during that disastrous *kahs-wan* ordeal twenty years ago, he had declared he was not fit to live or die on the Mother World and had accepted Exile.

Clearly, however, Rovalat had not left all emotional baggage behind him on Vulcan.

"What do you think you're doing, *T'Kehr?*" he demanded. "You're a civilized man! An Elder! How will we live if we're already snapping at each other like *le-matya* round a watering hole in a drought?"

Rovalat, bleeding from the mouth, spat. "Do you see his insignia, Karatek?" he demanded. "Match them against the spear your son Solor brought out of the desert, and then tell me I have no right to avenge my honor upon him!"

"Solor lived," Karatek said. "And, in any event, if a death judgment is to be passed, he should have a voice in it. He could have left this man for the *le-matya.* Instead, he unbound him."

Now that Karatek looked at Rovalat's victim more closely, he could see the scar from where his son had struck the man with a rock.

"You shame your student," he told Rovalat. "Solor chose mercy over vengeance. Granted, he made his choice twenty years ago, but that should have given you time to learn."

The old veteran flushed deep olive under a pallor—and a discomfort—he was fighting to conceal. This was Rovalat's first time offworld, let alone at heavy acceleration, so he was probably suffering the consequences and controlling himself admirably. Karatek felt a moment's regret at lecturing an Elder. Then, he recalled Torin's impatience with Rovalat's protracted mourning.

"You have remedies with you," he murmured to Rovalat. "Use them before you . . ."

Rovalat plunged his hand into pocket after pocket of his traveling cloak, emerging finally with a small, square white patch that he applied to the inside of his wrist. His color improved.

Bending over, Karatek relieved the te-Vikram of his dagger and whatever other sharp objects or trappings that could become weapons with a little ingenuity.

"Karatek!"

That was T'Partha. Efficient woman to have completed what she planned to do and return, in this confusion. Karatek braced himself for the next calamity. The voice that cut across T'Partha's took away his fears.

"My husband?"

T'Vysse!

At the familiar touch upon his mind, Karatek felt the strain upon him diminish. He gestured at several of the surrounding men—two in the utilitarian desert suits of Surak's disciples, a once-trim man in formal robes from the High Command's staff, and uniformed security—to watch the te-Vikram before he turned to greet his wife.

T'Vysse hurried across the deck to meet him. Taking Karatek's hand, she covered it in both of hers, as desperate for reassurance as he was. Through their bond, he shared her anguish at the sundering of their family. For now, she rejected the long view that one day the descendants of the children who were left behind and the children who went out into the long night of Exile might meet and greet each other as close kin.

That is for tomorrow, or a year of tomorrow's from now. But not for today.

T'Vysse might be an historian, but for now she had found no

perspective. Later, she would yield to the logic of the situation and endure what was: for now, however, she considered grief the appropriate and logical response, and she grieved.

Lovar, his younger son before he had adopted Solor, stood behind his mother. Then he heard rapid footsteps. Why was he not surprised? When in all her life had Sarissa not managed to be on the scene when there was trouble? And when did she and Solor not join forces?

A rhetorical question, as Surak would say.

Sarissa attempted to hold her brother back, but Solor shook free of his sister. Edging around the te-Vikram's guard to get a better view, he blinked, practically dropping the Veils of his inner eyelids in his surprise.

"N'Keth!" he exclaimed. "This is not why I spared you from becoming a feast for the *le-matya!*"

"You!" snapped the te-Vikram. "The brat I planned to take back to the Womb to be reborn as a child of my House! How did you learn my name?"

"I read it off the sigils on your spear," Solor said. "The one I took as a prize. I still have it. Would you like it back?"

To Karatek's astonishment, the te-Vikram laughed, a sharp brief bark. "Ingrate, I would have raised you as a son, schooled you to withstand any challenge, and instead, you trapped and struck me. Keep what you stole! And may it serve you as badly as it served me."

"It has served me well," Solor told him. "I had already lost one father and gained another. I did not wish a third. What's done is done," Solor said. "Now, we can accept what is, or we can die. You may prefer to die with honor, but I prefer to live with it."

"And what are we going to do about it?" Karatek saw his moment and seized it.

"For a start," came T'Partha's voice, "we could see what personnel and what supplies we have on board. I have here a roster of this shuttle's crew, passengers, and its cargo manifest. It cannot be correct: for one, I am not listed on it, nor are the other political representatives or our te-Vikram . . . guests. Do you not think it logical to correct these lists?"

The woman was stealing his thoughts, his plans, the leadership Torin had entrusted to him, Karatek thought, with an instant's furious resentment.

How could he compete with T'Partha? As the youngest person to win a seat on the High Council in fifty years, she knew politics.

In the next moment, T'Partha had walked over to him and put the lists into his hands.

"One of my roles in the High Command was to evaluate the consensus, confirm it, and then act upon what I found," she told him. "Here are the lists you asked for. Please let me know what else I can do to help."

Then he understood. Her talent was to evaluate the consensus, in effect, to gain the measure of how a group thought and felt, and to proceed accordingly. This group, however—here was a group whose core had chosen to break free of the High Council's authority, a group that had found itself tossed together with other groups that it had always considered to be enemies. A member of the High Council could not take command. But someone else might. Someone who understood how things worked. Who was backed by people with a knowledge of history, understanding of their mission, and even familiarity with the faces of their enemies.

T'Partha had placed power firmly in his hands.

And now he owed her. It promised an interesting dynamic going forward.

He leaned over. "Talk with T'Vysse, please. I've worked with the Technocrats. The hardcore Surakists, well, if they haven't yielded to the logic of the situation, they're probably spies, so we'll have to think of something else. Such as how to imprison them. What worries me now, however, is how to manage the te-Vikram."

T'Partha tilted her head and raised her eyebrow. This time, she didn't wince. *Note to self: T'Partha probably does not have a concussion, but should still be subjected to medical examination.* (He sensed the crystals of the coronet pressing into his flesh beneath his tunic, whispering at him to *remember.*)

"I think we should bring your son Solor into it," said T'Partha. "He seems to have had this prior relationship with that N'Keth. The man might be just malleable."

"A te-Vikram? Malleable?"

"A te-Vikram facing eternal exile from Vulcan," said T'Partha. Her voice broke on the words.

A little abruptly, she turned away from Karatek to speak with his son, who nodded, then sank on his heels to confront N'Keth. Solor had made a point, Karatek knew, of studying the te-Vikram. But how had T'Partha deduced that so quickly? She nodded and slipped away. Karatek suspected that the next time he saw her, she would have an updated list of passengers and cargo for him to present when they docked.

Again, Karatek reminded himself that T'Partha's special talent was for how a group ordered itself, just as one engineer's gift was for circuitry, another's for design, a third for visualizing the entire picture. He would have to learn all of those talents or at least how to make use of the people who possessed them.

With startling abruptness after so long on course, the shuttle yawed. Karatek gasped, gulped, and wondered if, this time, he would be sick. How long would it take for the shuttle to reach the vessel that would be their home until, should all go well, they made planetfall at New Vulcan? He was already beginning to hope that there would be older and wiser heads than he on board that ship, Elders who could advise him how to bear the responsibilities Torin had inflicted upon him.

Stop blaming Torin, he rebuked himself. *You have been preparing for this your entire adult life—or at least since you saw Surak walk out of the deep desert.*

"So, what are we to do with you and those of your brothers on board this shuttle? To say nothing of the other shuttles that are on their final approaches to the Great Ships?"

N'Keth lay silent, his eyes glinting.

"You know, a single explosion might take out a shuttle, but those ships are powerful beyond a personal bomb's capabilities. It would be a waste," Solor added meditatively. "As well as a betrayal of your deepest ethic."

"I am glad you tricked me and did not become my son," said N'Keth. "I would not have liked to expose my son in the Womb of Fire for blasphemy, but I would have done so and burned the glyph of shame into my own flesh."

" 'Blasphemy'?" Solor asked. "When I spared your life out of respect for the cycle of life itself, risking my own? And you call me an ingrate! N'Keth, I was a *child.* I knew you could track me and catch me, but I took the risk, rather than live with the certainty of having left you to die with no means of defending yourself!

"So I call life's debt on you. As payment, I claim your Right of Statement. Hear me, heed me: If you turn your back on life in this Journey, you betray your kind's greatest value!

"You value purity," said Solor. His voice almost cracked with tension, a throwback to the child he had been the first time he had faced N'Keth. "You see the Forge as an ordeal in which your people are passed through the fire and beaten on an anvil into something stronger and finer than anyone else. That fire is challenge."

"That fire is challenge," N'Keth repeated, as if it were a line in some ritual.

"And what do you think we face *but* challenge?" Solor demanded. "We cross the vastest desert we can imagine—the desert of stars. We do so to preserve the sanctity of the Mother World from conflict that might destroy it. And I tell you, that the lightest challenge we face on this Journey will be greater than the most severe ordeals in the Womb of Fire that the priest-kings can contrive!"

T'Vysse set two fingers on Karatek's arm. He nodded to her.

He too had not realized just how deeply his son had studied this strange and antagonistic offshoot of the Vulcan people—or how eloquent he was. A moment longer, and Solor and N'Keth might even agree—and on N'Keth's terms.

"My son is eloquent, isn't he?" Karatek stepped forward, putting himself between the two. "Young blood. But it seems to me that we must all hunt together or we shall all starve separately."

"There is no honor in that," said N'Keth.

"Indeed," Karatek agreed. "Shervon here, who gave his allegiance to Surak, would tell you that it is illogical to die when one might live. I simply think that it would be a waste."

"Now," he added, grateful for a gift for lightning calculation, "assuming we do not come under any more fire, I estimate that we shall arrive at the ship that will carry us into Exile in 5.4 hours. *T'Kehr* Torin entrusted this shuttle's welfare to me, and I think we would do well to organize ourselves for speed in processing so that the ships may leave on schedule."

"You, in charge?" asked T'hva. "But you're an engineer, not an administrator!"

Although she had lost her bid for a seat on the High Command, she held almost as much authority among the Technocrats as T'Partha held in the High Command. "What about the pilot?"

"The pilot flies the ship and defends us against attack. For that reason, I spare the pilot all other considerations. Or are you such a one," Karatek asked with a good imitation of disdain, "as brings petty complaints about the scarcity of scented towels to the caravan master himself as he tries to guide you across the Womb of Fire when the land is quaking?

"Let the pilot fly. I am ears and hands for the pilot. And, right now, I am her voice."

Abruptly, he felt his own voice faltering. He was the pilot's voice. He would be the shuttle's voice. But when would he be able to speak in his own voice for himself or on behalf of his family? He and his wife had just seen their son, daughter-in-law, and cherished only grandchild cut off from them forever. Did they not deserve time to mourn? They deserved to be whole, and never again would be.

We have not been whole since our daughter died, Karatek reminded himself. *And now, we know it for a fact.*

We are Exiles, and that knowledge will have to suffice.

With that realization, he felt his heart slow in his side. They had yielded to the logic of agonizing situations before, and they had survived. Yes, their daughter had died and could not be replaced. Not ever. But she had taught them to care, to want a daughter. As a result, they had known how to accept and value Sarissa, who was now a joy, a comfort, and a source of deep strength to them.

Karatek sensed T'Vysse's agreement in the bond they shared.

The crystals in the coronet hidden in his tunic murmured and whispered assent.

So, ultimately, did the people on board the shuttle.

The pilot had invited Karatek, as the representative of the shuttle's passengers, onto the bridge to watch its arrival at the docking bays of the *Shavokh*.

Schematics, he decided, had failed to prepare him for the majesty of the approach. He remembered the pilgrimage he had made in his youth to the sea, how his heart had lifted at the sight of the great statues built by the strand in days so far past that Vulcan had worshipped not gods, but omens scratched on the bones of *le-matya*. The statues had awed him, the earliest monumental work of Vulcans' hands, deep crimson jade sculpted flake upon flake by tiny stone chisels.

Even more impressive had been the cliffs themselves. Over the years, *shavokh* had turned the seaside cliffs into an eyrie: coming upon that eyrie at sunset and watching the *shavokh* come home had been the most impressive sight of Karatek's young life—except for dawn of the next day, when the *shavokh* flew out again to bring food to their mates and nestlings.

There was neither sunrise nor sunset in space, but Nevasa's light struck brilliant beads off the hull of the Great Ship named after Vulcan's birds of passage. The docking bays gaped open like immense metal eyries, all crimson and black and dulled bronze.

The ship edged into its berth.

"Docking complete, shuttle nine," came the voice from controls. *"Live long and prosper. And welcome on board."*

"We come to serve," replied the pilot. *"Standing down."*

As the pilot released the takehold signals, the immense gates of the airlocks slid across the docking bay, and air filled it, Karatek glanced out. In control rooms about the berth were Vulcans, work-ing to insure his shuttle's welfare. Waiting to receive its people.

Karatek nodded thanks at the pilot, then rose to lead the way out into the *Shavokh*.

This might be Exile.

But it would have to be home—for as long as the journey took.

TWENTY-FOUR

NOW

U.S.S. ALLIANCE

"Captain Saavik," Lieutenant Abrams paged from the bridge, her tone urgent. "More Watraii ships are arriving in the vicinity."

"So much for the luxury of ambivalence," Saavik said. "We make our decisions, and we make them now." To Abrams, she snapped, "On my way. Saavik out."

The four of them, Saavik, Spock, Chekov, and Ruanek returned to the bridge just as Lieutenant Abrams reported from her console, "There are ten new Watraii ships."

"Cowards," Ruanek muttered.

Their fleet had been successfully blocking the Watraii ships from any action until this moment. But now the sudden arrival of the newcomers threw everything off.

"Delta formation!" Saavik commanded sharply.

"Three-dimensional chess," Spock murmured to Ruanek as the ships shifted formation into a double polygon.

"Always hated that game," Ruanek shot back.

Now they had created a renewed stalemate, with ships still blocking ships. But the situation could not last. With so many different races forced into an immobility that was unfamiliar to many of them, with so many hands near the controls of so many weapons, the tension was growing so great that it prickled even along Vulcan nerves. There was utter silence, two fleets of ships hanging motionless in space . . .

And then someone, it wasn't clear who or on which side, suddenly could stand the suspense no longer and opened fire, one wild blast of red.

With that one blast, the perfectly balanced configuration was broken and the stalemate vanished into a full-out battle. Ships turned and swerved and fired without warning, according to their own captains' battle ideas, sending out blasts of blue or red or green fire that split the darkness of space, exploded against enemy shields—or sometimes the shields of friendly ships.

It had all at once become the most dangerous of situations, an open, three-dimensional melee, with the biggest problem that of not taking out a friendly ship while staying undamaged by an enemy ship. One Starfleet ship was enveloped in bright green, shields at full just barely holding off the direct hit. A Watraii vessel was hit by Romulan fire, to savage cheers from the Romulans, and veered sideways, a nacelle shorn off—

So easily? Spock wondered. *Do they not have efficient shielding? And why are they depending on standard-strength weaponry? Why are they not using the powerful weapon that destroyed the colony?*

But the *Alliance* banked sharply away before he could gain any further information. The white Klingon ship, the *Dragon's Wrath,* had almost cut too close to them for safety.

The Klingon captains, almost as one, shouted out, "Hegh-lu'meH QaQ jajvam!" *It is a good day to die.*

They sounded almost gleeful about it, Spock thought.

"Helm! Evasive action!" Saavik ordered. "Weapons armed— but do not fire! Repeat, *do not fire!"*

Now there was the terrible problem of a direct confrontation of Charvanek and her small Romulan fleet with the larger Watraii fleet. That would be a fatal encounter for the outnumbered Romulans.

Unfortunately, Spock thought with what would have been irony in a human, right now there was nothing he could do about it. He had all he could do to simply stay in his chair, the security strapping helping to keep him there, as Saavik sent her ship on a sharply darting, twisting evasive course that could not have been possible with an earlier design.

"Helm, keep us out of collisions! Weapons, fire only when you must to clear our path. You are not to make any direct attacks on anyone. Repeat: You are not to make any direct attacks!"

Even at that moment, the two Klingon ships got in two direct hits on a Watraii ship, both damaging enough to start a series of explosions that ended with the Watraii ship disappearing into a white-hot cloud. The Klingons let out earsplitting howls of triumph.

That was finally more than Ruanek could endure. All but abandoning every attempt at Vulcan calm, he cried, "How can we bear this dishonor?"

"There is no dishonor," Spock said.

"The Klingons fight, and we do not!"

"They are Klingons. It is their nature."

"But that first treacherous attack—"

"We do not know who began it."

"But we *must* fight them!"

"No. Think, Ruanek. Be logical."

"Akkh!" It was a purely Romulan sound of frustration. It was no simpler for Ruanek to be of two worlds than it had been for Spock.

But this is no time for him to revert to his warrior self.

Saavik either didn't hear the outburst or was simply too busy to pay it any attention. Chekov had his attention glued to the viewscreen, his eyes alive, his whole stance all at once not that of the deskbound admiral, but of the eager ensign of the *U.S.S. Enterprise.*

Meanwhile, Charvanek, even more furious than Ruanek, shouted out, "The Federation has betrayed us! Divert all power to weapons!"

Charvanek, no, do not do this.

Such an action would leave the Romulan ships with no power for a safe return to the homeworlds. The Romulans meant to take out the Watraii even if it cost them their lives.

It is a gallant if emotional move, the few sacrificing themselves for the many, Spock thought. *But there is no guarantee of their success. And suicide is never logical.*

But then Spock, ignoring everything but the cold, sharp call of logic, sat bolt upright, studying the viewscreen.

"Hold position."

Saavik, trusting her husband's logic, asked him no questions but simply echoed, "Helm! Hold position." Only then, when they were dead in space, did she ask, "Spock . . . ?"

"I point out that the leaders of both sides, Romulan and Watraii, are within range."

"So they are!" She shot Spock a quick, grateful glance of

understanding, and swiftly ordered, "Fire at both ships—and be sure to *just* miss!"

Twin blasts shot out into space, cutting so narrowly across the two ships that the Romulan received a line of scorch marks across its bow.

That instantly stopped those two ships dead in space.

It stopped every other ship as well. Every captain instantly realized the danger posed to the two leaders. Every captain instantly ordered his or her ship's shields up to full power if they hadn't been at full before, the orders snapping up and down the line. Every ship was fairly quivering with each crew's frustrated will to fight—but no captain on either side dared to give any other orders. No captain wanted to be the one who had caused the destruction of—depending on which side he or she was on—the Watraii or the Romulan leaders.

Saavik was taking advantage of the moment's silence to check damage and casualty reports throughout the fleet. A Zedali had taken three direct hits, but their captain proudly declared them to be still battleworthy. One Federation cruiser had lost two crewmen. Then Spock heard, "This is the *U.S.S. Verne.* We regret to announce that Captain Jack Butterworth is dead. He died at his station, struck by debris."

Spock heard Saavik draw in her breath ever so softly at that.

"He died with honor," Ruanek said gently.

Will his grandchildren be comforted with that? Spock wondered.

It was the Romulans—or at least Charvanek—who were the soonest to face up to the uncomfortable facts.

"There might be honor in sacrificing my life for the Empire," Charvanek said dryly over the still open com, "but if any Watraii survive such a battle, I am better off staying alive to fight them."

Excellent! Spock thought.

Unfastening his harness and leaving his seat, Spock took over a console, his fingers flying over the keys with practiced skill. Stop, pause, rescan, enlarge image . . . replay . . . focus . . . replay at half speed . . .

Spock raised an eyebrow. Yes, he *had* seen that: What had happened hadn't been a chance strike. The Watraii had, indeed, deliberately blown up their own damaged ship, the one that had lost a nacelle. Even after the fact, he was still able to capture a split-second scan that showed some most intriguing details. . . .

"Fascinating."

"Spock?" Saavik asked.

"The Watraii apparently have a rather terrifying capacity not just to combine firepower, but to boost it exponentially."

"But?"

"But there is a weakness: The source of this capacity seems to be located on the lead Watraii ship."

"Interesting," Saavik said thoughtfully.

"Here is the schematic." He called it up onto her screen. "We can pinpoint its exact location."

"Now, that is a very interesting device, indeed," Saavik agreed. "It surely can serve no other function, not with life-support nor with standard weaponry."

"Still," Spock said, "without sufficient data, I can but theorize."

"Understood."

"But what I do theorize is that this device, whatever it may prove to be, serves as a force multiplier. Not only does it strengthen the Watraii ships' shields, at least in certain configurations, it must also be the means by which the Watraii can concentrate their lethal energy weapon into one massively powerful beam of energy."

"Wery interesting indeed," Chekov commented. "Vhatever this amazing device may be, if ve can steal it off the Vatraii ship, the aliens vill be left in a wery sorry position."

"Indeed they will," Spock agreed. "They would not be able to combine their firepower or their shields."

"And that," Ruanek cut in, "would leave them vulnerable to conventional weaponry." He managed to give the impression of a fierce Romulan grin without actually grinning. "I like that idea. I like it very much." He glanced swiftly about the bridge, clearly considering and rejecting candidates. "Spock, my friend, I think this is going to be our job."

"It does seem logical."

But then Spock had a flash of memory: his first meeting with Charvanek so long ago, and the theft of a secret Romulan device— and if she was listening in, which she surely was, she would certainly be remembering the incident, too, and probably, being Charvanek, with a great deal of irony.

None of us ever could have postulated what would come from that incident. In a way, it led all the way up to this situation.

The past does have its own way of returning, it seems.

TWENTY-FIVE

MEMORY

The coronet rested on Karatek's temples, its bloodmetal almost pleasingly warm, the gems that were its storage units glowing. He cleared his throat and spoke softly.

"Personal record, the Fifth of Tasmeen.

"I am Karatek, formerly an engineer in the Vulcan Space Initiative, and now, it seems, one of the leaders of this ship. There is, of course, only one commander whose crew will continue to pilot this ship, one commander who will order the entire fleet. But T'Kehr Torin ordered me to assume leadership here, and Surak commanded me to keep records. I will attempt to perform both duties in a manner these men would have found satisfactory. I am not certain that I will succeed.

"Additional dissension has broken out on board—to be expected with the mixed population that thrust its way into the last shuttles during the attack on ShiKahr. It is logical that they cannot yet agree.

"Some say that it would be better to postpone the journey now that the station has been destroyed. Others say that the journey is the only memorial we can provide. I agree with the latter party. We will leave today. If all goes well, our exile will be permanent, although I hope that, one day, my children's children's children may return this record to Mount Seleya as they would my katra, *long after events have become history and history the stuff of story."*

Karatek shivered as he ceased recording. Using the coronet felt little different from the trance he entered when he meditated.

"T'Kehr *Karatek to the command center!"* came over the speakers.

"I come," he told them, and hastened past the men standing guard. They feared sabotage.

"Sir, a message is coming through from the surface."

Not the "Mother World." Not even the name of the planet. Already, the long forgetting that would help them survive Exile and build a new home had begun. Karatek studied the faces of the command crew for signs of anger and found none.

"I will take the call here," he said.

"Karatek?" He remembered the woman's voice despite the static that distorted it.

"Lady Mitrani?" Karatek had seen her consort, Torin, fighting at the barricades, offering his life so that others would have a chance to go into Exile. "Where is *T'Kehr* Torin?"

A long pause told Karatek that Torin's gift had been accepted.

"I grieve with thee," he said. Around him, the crew bowed their heads and nodded sympathy.

"I have taken up my husband's administrative duties," Mitrani told him. *"The High Command has asked me to tell you: The fleet will not be recalled."*

As if they would return!

"But I have a message to give you. Surak is dead."

Karatek had always heard that the most serious wounds didn't hurt at first. The pain came later. Now he had proof.

"All the more reason to grieve," said Karatek. He fought against the heaviness in his side, the ache in his eyes that wanted to turn itself into wasteful tears.

"*I would ask . . .*" Mitrani's voice broke, then steadied. "*. . . That you who go into the long night of space join with those of us who remain in one act at least: Whatever you remember, whatever you discard or forget, you must keep the Fifth of Tasmeen for reflection and remembrance, as we shall.*"

Karatek inclined his head, then realized Mitrani could not see him. "I will do my best," he said.

"*You must do more than your best,*" Mitrani's voice became crisp once again. "*You must succeed. You carry the hopes of a world and a people with you.*"

"The signal is breaking up, sir," a woman told Karatek. Her hands danced on her board, but the static increased.

"Mitrani!" he called. "What did you say?"

"*Live, Karatek,*" Mitrani raised her voice as if shouting would carry her words out into space. "*Live long. And prosper.*"

TWENTY-SIX

NOW

U.S.S. ALLIANCE

Chekov remained on the *Alliance*'s bridge with Saavik. Spock and Ruanek, however, hurried to the transporter room, where the transporter technicians stood waiting for them.

"The coordinates should be accurate enough," Ruanek said as they approached the transporter dais.

"'Should'?" Spock retorted. "The coordinates *must* be accurate."

"Why, Spock, have you no feel for a good gamble?"

"Ruanek, if that was meant to be humorous, I find it sadly misplaced humor. I, for one, do not wish to materialize within a Watraii bulkhead."

Ruanek sighed. "Neither do I, I assure you." He added after a half-second pause, "T'Selis would never forgive me."

Spock wisely ignored the deliberate illogic in that statement and let the subject drop. Together, he and Ruanek stepped onto the transporter dais.

"Energize," Spock commanded.

There was the familiar swirling of light, the familiar sensation of utter disassociation that lasted for no time and all time and—

—then there was the sudden equally familiar reality of being suddenly *there* in tangible reality again, with all senses returned.

Reality in this case was revealed as a narrow, dimly lit ship corridor that smelled faintly of what Spock quickly identified after decades of shipboard experience as a mixture of insulation materials and oil, the scent one found in less elegant vessels. The Watraii apparently wasted no funds on ship décor, or perhaps had no spare funds at all. Spock thoughtfully stored that possible bit of data away for future analysis.

As his eyes adjusted to the dim light, Spock checked the schematics on his tiny padd, orienting himself. He pointed. That was the right way, down the corridor—once they could get past the looming figures of two dark-robed and masked Watraii who were just ahead of them in the corridor.

Ruanek nodded curtly. The years of practicing martial arts clearly had kept his Romulan warrior skills honed. Moving with a professional soldier's speed, he leaped, bringing down the two Watraii with two blows, swiftly, silently, and efficiently.

A third Watraii, who had been hidden from them by the bulk of the first two, turned sharply to see what had just happened to the others. Spock heard him draw in a breath for a shout. But before the Watraii could sound an alarm, Spock gestured. Ruanek caught the Watraii, pulling him off balance and dragging him helplessly backward. Spock calmly brought the Watraii down with the quick grip that humans had once dubbed "the Vulcan nerve pinch."

As the Watraii went limp, Ruanek lowered him soundlessly to the floor, then gave Spock an approving nod.

Unfortunately, though, the walls of the corridor were smooth. There were no convenient alcoves or vents, no places in which to hide the three unconscious Watraii. They would just have to lie where they had fallen.

Now we are *gambling like Romulans,* Spock thought, *gambling that we can get the device and be gone before they—and we—are found.*

He gestured to Ruanek: onward. Together, they moved forward in utter silence, since the schematics told Spock that the amplification device would be in the antechamber to the main power drive, just ahead.

Spock stopped short. Ah. There were complications.

Of course there would be complications, he told himself sternly. Yes, it was true that the Romulans, back in the time of Kirk's *Enterprise* and Spock's mission of espionage, had been amazingly careless about the way they'd been guarding what was then a top-secret cloaking device (for which laxity, of course, Charvanek had paid dearly). But that didn't mean that the Watraii would be so . . . conveniently careless as well.

The amplification device itself seemed to be quite unremarkable, a featureless, rectangular box of some matte black material. Judging from its small size, no larger than that long-ago cloaking device, it looked, fortunately, reasonably portable. And even more fortunately, it clearly wasn't welded into the rest of the power drive. Spock didn't doubt that he could detach it from its connections, hopefully without damaging it or himself in the process, if only he had the time in which to do it.

Unfortunately, though, a double circle of fifteen Watraii surrounded the device.

He gestured to Ruanek: *Can you . . . ?*

Ruanek gave him a raised eyebrow *you must be joking* look back.

There is little time for logical conclusions. In brief, all I need to do is get near enough to the device to detach it. But how am I going to . . . ?

Then inspiration struck. Spock backed off from the chamber full of Watraii just enough to let him send a whispered message to Saavik without being overheard. "Ready the transporter-room personnel. Have them beam up and hold in the pattern buffers everyone in this chamber save Ruanek and me. Hold but *do not* materialize them!"

She must truly have been wondering what her husband could possibly be thinking, but Saavik merely said, "Understood."

In only a few moments, a shimmering filled the room. In only a few moments more, the Watraii guards were . . . gone.

Ruanek gave Spock an Earthly thumbs-up gesture of appreciation. Spock nodded gravely and hurried to the amplification device. There was only a finite amount of time before someone came to check on the guards, and another finite amount of time that so many could be held in stasis.

With Ruanek standing watch, Spock studied the housings. No, he definitely could not simply detach them at random. As he'd suspected, a security system had been at work here, too, creating a specific pattern of color and shape that had to be followed as each housing was released. What would happen if the pattern was broken, an explosion, a lethal gas, an equally lethal shock—illogical to consider what might or might not happen, logical to assume that it would be suitably unpleasant.

Closing his mind to the fact that precious seconds were passing, Spock carefully studied the pattern, swiftly analyzing possibilities and mathematical progressions. Then, working with deliberate care, he began to delicately detach the housings . . . yes, he did have the correct pattern, but he was not sure what even the smallest slip, the slightest stray spark might trigger.

One more connection . . . there. Now, one last connection remains. . . .

"Here they come," Ruanek snapped.

"Finished."

"Good timing! Wait, here, let me."

The device was definitely heavier than it looked. With a grunt of effort, Ruanek hoisted it into his arms and Spock told Saavik, "Return the Watraii and be prepared to beam us up precisely after that."

It was perfectly timed. The startled guards found themselves suddenly back in reality, not sure what had just happened to them, even as the new guards came rushing in—and Spock, Ruanek, and the amplification device vanished into sparkling air.

And then they were back in reality.

As the transporter room of the *Alliance* formed about them again, Ruanek stepped down from the dais, staggering a little, and gladly handed his heavy burden to the waiting engineers, who had an antigrav pallet waiting for it.

"We have it, sir."

They quickly began shielding the device to keep it from attempting an interface with Saavik's ship and a possible lethal explosion.

While the engineers continued their work, Spock and Ruanek hurried back to the bridge.

" 'Sir,' " Ruanek said wryly.

"He was uncertain of what rank you held."

"Commander of the Romulan Star Empire, last time I actually was in service. Not exactly useful here."

With a nod to Saavik, who nodded approval back at him, Spock opened hailing frequencies between the Watraii, the Federation ships, and the Romulans.

Without preamble, Spock began, "We have aboard our ship a certain vital weapons device formerly belonging to the Watraii. I am certain that they will be willing to verify this fact."

There was heavy silence from the Watraii. *Embarrassed silence, presumably,* Spock thought.

He didn't wait. Instead, he then told Charvanek, "I would find it quite agreeable to use the device to save the Romulans—but only if you are willing to order your fleet to drop their shields as well."

"What are you suggesting?"

Instead of answering, Spock said to the Watraii, "I would be willing to return your property to you—but again, only if you are willing to order your fleet to drop their shields."

"What madness is this?" Charvanek snapped.

"No madness. Merely logic."

"You dare to call it logic? I call it cunning, and were it anyone other than you, I would think myself betrayed! Romulan honor works against me, no thanks to you, Spock. If I promise not to shoot, my honor is pledged."

"What nonsense is this?" cried the Watraii leader, unable to keep silent any longer. "You know that this matter cannot be resolved! If we open fire, the murderer race retaliates. And neither side can know which side a thief and trickster will favor."

"Now, which of the two of us, I wonder, is the thief and which one is the trickster?" Ruanek commented wryly. "Not that it matters. The only ones left with functioning shields after all this maneuvering are our nice, friendly Federation ships."

"Exactly so," said Saavik. In what Ruanek had once ironically dubbed full Starfleet Bluffing Mode, she swore to all listening, "I will open fire on whoever shoots first."

Spock wondered, with the slightest touch of humor, just how much of that proclamation actually was bluff.

But the facts were the facts. The Romulans and the Watraii really did have no choice but to accept the reality of the stalemate, Spock thought. They would have to agree—

Did they, though? No matter what she might be thinking, Charvanek was too honorable for anything like trickery. But this was still all suddenly a little too easy to be logically credible. Why was there no more resistance from the Watraii than a few harsh words?

"To the transporter room!" Spock snapped.

Ruanek hurried after him—and so did Chekov.

"Admiral!" Saavik shouted.

"No! I'm not being left behind this time."

Closely followed by both Ruanek and Chekov—who was moving with a younger man's speed and determination—Spock reached the transporter room just as someone dark-clad and masked beamed aboard from the Watraii ship. The Watraii leaped straight at the device, wrestling with it, trying to tear off its shielding.

Chekov, who was nearest to the intruder, threw himself at the alien, not trying anything as foolish as fighting, since a younger warrior was bound to be stronger, but just hanging on with all his might, trying to drag the Watraii away from the device.

"Chekov, get back!" Spock shouted.

"No, dammit! Just help me hold him!"

"Pavel, *now!* A transporter beam is activating—*get back!*"

But the Watraii and Chekov were now tangled up in the Watraii's flowing robes. Chekov, struggling, couldn't pull free in time. The Watraii transporter beam caught him as well as the Watraii intruder, and they both faded out in a shower of sparks.

Spock raced to the transporter controls, struggling to recover Chekov, refusing to let himself feel anything but calm determination . . . logic . . . The Watraii program was similar to that used by the Federation, since there were only so many ways to use a scientific principle, but it wasn't identical. The frequencies weren't quite the same—and there was no time to puzzle out the differences.

For a moment, he thought he'd succeeded. Chekov and the Watraii rematerialized on the transporter platform, struggling fiercely. But then the image wavered, distorting, breaking up—

Spock heard a hoarse scream of agony.

Then the figures were—gone.

Spock's hands tightened on the console so fiercely that the composite cracked. Ruanek, after a stunned moment of silence, began to murmur a prayer in Romulan.

It seemed the only thing that could be done. Spock could only, logically, deduce that Chekov and his enemy had both died in a transporter malfunction, possibly the result of incompatible energies between the Starfleet and the Watraii ships.

What had seemed a victory had just been turned into a stunning personal loss.

He chose this, Spock told himself. *There is no blame.*

His voice sternly under control, Spock reported what he had

witnessed to the bridge, speaking formally to Saavik, saying the words he had never thought to speak:

"Admiral Pavel Chekov is dead."

TO BE CONTINUED IN
VULCAN'S SOUL, BOOK II
EXILES

ABOUT THE AUTHORS

JOSEPHA SHERMAN is a fantasy novelist, folklorist, and the owner of Sherman Editorial Services. She has written everything from *Star Trek* novels *Vulcan's Forge* and *Vulcan's Heart* with co-author Susan Shwartz, to biographies of Bill Gates and Jeff Bezos (founder of Amazon.com), folklore titles such as *Mythology for Storytellers* (from M. E. Sharpe) and *Trickster Tales* (August House), and fantasy novels such as the forthcoming *Stoned Souls* (Baen Books) with Mercedes Lackey. She is the winner of the Compton Crook Award for best fantasy novel, and has had many titles on the New York Public Library Books for the Teen Reader list.

As of this writing, Sherman is editing *The Encyclopedia of Storytelling* for M. E. Sharpe. For her editorial projects, you can check out www.ShermanEditorialServices.com. When she isn't busy writing, editing, or gathering folklore, Sherman loves to travel, knows how to do horse whispering, and has had a newborn foal fall asleep on her foot. You can visit her at www.JosephaSherman.com.

SUSAN SHWARTZ's most recent books are *Second Chances,* a retelling of *Lord Jim;* a collection of short fiction called *Suppose They Gave a Peace and Other Stories; Shards of Empire* (Tor), and *Cross and Crescent* (Tor), set in Byzantium; along with the *Star Trek* novels (written with Josepha Sherman) *Vulcan's Forge* and *Vulcan's Heart.* Other works include *The Grail of Hearts,* a revisionist retelling of Wagner's *Parsifal,* and more than seventy pieces of short fiction. She has been nominated for the Hugo twice, the Nebula five times, the Edgar and World Fantasy Award once, and has won the HOMer, an award for science fiction given by Compuserve.

Her next novel will be *Hostile Takeovers,* also from Tor. It draws on more than twenty years of writing science fiction and almost twenty years of working in various Wall Street firms; it combines enemy aliens, mergers and acquisitions, insider trading, and the asteroid belt.

She received her B.A., *magna cum laude* and Phi Beta Kappa from Mount Holyoke and earned her doctorate in English from Harvard University. She has also attended summer school at Trinity College, Oxford, and has held a National Endowment for the Humanities grant for postdoctoral study in conjunction with Dartmouth College.

For three years, she taught at Ithaca College in upstate New York, but for the past twenty years, she's worked on Wall Street at various brokerages, a leading bond-rating agency, and an asset management firm. She is now Vice President of Communications at an alternative investments firm in New York.

Her nonfiction has appeared in *Vogue, The New York Times,*

Analog, Amazing, various encyclopedias, and collections of critical work. She is a frequent public speaker, most recently at the NSA, but also at Harvard, Princeton, Mount Holyoke, the University of Connecticut, the State University of New York at Binghamton, Smith College, the Naval War College, and the United States Military Academy.

Some time back, you may have seen her on TV selling Borg dolls for IBM, a gig for which she actually got paid. She lives in Forest Hills, New York.